ON BLACK SISTERS STREET

MODERN African Writing

from Ohio University Press

This new series brings the best African writing to an international audience. These groundbreaking novels, memoirs, and other literary works showcase the most talented writers of the African continent. The series will also feature works of significant historical and literary value translated into English for the first time. Moderately priced, the books chosen for the series are well crafted, original, and ideally suited for African studies classes, world literature classes, or any reader looking for compelling voices of diverse African perspectives.

Welcome to Our Hillbrow: A Novel of Postapartheid South Africa
by Phaswane Mpe
ISBN: 978-0-8214-1962-5

Dog Eat Dog: A Novel
by Niq Mhlongo
ISBN: 978-0-8214-1994-6

After Tears: A Novel
by Niq Mhlongo
ISBN: 978-0-8214-1984-7

From Sleep Unbound
Andrée Chedid
ISBN: 978-0-8040-0837-2

On Black Sisters' Street: A Novel
Chika Unigwe
ISBN: 978-0-8214-1992-2

OHIO UNIVERSITY PRESS • ATHENS

ON BLACK SISTERS STREET

A NOVEL

CHIKA UNIGWE

First U.S. paperback edition 2012

Ohio University Press, Athens, Ohio 45701
ohioswallow.com
Published by arrangement with Random House,
an imprint of The Random House Publishing Group, a division of Random House, Inc.

Printed in the United States of America
Ohio University Press books are printed on acid-free paper ⊗ ™

20 19 18 17 16 15 14 13 12   5 4 3 2 1

First published in the United States by Random House, an imprint of The Random House
Publishing Group, a division of Random House, Inc., New York.

Random House and colophon are registered trademarks of Random House, Inc.

This work was originally published in Dutch as *Fata Morgana* by Meulenhoff/Manteau,
Antwerp, Belgium, in 2007. This English translation was previously published in slightly
different form in the United Kingdom by Jonathan Cape, a member of The Random House
Group Limited, in 2009.

Library of Congress Cataloging-in-Publication Data
Unigwe, Chika.
[Fata Morgana. English]
On Black Sisters' Street : a novel / Chika Unigwe.
   p. cm.
"This work was originally published in Dutch as Fata Morgana by Meulenhoff/Manteau,
Antwerp, Belgium, in 2007."
ISBN 978-0-8214-1992-2 (pb : alk. paper)
1. Prostitutes—Belgium—Antwerp—Fiction. 2. Female friendship—Fiction. 3. Africans—
Belgium—Antwerp—Fiction. 4. Antwerp (Belgium)—Social conditions—Fiction. 5.
Unigwe, Chika—Translations into English. I. Title.
 PR9387.9.U52O5313 2012
 839.3137—dc23

                         2011047980

To Jan and our four sons:
for their incredible capacity
to tolerate my moods

To the ABC Triumvirate—
Arac de Nyeko, Monica; Batanda Budesta,
Jackee; and Chikwava, Brian—
for being there from A to Z

Armed with a vagina and the will to survive, she knew that destitution would never lay claim to her.

Brian Chikwava, *Seventh Street Alchemy*

ON BLACK SISTERS STREET

MAY 12, 2006

THE WORLD WAS EXACTLY AS IT SHOULD BE. NO MORE AND DEFINITELY no less. She had the love of a good man. A house. And her own money—still new and fresh and the healthiest shade of green—the thought of it buoyed her and gave her a rush that made her hum.

These same streets she had walked before seemed to have acquired a certain newness. Humming, relishing the notion of new beginnings, she thought of how much her life was changing: Luc. Money. A house. She was already becoming someone else. Metamorphosing, she told herself, recalling the word from a biology class. Sloughing off a life that no longer suited her.

What she did not know, what she would find out only hours from now, was just how absolute the transition would be.

Sisi navigated the Keyserlei and imagined everything she could buy with her brand-new wealth. It would buy her forgetfulness, even from those memories that did not permit silence, making her yell in her sleep so that she woke up restless, wanting to cry. Now the shops sparkled and called to her, and she answered, touching things that took her fancy, marveling in the snatches of freedom, heady with a joy that emitted light around her and made her surer than ever that the Prophecy was undoubtedly true. This was the true epiphany. Not the one she had on a certain Wednesday night on the Vingerlingstraat. That one was a pseudo-epiphany. She knew that now.

She was hungry and stood undecided between the Panos and the Ekxi on the Keyserlei. Her new life smiled at her, benevolent and lush. It nudged her toward the Ekxi, with its price a notch higher than Panos's. She went in and bought a sandwich with lettuce spilling out the sides, ruffled and moist. To go with it, a bottle of thick fruit cocktail. She sat at a table outside, her shopping bags at her feet; the bags shimmied in the light spring breeze, evidence of her break from a parsimonious past. What should she get? Maybe a gift for Luc. A curtain for his doorless room. *Imagine a room without a door! Ha!* The architect who designed the house had a thing for space and light, and since Luc was coming out of a depression when he bought the house, he had been certain that space and light were the very things he needed. The lack of a door had not disturbed him in the least. "Rooms must have doors," Sisi told him when he showed her around the house. "Or curtains, at the very least!" Luc had said nothing in response. And silence was acquiescence. Certainly. Curtains with a frenetic design of triangles and squares, bold purple and white splashes against a cocoa brown, found in the HEMA. She imagined what the other women would say of Luc's doorless bedroom. She imagined their incredulous laughter. And that was enough to feed a guilt that she was trying hard to stop. She hadn't abandoned them. Had she? She had just . . . well, moved on. Surely, surely, she had that right. Still, she wondered: What were they doing now? When would they notice that she was gone?

IN A HOUSE ON THE ZWARTEZUSTERSTRAAT, THE WOMEN SISI WAS thinking of—Ama, Joyce, and Efe—were at that very moment preparing for work, rushing in and out of the bathroom, swelling its walls with their expectations: that tonight they would do well; that the men who came would be a multitude; that they would not be too demanding. And more than that, that they would be generous.

"Who has my mascara? Where's my fucking mascara?" Ama shouted, emptying a makeup bag on the tile floor. Joyce was at the same time stuffing a denim duffel bag with a deodorant spray, a beach towel, a duster, and her Smiley, so nicknamed by Sisi. Smiley was a lubricant gel, innocuously packaged in a plastic see-through teddy bear with an orange conical hat and a wide smile; it might have been a child's bottle of glue. She blocked her mother's face, looking aghast at Smiley, her lips rounding to form a name that was not Joyce.

"Where's Sisi?" she asked.

"I haven't seen her. Maybe she don' leave already," Efe said, putting an electric toothbrush into a toilet bag. In an inner pocket of the bag was a picture of a boy in a baseball cap. On the back of the photograph were the initials L.I. The picture was wrinkled and the gloss had worn off, but when it was first sent to her it would have been easy to see (in the shine of the gloss that highlighted a broad forehead) that the boy bore a close semblance to her. The way a son might his mother. She carried this picture everywhere.

They still had a bit of time before they had to leave, but they liked to get ready early. There were things that could not be rushed. Looking good was one. They did not want to turn up at work looking half asleep and with half of their gear forgotten.

"How come Sisi left so early?" Joyce asked.

"Who knows?" Ama answered, running her hand quickly across her neck as if to assure herself that the gold chain that she always wore was still there. "All this Sisi, Sisi, Sisi, are you lovers? Maybe she's gone on one of her walks."

Ama laughed, slitting her eyes to brush on mascara.

Sisi went out alone at least twice a week, refusing company when it was offered. Nobody knew where she went except that she sometimes came back with boxes of chocolate and bags of Japanese fans and baby booties embroidered in lace, fridge magnets and T-shirts with Belgian beer logos printed on them. "Gifts," she mumbled angrily when Joyce asked her once who they were for.

Joyce was already out of the bathroom. She had hoped Sisi would help her cornrow her hair. In between perm and braids, her hair was a wilderness that would not be subdued. Neither Ama nor Efe could braid. Nothing for it now, she would have to hold it in a bun and hope that Madam would not notice that the bun was an island in the middle of her head, surrounded by insubordinate hair that scattered every which way. If Sisi had not left, if she was simply running late, she would have Madam to answer to. For Sisi's sake, Joyce hoped she would be back on time. How could anyone forget what Madam had done to Efe the night she turned up for work late? Nothing could excuse her behavior, Madam said. Not even the fact of her grandmother's death.

ZWART

ZWARTEZUSTERSTRAAT

IT WAS NOT EVERY DEATH THAT EARNED A PARTY. BUT IF THE DEPARTED was old and beloved, then a party was very much in order. Efe's grandmother was both. And since she was too far away to attend the burial herself, the next best thing, the expected thing, was a big party. Plus, in dismal November, nothing could beat a good party.

Efe did not tell Madam of the death. Or of the party. Nobody told Madam anything. It was not like, if she were invited, she would attend anyway.

The girls had started the day in the kitchen doing dishes from the previous day. Sisi's laughter was the loudest, rising and drowning out the voices of the other women. She slapped her thighs with a damp kitchen towel, and the strength of the laughter shut her eyes. "Tell me, Efe, your aunty really believed her husband?"

"Yes. She did. He told her she could not go abroad with him because the British embassy required her GCSE results before they would give her a visa. Dat na de only way he could tink of to stop her *wahalaing* him about traveling with him. Four wives, and she wanted him to pick her above the rest? And she no be even the chief wife. Imagine! De woman just dey craze!"

"Your uncle handled it well. Sometimes it's just easier to lie to people. Saves you a lot of trouble and time," Joyce said, placing a drinking glass she had just dried in the cupboard above her head.

"Men are bastards," Ama said.

"Ama, lighten up. Since when did this story become about men being bastards, eh? Everything has to be so serious with you; you know how to spoil a good day. You just have to get worked up over nothing!" Sisi wiped a plate dry, examined it for smudges, and finding none, placed it on top of another on the work surface beside the sink.

Ama turned toward Sisi and hissed. "Move the plates, *abeg*. If you leave them there, they'll only get wet again. Why don't you put them away as soon as you've dried?" She hissed again and went to work scrubbing a pot in the kitchen sink. "How could you burn rice, Sisi? I can't get the fucking pot clean!"

"I don't know what's eating you up, Ama, but I don't want any part of it. Whoever sent you, tell them you didn't see me, I beg of you."

"Fuck off. Why don't you fuck off on one of your long walks?" Ama's voice was a storm building.

Efe tried to calm the storm. "Girls, girls, it's a beautiful day. Make una no ruin am!" She hoped it would not rain. It was a beautiful day for November: leaves turned aubergine-purple and yellow and white by a mild autumn and a sky that did not forebode rain. A minor miracle for the time of year. "See as de day just dey like fine picture, and una wan spoil am?"

"Nobody's ruining anything. Anyway, I'm done here." Ama pulled out the now gleaming pot and walked out of the kitchen into the sitting room. She flooded the room with the *twang boom bam* of a Highlife tune. She lit a cigarette and began to dance.

Efe, swishing a kitchen towel over her head, sighed and followed her into the sitting room. "I can see you don' dey get ready for the party, Ama. Oooh, shake that booty, girl! Shake am like your mama teach you!"

"Oh, shut it! What has my mother got to do with my dancing?"

Ama moved away from Efe, the crucifix around her neck glinting. Her anger seemed blown up. Exaggerated. But Efe let it pass. She had other things on her mind.

The party, for starters. The Moroccan man who had promised to get her cartons of beer at a discount had just called to say that his contact had not come through. Now the drinks would cost her a lot more than she had budgeted for. The girls had promised to help her with the food, but with Ama in this mood, she might have one fewer pair of hands. Everything had to go to plan today. A burial ceremony for her grandmother had to be talked about for months to come. That was how much she loved the woman. And they were not even related. She wanted a party that would last all night.

And that would be what would put her in trouble with Madam. The party was a success, so much so that Efe could not leave until almost midnight. Madam's anger manifested itself in a laughter that was dry like a cough and a sneering "Ah, so you've earned enough money to waltz in to work whenever you want?" For a week she refused to let Efe use her booth. One week of not earning money was enough to put anyone off getting into Madam's bad books.

Still, Iya Ijebu got a party deserving of her. "She is not even my real grandmother," Efe told the women when she told them of her death. "I been dey call her granny, but she be just dis woman wey live near our house. On Sundays, she made me *moi-moi*. When I was in primary school, if my mother wasn't home, she'd make lunch for my younger ones and me. Ah, the woman was nice to us. Which kin' granny pass dat one? Goodbye, Granny. Rest in peace."

"What killed her?" Joyce asked.

Even Efe did not know how the woman had died. The news of her death had been an interspersion between "Buy me a Motorola mobile phone" and a "Papa Eugene wants to know how easy it is to ship a car from there to here." A distant "Iya Ijebu died two weeks ago" carried along a faint and crackling telephone line from a telephone cabin in Lagos to a glass-doored booth in a Pakistani Internet/telephone café in Antwerp.

"She died? Iya Ijebu? *Osalobua!* What killed her?" A voice loud enough to reach the other end. She had tried to drag her sister back to the news she had just delivered. "How? What happened?"

"What? I can't hear you. Did you hear what I said about the Motorola?"

And then the line had whined and died, and Efe went around in a frenzy organizing a party.

She did not know the details of the death, but at the party she would distribute badly xeroxed pictures of the deceased: a woman in a huge head scarf, looking solemn and already dead, against a backdrop of palm trees painted wildly on a prop behind her. Below it would be the announcement that she had died after a "sudden" illness at the age of seventy-five (which was an estimation; who cared, really, about exact ages?). And that Efe, her granddaughter, was "Grateful to God for a life well spent." Summer would have been a better choice, its temperament better suited to feasting, but a party was what dreary November needed to cheer it up. She had a lot to worry about. What to cook. What to play. Who to have. There would be lots of Ghanaians; those people were everywhere. Nigerians, of course, went without saying. A sprinkling of East Africans—Kenyans who ate samosas and had no traditional clothes and complained about the pepper in Nigerian food, not really African. The three Ugandan women she knew who stumbled over their words, *brackening* black and *renthening* long. And the only Zimbabwean she knew, a woman who shuffled when she danced. Those guests would spawn other guests, multiplying the guest list to infinity, so that she was glad she had the foresight to hire a huge abandoned warehouse close to the Central Station, not the parish hall of a church she had rented last year to celebrate her birthday.

Here she had enough space not to worry about the number of people who would eventually turn up. And unlike the floor of the parish hall, which she had to ensure was spotless at the end of the party, this place had no such obligation. The tiles had come off in some places, exposing dark earth, like half-peeled scabs over old wounds. Against the walls were high metal racks, most of which were already corroded. The racks would come in handy for stacking crates of beer and cool boxes of food, so Efe did not need to borrow tables. In front of the racks were white picnic chairs. The space in the middle provided ample dancing room.

By the time Sisi, Joyce, and Ama arrived, the party was in full swing. Music blared and a lady in bright orange stilettos pulled off her shoes, held them over her head, and yodeled at the very high ceiling. Joyce, radiant in a black minidress that showed off her endless legs, edged farther into the room and began to dance with a man in an oversize shirt. Several times that day she would be told that with her height and good looks she could have been a model. It was not anything she had not heard before. So she would laugh it off and say, "Now, that's my plan B."

Ama spied two Ghanaian guests going back for a third helping of rice and smirked to Sisi that surely, surely, Nigerians cooked better, made tastier fried rice than Ghanaians (people who threw whole tomatoes in sauces could not really cook, could they?). And both women agreed that Ghanaians were just wannabe Nigerians and Antwerp was, for all its faults, the best city in the world and Belgium had the best beers, the Leffe and the Westmalle and the Stella Artois. You could not find those anywhere else, could you?

Efe toddled up to them, complaining that the soles of her feet hurt from too much dancing. She should not have worn such high-heeled shoes, she said.

"But you always wear high heels! You'll complain today, and tomorrow you'll be in them again," Sisi teased.

"With my height, if I no wear heels, I go be like full stop on the ground."

Efe was not really short. At least not much shorter than Sisi, who described her height as average. "Average" translated in her passport to five feet seven. But of all four women, Efe was the shortest, and this gave her a complex.

"You're not short, Efe. You just like your heels high!"

High-heeled shoes and wigs were Efe's trademark. Ama called her the Imelda Marcos of wigs. Today she wore a bobbed black wig, so it looked as if she were wearing a beret. It was not a wig her housemates had seen, so it must be new. Bought for the occasion. It was not as voluminous as the wigs she normally wore, and the effect was that her features looked exaggerated: her nose, her lips, her eyes looked blown up, as if they were under a magnifying glass.

Ama tapped her feet impatiently to the music.

"These your bowlegs dey always itch to dance," Efe teased her.

"Where's the fucking booze?" Feet still tapping to the music.

Before Efe could answer, Ama was already off. She found her way to the beer and grabbed a bottle of her favorite blond beer. Swigging the beer, she danced alone in the middle of the floor, bumping into other dancers, shouting out at intervals that life was good. GOOD! A black man in short, angry dreads swayed effeminately toward her, and Ama moved back. He tried to grasp her hand, and she snatched it away and gave him an evil eye.

"What's wrong with ya, sister?" he said, in what she could only guess was meant to be an American accent.

"I'm not your sister," and she twirled and danced away.

The man shrugged and went in search of a more willing dance partner, grumbling "Bloody Africans" under his breath. He found his way to Efe, who was sipping a glass of apple juice, and dragged her to the dance floor. Efe was a lot more obliging. She downed her juice and glided onto the dance floor, which was fast filling up. "*Wema*, you're an awright sister! You Africans can really *pardy*!"

"Where're you from?" Efe asked, amused.

"*Seth* Africa. The real deal. You Ghanaian, too?"

"Nigerian."

"Oh, Nigerian? We got a lotta those *makwerekweres* in Jo'burg. Lots of Nigerians. They in the news all the time back home in *Seth Africa.*"

Efe said she had to get back to her drink. What was it with the South Africans she met claiming another continent for their country? Especially the black South Africans. She saw Joyce, her black hair extensions moving furiously as she danced with a light-skinned man in a kente shirt. Efe smiled and mouthed "jerk" to Joyce and pointed at the South African, who was now talking to a woman with braids down to her shoulders. Sisi danced behind Joyce, a bottle of beer in one hand and the other waving wildly in the air, two gold rings catching and dispelling light like magic.

Sisi moved close to Joyce and whispered that Ama seemed to be in a much better mood. "That Ama. She can be tiresome sometimes. What does she want us to do? Walk on tiptoe in our own house?" Sisi and Joyce had joined the women only two months before.

Joyce shrugged. She was out to have a good time, not worry about Ama. Of all the women in the house, Sisi was the only one she was remotely close to. Sisi was the most beautiful of the other three, she thought. Her beauty was all the more striking for being unexpected; she had thin legs, a low waist, and a short neck. When you saw her from behind—which was how Joyce saw her the first time—you did not expect to see a beautiful face, flawless skin. She also seemed genuinely nice. Ama was a basket case given to bellicosity; everything set her off. Efe, she was not sure about. Perhaps, given time, she would like her. Efe was definitely more likable than Ama, although she had her own issues. Yesterday Joyce had called her Mother because she had tried to mediate between Sisi and Ama, who were having a quarrel over what TV program to watch. Everybody could tell it was a joke— even Ama (even Ama!) laughed—but Efe had not been amused. "I'm nobody's mother," she had said, her voice wan, as if in disappointment at a betrayal. Still, she was more affable than Ama.

"I need to pee," Sisi said, and went off in search of a bathroom.

Ama saw her pushing her way through the people on the dance floor and went up to her. "Not off, are you?" Ama asked with a wink.

Sisi's lips pursed. "I'm just looking for the toilet. Not like it's any of your business."

"What's your fucking problem? Geez!" Ama hissed. She had a bottle of beer in one hand.

"My problem is you," Sisi responded.

"Oh, get over it! Are you still upset about Segun?" Ama quaffed some beer. "If it's a lie, why are you so bloody worked up?"

"Shut up, Ama!" Sisi's voice was raised. Ever since the incident with Segun, Ama had been frustratingly smug. Winking and making silly comments. Screeching songs around the house about Segun and Sisi.

"You think you know it all."

"So why don't you tell me, then?" Ama bridged the gap between them so that their shoulders touched. Sisi was the taller, bigger woman, but if it came to blows, she would bet on Ama. The regularity with which she picked fights suggested brawn of such superiority as to instill dread. Sisi took a step back. Ama took one step forward. Efe appeared at their side. "I hope you girls dey enjoy my party?" Chance. Luck. Whatever it was that had brought Efe, Sisi grabbed it and walked away.

When Sisi got back from the bathroom, Joyce was still on the dance floor. Sisi went over to her and tapped her on the shoulder. "What time do we leave?" Joyce asked, turning away from the man in kente. They had to be in their booths by eight.

"Around seven. I'd still like to clean up a bit before work tonight."

"I've eaten so much at this party that I worry I'll just snooze at work," Joyce said, and laughed, a bit of tongue showing through the gap in her front teeth, white teeth that contrasted so sharply with her dark lips.

"Sleep *ke*? Me, my eyes are on the money, baby! I've got no time to sleep, and neither do you!" Sisi mock-scolded. "I want a gold ring on each finger."

She danced away to the racks for a piece of chicken leg fried an incandescent brown, hoping she did not run into Ama again. She picked out a leg, bit into it, and thought, *I'm very lucky to be here, living my dream. If I'd stayed back in Lagos, God knows where I'd have ended up.*

She banished the thought. Lagos was not a memory she liked to dredge up. Not the house in Ogba and not Peter. She tried to think instead of hurtling toward a prophecy that would rinse her life in a Technicolor glow of the most amazing beauty.

But memories are obstinate.

SISI

ON THE WALLS OF THE OGBA FLAT, THREE FRAMED PICTURES HUNG. The first was the wedding photograph of Chisom's parents: the bride, beautiful in a short, curly wig (the rage at the time) and a shy smile. The groom, hair parted in the middle and daring eyes that looked into the camera. One hand proprietarily placed on his seated bride's shoulder, the other in the pocket of his trousers: a pose that said quite clearly, "I own the world." A happy couple drenched in fashionable sepia that gave the picture an ethereal look. The second picture, the one in the middle, was of Chisom in a graduation gown that touched the ground, flanked by her parents. Her father's head was slightly bent, but a smile was visible. Her mother's smile was more obvious, a show of teeth. Chisom's was the widest. This was the beginning. In her new shoes, bought especially for the occasion, she knew that her life was starting to change. The third picture was the largest, its frame an elaborate marquetry of seashells and beads commissioned by her father specifically for this photo: "The very best! The very best! Today money is no issue." Taken on the day of Chisom's graduation, it showed all three with bigger smiles. With wider eyes than in the previous picture. After the photographer had arranged them for the shot, Papa Chisom said he wished the woman who had spoken for the gods when Chisom was born were around.

"It'd have been nice to have her in the picture. Her words gave us hope."

Chisom's mother said, "Yes, indeed. It's a pity that she's moved. If only we had kept in touch."

Chisom said, "I'm just glad I've graduated." She was looking forward to a realization of everything dreamed. To a going-to-bed and a waking-up in the dreams she had carried with her since she was old enough to want a life different from her parents'. She did not need a clairvoyant to predict her own future; not when she had a degree from a good university. She would get a house for herself. Rent somewhere big for her parents. Living with three people in two rooms, she wanted a massive house where she had the space to romp and throw Saturday-night parties.

The Prophecy haloed their heads and shone with a luminescence that shimmered the glass. By the time Chisom visited her parents from Antwerp, she would have acquired the wisdom to see beyond the luminescence, a certain wrinkling of the photograph, a subtle foreshadowing of a calamity that would leave them all spent.

Chisom dreamed of leaving Lagos. *This place has no future.* She tried to imagine another year in this flat her father rented in Ogba. Walls stained yellow over time—the color of pap—that she could no longer stand, their yellowness wrapping their hands around her neck, their hold on her life tenacious. She tried not to breathe, because doing so would be inhaling the stench of mildewed dreams. And so, in the house, she held her breath. A swimmer under water. Breathing in would kill her.

"The only way to a better life is education. *Akwukwo.* Face your books, and the sky will be your limit. It's in your hands." Her father's eternal words. The first time Sisi would return to the flat after she had left, she would go up to her father and whisper in his ear, "You were wrong about that, Papa," she would say. He would not hear her.

Her father had not studied beyond secondary school and often blamed that for his stagnant career. Destiny had not lent him an extra hand, either, by providing him with a peep into a sure future.

"I am giving you the opportunity I never had; use it wisely." As if opportunity were a gift, something precious, wrapped up carefully in bubble to keep it from breaking, and all Chisom had to do was un- wrap it and it would hurtle her to dizzying heights of glory.

His parents had needed him to get a job and help out with his brothers and sisters, school fees to be paid. Clothes to be bought. Mouths to be fed. We have trained you, now it's your turn to train the rest. Take your nine siblings off our hands. Train them well, and in two years the twins will have a school leaving certificate and get jobs, too. Why have children if they cannot look after you in old age? It's time for us to reap the benefits of having a grown-up son! But he had not felt very grown up at nineteen. Had hoped to go on to university at Ife. To wear the ties and smart shirts of a scholar. Not work as an ad- ministrative clerk for a company he did not care much for, being a "yes sir, no sir" subordinate to men who were not much smarter than he was. "I had the head for it. I had bookhead, *isi akwukwo*. I could have been a doctor. Or an engineer. I could have been a *big* man."

He would often look around him in disdain, at the walls, at the three mismatched chairs with worn cushion slips, at the stereo that no longer worked (symbol of a time when he had believed that he could become prosperous: a raise that taunted him with the promise of prosperity), and he would sigh as if those were the stumbling blocks to his progress, as though all he needed to do was get rid of them and *whoosh*! His life would take a different path.

Chisom studied hard at school, mindful of her father's hopes for her: a good job once she graduated from the University of Lagos. She had envisioned her four years of studying finance and business ad- ministration culminating, quite logically, in a job at a bank, one of those new banks dotting Lagos like a colony of palm trees. She might even be given a company car, with a company driver to boot, her father said. Her mother said, "I shall sit in the back of your car with you. You in the owner's corner. Me beside you. And your driver shall drive us *fia fia fia* around Lagos." All three laughed at the happy image of the car. (A Ford? A Daewoo? A Peugeot? "I hope it's a Peugeot; that brand has served this country loyally since the beginning of time. When I worked for UTC . . .") The mother's mock plea that Papa Chisom should save them from another trip down memory lane would gently hush Chisom's father, and then Chisom herself would say, "I don't really care what brand of car I get as long as it gets me to work and back!"

"Wise. Wise. Our wise daughter has spoken," the father would say casually, but his voice would betray the weight of his pride, the depth of his hopes for her, his respect for her wisdom, all that wisdom she was acquiring at university; their one-way ticket out of the cramped two-room flat to more elegant surroundings. In addition to the car, Chisom was expected to have a house with room enough for her parents. A bedroom for them. A bedroom for herself. A sitting room with a large color TV. A kitchen with an electric cooker. And cupboards for all the pots and pans and plates that they would need. No more storing pots under the bed! A kitchen painted lavender or beige, a soft, subtle color that would make them forget this Ogba kitchen that was black with the smoke of many kerosene fires. A generator. No more at the mercy of NEPA. A gateman. A steward. A high gate with heavy locks. A high fence with jagged pieces of bottle sticking out of it to deter even the most hardened thieves. A garden with flowers. No. Not flowers. A garden with vegetables. Why have a garden with nothing you can eat? But flowers are beautiful. Spinach is beautiful, too. Tomatoes are beautiful. Okay. A garden with flowers and food. Okay. Good. They laughed and dreamed, spurred on by Chisom's good grades, which, while not excellent, were good enough to encourage dreams.

The days after graduation were filled with easy laughter and application letters, plans, and a list of things to do (the last always preceded by "Once Chisom gets a job," "As soon as Chisom gets a job," "Once I get a job"). As her father would say, there were only two certainties in their lives: death and Chisom's good job. Death was a given (many, many years from now, by God's grace, amen!), and with her university degree, nothing should stand in the way of the good job (very soon—only a matter of time—university graduates are in high demand! high demand!). His belief in a university education was so intrinsically tied to his belief in his daughter's destined future as to be irrevocable.

Yet two years after leaving school, Chisom was still mainly unemployed (she had done a three-month stint teaching economics at a holiday school: the principles of scarcity and want, law of demand and supply), and had spent the better part of the two years scripting meticulous application letters and mailing them along with her résumé to the many different banks in Lagos.

Dear Mr. Uloko:
With reference to the advertisement placed in the Daily Times
of June 12, I am writing to—

Dear Alhaji Musa Gani:
With reference to the advertisement placed in The Guardian *of*
July 28, I am writing to apply—

But she was never even invited to an interview. Diamond Bank. First Bank. Standard Bank. Then the smaller ones. And then the ones that many people seemed never to have heard of. Lokpanta National Bank. *Is that a bank? Here in Lagos? Is it a new one? Where? Since when?*

Even in their obscurity, they had no place for her. No envelopes came addressed to her, offering her a job in a bank considerably humbler than the banks she had eyed while at school, and in which less intelligent classmates with better connections worked. It was as if her résumés were being swallowed up by the many potholes on Lagos roads. Sometimes she imagined that the postmen never even mailed them, that maybe they sold them to roadside food sellers to use in wrapping food for their customers. Maybe, she thought sometimes, her résumé had wrapped ten naira worth of peanuts for a civil servant on his way home from work. Or five naira worth of fried yam for a hungry pupil on the way to school. She sought to find humor in the thought, to laugh off the fear of an ineluctable destiny that she had contracted from her parents. The Prophecy by now meant nothing to her. Of course.

There was no longer talk of a company car. Or a company driver. No arguments about a garden with food or flowers. And as the years rolled on, no more letters of application.

"Why bother?" Chisom asked her father when he tried to egg her on. "Unless you have found out that one of your friends is the director of any of the banks, because that is how things work, you know?"

She did not tell her father that she had also tried applying for other jobs, sometimes jobs she was hardly qualified for, but as she reasoned, she stood as good a chance with those as she stood with a job at the bank. A flight attendant with Triax Airlines (must be an excellent swimmer; Chisom had never learned to swim); an administrative assistant with Air France (excellent French required; Chisom knew as much French as she did Yoruba, which was not much, if at all: words she had learned by rote from a zealous French tutor— *Comment tu t'appelle? Je m'appelle* Chisom, *et vous? Comme ci, comme ça. Voilà* Monsieur Mayaki. Monsieur Mayaki *est fort*"). And she was right. No requests for interviews came from those quarters, either. Still, she scanned the newspapers, sending off arbitrary applications for jobs announced, finding satisfaction in the recklessness of the arbitration, watching with anger as life laughed at the grandiosity of her dreams.

So, when she got the offer that she did, she was determined to get her own back on life, to grab life by the ankles and scoff in its face. There was no way she was going to turn it down. Not even for Peter.

ZWARTEZUSTERSTRAAT

BEFORE EFE CAME TO BELGIUM, SHE IMAGINED CASTLES AND CLEAN streets and snow as white as salt. But now, when she thinks of it, when she talks of where she lives in Antwerp, she describes it as a botched dream. She talks about it in much the same way as she talks about Joyce in her absence: created for elegance but never quite accomplishing it. In her part of Antwerp, huge offices stand alongside grotty warehouses and desolate fruit stalls run by effusive Turks and Moroccans. On dark streets carved with tram lines, houses with narrow doors and high windows nestle against one another. The house the women share has an antiquated brass knocker and a cat flap taped over with brown heavy-duty sticky tape.

Outside, a neighbor's dog barks. Its owner shouts for it. Tells it to be calm, he's almost ready for their walk. The ladies might still be sleeping, he says. *Shh*.

But the ladies are not sleeping. Inside, Efe, Ama, and Joyce are gathered in a room painted in tongues of fire. They are sitting on a long couch, its black color fading with age, its frame almost giving way underneath their combined weight. The wall against which their couch is placed is slightly cool, and if they lean back, their necks press against the coolness. They are mostly silent, a deep quiet entombing them, filling up the room, so that there is hardly room for anything else. The silence is a huge sponge soaking up air, and all three of them have thought at different times this morning that perhaps they should open the door. But they do not, because they know that would not have helped, as the door opens onto a short carpeted hallway. They think about the air that seems vile and rub their necks and their temples. Still, no one says a word. They will not talk about it. Their eyes are mainly on their laps, their arms folded across their chests. Sisi is everywhere. She is not here, but they cannot escape her, even in their thoughts. Joyce says the room is dusty. She grabs a rag from the kitchen—one of the many that she stocks in a cupboard—and starts to dust the walls. The table. The mantelpiece above the fake fireplace with logs that never burned.

Efe says, "Stop. It's not dusty."

Joyce continues dusting. Frantically. Her rag performing a crazed dance, like one possessed. The same way she dusts her bedposts in the Vingerlingstraat every morning, after the men have gone.

Ama has a bottle of Leffe on the floor between her legs. She picks it up and starts to drink. The sound of her gulping the beer takes over the silence for a while. *Glup. Glup. Glup.* Until it's finished. She flings the bottle onto the floor. Efe eyes it as it rolls, slows down, and finally stops.

"Isn't it too early to be drinking, Ama? Day never even break finish!" Efe tells her.

"It's early, and so fucking what?" Ama burps. Tugs at her crucifix. "You dey always get ant for your arse. Every day na so so annoyance you dey carry around."

"Fuck off."

Another burp.

Joyce keeps dusting. Maniacally.

The women are not sure what they are to one another. Thrown together by a conspiracy of fate and a loud man called Dele, they are bound in a sort of unobtrusive friendship, comfortable with whatever little they know of one another, asking no questions unless they are prompted to, sharing deep laughter and music in their sitting room, making light of the life that has taught them to make the most of the trump card that God has wedged in between their legs, dissecting the men who come to them (men who spend nights lying on top of them or under them, shoving and fiddling and clenching their brown buttocks and finally [mostly] using their fingers to shove their own pale meat in) in voices loud and deprecating. And now, with the news that they have just received, they have become bound by something so surreal that they are afraid of talking about it. It is as if, by skirting around it, by avoiding it, they can pretend it never happened.

Yet Sisi is on their minds.

SISI

"THERE IS NO ROOM TO BREATHE HERE!" CHISOM DROPPED THE MIRROR
and turned to Peter, her boyfriend of three years. She had left her parents in the middle of an argument and gone to Peter's flat, not too
far from theirs. Peter with a bachelor's degree in mathematics. The
framed certificate had pride of place in his cluttered sitting room, on
top of his small black-and-white television. Since the television faced
the door, the certificate was usually the first thing a guest saw. Above
it on the wall, another framed certificate announced that Peter was
teacher of the year. Beside that, a framed photograph of Peter with
stars in his eyes, shaking the hand of a bored-looking man in a stiff
black coat. Under the photograph, the inscription TEACHER OF THE
YEAR, with the commissioner for education, Chief Dr. R. C. Muno-
nye. There were identically framed photographs in Peter's bedroom.
Peter with eyes that sparkled, shaking the hands of men (and occasionally women) in flamboyant suits who always looked bored. Or
busy. And very often both. Peter's flat was a shrine to an accumulation
of incremental successes that did not camouflage, as far as Chisom was
concerned, the fallacies of those successes. Peter's life was a cul-de-sac.
He did not have the passion to dream like Chisom did, did not aspire
to break down the walls that kept him in.

And this made her think that she was outgrowing him.

"I'll marry you one day, and I shall take you away from here," Peter swore, his voice firm like a schoolteacher's, as he wet his right index finger and pointed it up to the ceiling to accompany his oath. He walked toward her and held her around her waist, nuzzled the side of her face with the side of his. "I promise you. I'll take you away from all this, baby!" Another nuzzle.

In Europe, when she would no longer be Chisom and before Luc, this was what she would miss most about him. His hands around her waist. His breath warm against her face. His stubble scratching her cheek. She would believe that she would never find that kind of love again. That she would never hanker after the sort of intimacy that made her want to be completely subsumed by the other. She would be wrong on both counts.

"I don't want to become like my mother," Chisom said, gently unlocking his hands around her and turning around to look earnestly at this young man who thought he could rescue her. What did he have? she thought. He had a job teaching at a local school. The months he got paid, his salary was barely enough to cover the rent on this flat where his five siblings lived with him. The months he did not get paid, he begged his landlord to allow him to live on credit. His eyes looked into hers, and their solemnity pained her. She looked away. His patience, of rather heroic proportions, aggravated her.

"Peter, you have to save yourself from drowning before you start promising to save others!" Her voice came out angrier than she had intended. What right did he have to make promises he could not keep? What right did he have to ask her to wait here, to wait for him, while she got pulled further underwater?

There had been a time when she had looked up to him. Her whiz kid with the soft hands and a brain that could make sense of any mathematical equation, $(a \times b) \times c = a \times (b \times c) = a \times b \times c$, decipher words that made no sense to her: polynomial, exponential, trigonometric. Algebraic identities. Laplace transform table. Scribbling magic in his notebook that fascinated her to no end and gave certainty to a future that included him.

It was not as if she no longer loved him. She did. She loved the way his left eye half shut when he smiled. She loved the way he cradled her when they made love, breathing into her skin. She loved the way he grinned while he ate, as if the very act of eating, the thoughtful chewing, never mind what was being eaten, was pleasurable; an art to be cultivated, elevated, and enjoyed. But love had its limits. Peter did not have the means to turn her life around. Had she had foresight, she often thought, she would have done a nursing degree. At Christmas most of the men returning home from Europe and America with wallets full of foreign currency, to scout for wives, always went for the nurses. They said it was easier for nurses to get a job abroad. "The British NHS depends on our fucking nurses, innit?" Ed, her friend and Ezimma's cousin, told her. Ed also had come to get a wife. He lived in England—somewhere unpronounceable that ended in "Shire"—but so unmistakably English that it made him attractive, and within three weeks of being in Nigeria and parading both himself and his pounds, he found himself a willing nurse. Even though Chisom did not like the way he marinated his sentences in "shit" and "bloodyfucking" and "innit," she knew that had he asked her to marry him, she would have. Because by then she had given up on love as a prerequisite for marriage. She would discover this yearning, this want to marry for love, a year later, abroad.

"We are all stuck here, baby," Peter told her, his arms around her again. He took her ear in his mouth and bit on it gently. She liked it when he did that.

"And I am tired of being stuck." She let him hold her, regretting her earlier outburst. It was not Peter's fault, after all, that she had no job or that he did not earn enough or that the entire economy was in a mess, so her father had nothing to show for his many years in the civil service, or that she did not see Peter as part of the bright future that was hers. She closed her eyes and let the smell of his cologne take her away. "I wish life were like this," she muttered. "I wish life smelled this good."

Even as she said that, she knew she could not stand another year in Lagos. Not like this. *I must escape*. Perhaps it was this vow that made her recoil when Peter teased her mouth open and snaked his tongue in, running it across her teeth. She put a hand on his chest and gently pushed him away. She was not in the mood, she grumbled.

She would think, a few weeks later, that it was the vow that threw her directly in the path of providence. It would make leaving Peter easier. As for leaving her parents, she would be doing it for them as much as for herself.

CHISOM WAS AT THE HAIR SALON ON ADENIRAN OGUNSANYA STREET, getting her perm retouched, when a man with a protuberant stomach walked in with a young girl who could not have been older than seventeen. It was obvious from the way he held her with his left hand, casually touching her buttocks, that there was nothing innocent about their relationship.

"*Oya!* Make am beautiful. She dey go abroad. Today! Beautify am!" he shouted, almost pushing her toward one of the hairdressers. He brought out a white handkerchief and wiped sweat off his forehead. His breath came in loud pants, the *hmph hmph hmph* of someone who had just run a marathon. It occurred to Chisom that it was probably the talking that wore him out. The young girl—all bones mainly, except for a humongous pair of breasts—was quiet. There was an uncertain smile on her face as she stood while Tina the hairdresser, toward whom she was pushed, touched her hair to determine what to do with it.

"You wan braid am? You get good hair," Tina complimented as she raked professional fingers through the girl's hair.

"Braid? I tell you say she dey go abroad, you wan' do *shuku* for am? Perm am. Put relaxer. Make she look like *oyibo* woman! I wan' make she look like white woman!" The man wiped his forehead again. He looked around for a chair and, finding a wooden stool, drew it closer and started to sit. With his massive buttocks hovering over the chair, he shouted out at one of the hairdressers, his voice like a madman's: "Una butcher meat for dis chair? Dis chair dirty plenty!"

The hairdresser rolled her eyes and grabbed a tattered towel from a client's head. Standing behind the man, she spat on the towel and then proceeded to wipe the stool, rubbing slowly. Chisom, who had seen what the hairdresser did, snickered.

"It's clean now, sir," the hairdresser said to the man's back with a self-satisfied grin as she watched him groan and settle into it.

Tina touched the young girl's hair again. "You get good hair." She sat the girl down in an empty chair beside Chisom's. As soon as she was done with her client she would attend to the girl, she promised.

Chisom felt compelled to talk to the girl. Her silence bothered her. "So you dey go abroad?"

"Yes." The girl nodded. Then added, almost as an afterthought, "Spain." Her voice sounded garrotted, as if it hurt her to use it.

"Wetin you dey go abroad go do?"

"She dey go work. You wan' go, too? You wan' go abroad, too?" The man walked up to where Chisom and the girl sat, inserting himself, incredibly, into the space between their chairs. He brought out his handkerchief again and sighed as he wiped sweat off his neck. On the side of his neck, Chisom noticed a tattoo: a small dark drawing of a hammer. This was what Sisi would remember as she died. Dele and the tattoo on the side of his neck.

"If you wan' comot from dis our nonsense country, come see me, make we talk," he continued loudly, not giving the girl a chance to say anything. He brought out a wallet from the front pocket of his shirt and drew a card from it. "Here. Take." He stretched out the hand with the card. Chisom took it out of politeness. She did not think she could take him seriously. Who offered a total stranger the chance to go abroad? She put the gold-edged card in her purse.

Chisom did not talk to the girl again, because she did not want to hear the man answer for her. His manner irritated her, and she half wished she had been rude to him, refused to take the card. She would never use it anyway.

When she got home that night and she had to eat *gari* and soup for the third day in a row, she thought nothing of the man's offer. The next day, when her father came home to announce that there were rumors of job cuts in the civil service—"They're likely to let me go. Twenty-four years and *pfa*, to go because I am not from Lagos State!"—Chisom merely brought out the card and fingered it. Like she would something beautiful, a pair of silk underwear, perhaps, and put it back in her purse. When she went to the toilet and found it broken and overrun with squirmy maggots and a day's load of waste— there was a citywide water shortage—she felt short of breath. She needed to get out of the house. Go for a walk. A breath of fresh air. And even then she had no destination in mind until she found her- self at an office on Randle Avenue, standing at the address on the gold-edged card, which she had somehow, without meaning to, memorized.

The office was large, with carpeting that yielded like quicksand under her feet and air-conditioning that kept out Lagos's oppressive heat, keeping her skin as fresh as if she had just taken an evening bath. He smiled at her as if he'd been expecting her, which made Chisom wonder what she was doing there. Why had she come to see this stranger with a leer on his face and folds of flesh under his chin?

In his office, Dele's voice was not as loud as it had been in the salon. Perhaps, Chisom thought, the rug and the air conditioner swal- lowed up the noise, so that when he spoke he did not sound loud. Or perhaps it was the sheer distance put between them by the massive wooden table he sat behind, his stomach tucked neatly away from sight.

"I dey get girls everywhere. Italy. Spain. I fit get you inside Belgium. Antwerp. I get plenty connections there. Plenty, plenty!" He panted with the effort of talking. *Hmph, hmph.*

A phone rang, and he picked up one of the seven mobile phones on the table. "Wrong one," he muttered, and picked up another. He barked into it for a few minutes in rapid Yoruba and hung up. "Ah, these people just dey disturb me! 'Oga Dele dis,' 'Oga Dele dat.' Ah, to be big man no easy at all!" He grunted and continued talking to Chisom. "But I no dey do charity o. So it go cost you. Taty t'ousand euro it go cost you o." He smiled. His gums the black of smoked fish.

The amount spun in Chisom's head and almost knocked her out. Was this man serious?

"If I had that kind of *owo*, sir, I for no dey here. I for done buil' house for my papa and my mama!" she protested angrily. For that amount of money, she could not only buy a house for her parents, she could buy an entire city. Why would she be desperate to leave the country if she could miss thirty thousand euros? It hurt her head even to do the math of how much that would amount to in naira. Millions! The kind of money she only read about in the papers, especially when there was a politician and a scandal involved. Was this man completely mad?

"Ah ah?" the man asked. "You tink say na one time you go pay? No be one time oo."

He bit into a corncob, and Chisom watched him munch with his mouth open, his jaws working the corn like a mini grinding machine.

"Na, when you get there, begin work, you go begin dey pay. Installmental payment, we dey call am! Mont' by mont' you go dey pay me." He spoke through a mouthful, and she watched half-masticated corn and spittle splatter onto the table, minuscule yellow and white grains that made her think of coarse *gari*. Why couldn't the man eat properly? Did he not grow up with a mother? She fixed her eyes on the clock above his head so that she did not have to see him chew. What was she doing here, by the way? What did she think Dele was going to do for her? Grant her a miraculous consummation of a vision that even her father was losing faith in? Chisom picked up her handbag. She ought to be going back home. There was nothing for her here.

ZWART

ZWARTEZUSTERSTRAAT, MAY 13, 2006

NOBODY KNOWS SISI'S REAL NAME, NEVER HAVING USED IT. NOT THESE women gathered in this room without her. And not the men who had shared her bed, entangling their legs with hers. Mixing their sweat with hers. Moaning and telling her, "Yes. Yes. You Africans are soooooo good at this. Don't stop. Don't stop. Please. You. Are. Killing. Me. *Mmmmm. Mooi!*" Asking her, "You like it here?," as if she had a choice.

The silence is unnatural. Shrieks and tearing of clothes should accompany such news, Joyce thinks. Noise. Loud yells. Something. Anything but this silence that closes up on you, not even needing to tug at your sleeves to be noticed. But Sisi's death is not natural, either. So perhaps silence is the best way to mourn her. There is dust everywhere, Joyce thinks, dusting hard, clutching her rag tight, imagining it is Madam's neck.

Ama, the slim, light-skinned woman in the middle, coughs. She wants to bring some noise into the room. Her cough hangs alone and then disappears, sucked into the enormous quietness. She toys with the tiny gold crucifix around her neck, tugging at it as if demanding answers from it. Efe watches her movement and wants to ask her again why she wears a crucifix, being the way she is, but she does not. The last time Efe asked her, Ama had told her, "Mind your own fucking business!"

The flat-screen TV facing the women is on, but the sound is muted. There is a soap on, probably American. Impossibly beautiful blond women wearing huge volumnized hair and men with well-toned bodies and stormy eyes flit on and off. Nobody is watching. The CD player in a corner of the room right of the women is uncharacteristically off. On any normal day, Ama would have some music on, a cigarette in one hand and a glass of liquor in the other as she danced to Makossa or hip-hop, swearing that life could not be better. The other women might have joined her, smoking and downing liquor, twisting their waists to the music, except for Efe. She never drinks alcohol, and the others often tease her about her juvenile taste buds.

"Who found her?" Efe asks. She pats her head and, discovering that all is not well up there, inserts her thumbs under her blond wig to pull it in place. She crosses her legs. In the silence the squeak of her nylon spandex trousers as she lifts her left ankle onto her right knee is a loud hiss.

The story has been repeated many times, but Ama suspects that the owner of the voice is as oppressed by the noiselessness as everyone else and just needs to fill the void with sound, even if it is the sound of her own voice.

"A man. Didn't Madam say the police told her it was an early-morning jogger?" Joyce responds.

Joyce sounds different. Younger. Ama has a sudden suspicion that she is not twenty-eight, as she claims. She is still walking around, finding things to dust, muttering about the dirt that is taking over the house.

"What do we do now?" Efe asks, wobbling her buttocks so that she sits more comfortably. She is sitting to the right of Ama and is the heaviest of the three. She pats her head again and scratches her neck. The skin on her neck looks burned, flaky ocher with interspersions of a darker shade of brown. It is her neck that hints at the fact that at some point in her life she was darker.

"'What do we do now?'" Joyce mocks. She shakes her head and rolls her eyes up to the ceiling. "What can we do, Efe? What on earth can we do? You know her people? Who will you send the body to? And even if you knew her people, can you afford to pay for her body to be sent back to Nigeria? What can any of us do? What? Have the police even released the body? What do we do now, indeed!" Joyce's voice is loud, bigger than her body, but if stretched she might be seen to be as tall as she is: six feet and then some. It is sharp. A whip. But it tells the truth. They do not know Sisi's people. Joyce is stooped, dusting the top of the CD player.

"Why you dey vex now? Simple question. I just asked simple question and you start to foam for mouth."

"Who's foaming at the mouth, Efe? I ask you, who's foaming at the mouth?" Joyce stands up—with a velocity that befits her trim size—and in one swift movement reaches across Ama and jerks Efe up, knocking the blond wig off to reveal thinning hair held in a ponytail. "I say, who is foaming at the mouth?" she asks again, tightening her grip around the collar of the other woman. "I'll beat the foam out of your useless body today!"

It is Ama who pulls her away. "Somebody has just died, a human being, and you are all bloody ready to tear yourself to pieces. Sisi's body has not even turned completely cold yet, and you want to kill each other. *Tufia!*" She sighs and sits down, handing the wig she has retrieved back to Efe.

Her sigh restores the silence, which has again become the community they share. Everybody is lost in her own thoughts. Sisi's death brings their own mortality close to them. The same questions go through their heads, speech bubbles rising in front of each of them.

Who is going to die next? To lie like a sheet of paper unnoticed on the floor? Unmourned. Unloved. Unknown. Who will be the next ghost Madam will try to keep away with the power of her incense?

Nobody says it, but they are all aware that the fact that Madam is going about her normal business, no matter what they are, is upsetting them. There is bitterness at the realization that for her, Sisi's death is nothing more than a temporary discomfort. They watched her eat a hearty breakfast, toast and eggs chewed with gusto and washed down with a huge mug of tea, and thought her appetite, her calm, tactless.

Joyce thinks: When she told them of the death, she did not even have the decency to assume the sad face that the gravity of the news demanded. She did not try to soften the blow—did not couch the news in a long story about how death was a must, an escape, an entry into a better world—the proper way to do it. No. She just told of the discovery of the body. And: "The police might want to talk to you, but I shall try and stop it. I don't want anything spoiling business for us."

When she added, "Another one bites the dust," in a voice that she might have used to talk about the death of a dog or a cockroach, Joyce felt the urge to slap her. Or to stuff her mouth with dust until she begged for mercy. But Joyce did neither. She could not. Instead, she tensed her muscles and bit into her cheeks until she drew blood. Her helplessness, desolate in its totality.

Ama lets out another drawn-out sigh that blankets them all, and they sit, subdued. Their different thoughts sometimes converge and meet in the present, causing them to share the same fear. But when they think about their past, they have different memories.

Years later, Efe will claim to understand why Madam is the way she is: detached, cold, superior. "If you're not like that, your girls will walk all over you," Efe will tell Joyce. "If you become too involved, you won't last a day. And it's not just the girls. The police, too. If you're too soft, they'll demand more than you're willing to give. *Oyibo* policemen are greedy. They have big eye, not like the Nigerian ones, who are happy with a hundred-naira bill. They ask for free girls. A thousand euros. Ah!"

Efe adjusts her wig, pulling it down so that the fringe almost covers her eyebrows. Her eyes are far away, fixed on a memory that starts to rise and gain shape in front of her. "I used to know a man who sold good-quality weave-on."

Ama and Joyce twist their bodies so they can look at her. It is the first time Efe has spoken about her life before Antwerp. The first time, as far as they can tell, that any of them has offered a glimpse into her past. Efe clears her throat. She does not know why she feels the urgency to tell her story, but she feels an affinity with these women in a way she never has before. Sisi's death has somewhat reinforced what she already knew: that the women are all she has. They are all the family she has in Europe. And families who know so little of one another are bound to be dysfunctional.

"Titus was his name," she continues, patting her wig. Joyce wipes the speakers of the CD player. Ama lights a cigarette. Efe's voice hems them in. "I was sixteen. I met him long before I met Dele."

SISI

CHISOM THOUGHT MAYBE SHE SHOULD GO. JUST WALK OUT THE DOOR, because the man was obviously a joke.

Every month she would send five hundred euros. "Or any amount you get, minimum of a hundred, without fail."

The "without fail" came out hard. A piece of heavy wood, it rolled across the table and fell with a thud. Any failure would result in unpleasantness, he warned.

"No try cross me o. Nobody dey cross Senghor Dele!"

He let out a cackle, a laughter that expanded and filled the room before petering out and burying itself into the deep rug.

"But how I go make dat kin' money?" Chisom asked, more out of curiosity than out of the belief that she could, if she wanted, earn that much. She was not even going to go through with it, whatever it was, with this man who made threats. She was just curious, nothing more.

"I get connections. Dat one no be your worry. As long as you dey ready to work, you go make am. You work hard and five hundred euros every month no go hard for you to pay. Every month I send gals to Europe. Antwerp. Milan. Madrid. My gals dey there. Every month, four gals. Sometimes five or more. You be fine gal now. *Abi*, see your backside, *kai*! Who talk say na dat Jennifer Lopez get the finest *nyansh*? Make dem come here, come see your assets! As for those melons wey you carry for chest, *omo*, how you no go fin' work?" He fixed his eyes, beady and moist and greedy, on her breasts.

When his words sank in, she expected to be furious. To ask him what type of girl he thought she was. To say, "Do you know I have a university degree? Do you know I am a graduate?"

She expected that her anger would give her the courage to slap his fat face. She expected to want to smash his mobile phones through his double-glazed windows. She waited for the hurricane of anger that would drive her to start breaking things and shout, "Stupid, useless man. *Oloshi!* Old man wey no get shame." Instead, images flashed in front of her like pictures from a TV show: the living room with the pap-colored walls. A shared toilet with a cistern that never contained water; anyone wishing to use the latrine had to first of all fetch a bucket of water from the tap in the middle of the compound. A kitchen that did not belong to her family alone. Her father folded, trying to be invisible. Her mother's vacant eyes interested in nothing. Finally, she saw Peter and the way he was easing into the lot life had thrown at him, floating on clammy handshakes with government officials who presented him with the Employee of the Year award. She knew that he would, like her father, never move beyond where he was. She did not want to be sucked into that life. She imagined her life, one year from now, if she stayed in Lagos. But could she really resort to *that*? She was not that sort of girl. She turned to go, but her feet stuck in the quicksand. They would not move.

Dele looked up at her. Smiled. "You fit sleep on it. No need to decide now. But I swear, with your melons, you go dey mint money anyhow!"

Rather than rant and rave, she took in his words with a calm that assured her she would do as he said. Staying on in Ogba was biding time until what? Until she married Peter and moved in with him and the rest of his family? That was worse than Dele's proposition.

Certainly. But was she really capable of *this*? There had to be another way. Something else she could do.

She did not tell Peter or her family the details of her meeting with Dele. She told them that he was a benevolent uncle of one of her friends. *Ezinne. You remember Ezinne? The girl with buckteeth. You must remember her. We used to study together every Wednesday evening to prepare for our SSCEs.* No one seemed to recollect Ezinne, the girl with the buckteeth, but it did not matter. She went on with the story she had ready. Ezinne's uncle had arranged for her to go abroad, and he would help her get work, and she would pay him monthly. She did not tell them that she had decided already to adopt a name that she would wear in her new life. Sisi. "Sister" in Shona. Roland, one of her classmates at the university, had told her that she reminded him of his sister back in Bulawayo. Roland, nostalgic for his home and missing his sister, had called Chisom Sisi throughout the four years they were classmates. She would rename herself. She would go through a baptism of fire and be reborn as Sisi: a stranger yet familiar. Chisom would be airbrushed out of existence, at least for a while, and in her place would be Sisi. She would earn her money by using her *punani*. And once she hit it big, she would reincarnate as Chisom. She would set up a business or two. She could go into the business of importing fairly used luxury cars into Nigeria.

That night her mother thanked God in a voice that brought in the neighbors from both sides. And the white-wearing churchgoing young couple did a dance around the room, clapping and calling on God by twenty-nine different names to let the blessings that had fallen on Chisom fall on them, too. When the woman said "fallen," she made Chisom think of blessings as something heavy that could crush you, something that could kill. And even though her parents sat in the sitting room, welcoming their guests and shouting a fierce "Amen" at the end of each prayer and singing and dancing, Chisom caught them looking at each other with defeated eyes, as if they had let down their only daughter. She sensed that they suspected her story was made up, but feared to know the truth, as if they feared the culpability that came with full knowledge. Chisom tried to nudge them into belief by reminding them of what the woman with the future in her eyes had seen. "This is it! How many people get opportunities like this? This is *it!*"

Her father nodded. "Yes. Yes. Indeed, this is *it!*"

Her mother nodded. "Yes. Yes. Very true. Very true."

Vigorous nodding. Yes! Yes! And behind the ferocious yes-yes nods were thoughts and questions that swirled and eddied and threatened to drag them down.

Her mother rushed into the kitchen. "The mortar cannot wait until tomorrow to be washed. If I don't do it now, I'll never get around to it."

Her father went to bed. "Long day tomorrow at the office." And in the morning he left for work, his breakfast of yam porridge untouched on the table.

Peter came a lot more often in the coming weeks, shoes dusty from the walk, cheeks bulging with the same plea. "Don't go. Please. Forget this uncle of your friend's." His voice growing fangs at "uncle." "We shall somehow muddle through. I promise you. I will look after you. I will take you abroad. London. Holland. America. Spain. Whichever one you choose. You know, no condition is permanent. We will make it. I'll marry you, give you children."

Chisom said none of the things she wanted to say, like how would he make it, how much would his condition change if he stayed on working at the same school and looked after his five siblings? How would he begin to raise a family?

It was almost as if he were afraid that once she went, he would lose her forever. "I love you and I don't want to lose you," he tried.

Peter, she thought but did not say for fear of hurting him, *right now you're not the man for me.* She hoped he would not see the impatient excitement in her eyes, the way they twitched with the thoughts of somewhere far from both him and Ogba.

THE DAY CHISOM LEFT, NO ONE SAW HER OFF AT THE AIRPORT. PETER had simply stayed away, sending a nine-year-old neighbor of his with a letter that Chisom accepted but refused to read, stuffing it into her handbag. She did not want to have to deal with Peter's declaration of love as well as the anxiety that was making her cling to her handbag tighter than she needed to. She had not realized that leaving would be this brutal. That she would want, almost harbor a wish, that a hand would stay her. Lagos was a wicked place to be at night, her father said. Especially in a taxi. And her mother concurred. So the taxi that Chisom chartered to take her to the Murtala Muhammed Airport had just her and her meticulously packed suitcase in it. The driver—a man with an Afro that was so high, Chisom feared it would tip him over—was very talkative. He complained of the difficulties of living with two wives and eight children, all of school age. He had inherited the second wife from his dead brother. "Practically *chassis*, almost a virgin. They had not even been married for a year when he died. And the girl is beautiful. Very beautiful. My brother had a sweeteye. But a beautiful woman is expensive to maintain, sista."

He seemed to think that if Chisom was traveling abroad, she must have money to spare. "My boy is sharp," he announced proudly. "Six years old, but you should hear the things he says! He is sharp, and I want him to go to school, but how? I can't pay his school fees with my spittle." His other children, all girls, went to the government school close to his house. "Cheap but rubbish. That school is not good enough for my son. At all!" He was breaking his back driving round the clock, because a son deserved the best. "You girls are lucky. All you need is a rich man to snap you up, and you are made. But boys? Their life is hard. God punishes us for the sins of Adam." He gave a self-mocking laugh and started to turn the knobs on the radio. There was a crackle and Fela's "Teacher Teacher" came on, hardly audible over the pitter-patter of rain on the windshield. The driver hummed and swayed slightly in his seat, breaking his humming to shout insults at other drivers for almost hitting his car, for cutting in front of him, for driving too slow. "You steal your license? *Oloshi!* T'ief man. Madman. You dey craze?"

Chisom stayed quiet through the journey. She had too much going on in her head to engage in banal conversation with this stranger. Let him sort out whatever mess was going on in his life, what did she have to do with it? Besides, despite all her years of living in Lagos, her Yoruba had never been sure. She still stammered her way through the language. She brought out the letter from Peter and crumpled it up. She reached behind her and stuffed it into the wedge between the backrest and the seat. Let it stay there. She was heading into the lights of her future. She put her hand into the wedge and pushed the letter deeper in, at the same time feeling a release from Peter, so that while she sat there in the taxi, her hand digging deeper and deeper, she suddenly felt immortal. The energy she felt oozing from her, enough to defeat love, enough to repel even death. She was ready to set forth bravely into her future. And it was all thanks to Dele. She owed him her life.

ZWART

ZWARTEZUSTERSTRAAT | EFE

EFE DISCOVERED SEX AT SIXTEEN BEHIND HER FATHER'S HOUSE. THAT first experience was so painful in its ordinariness that she had spent days wanting to cry. She'd had no notion of what to expect, yet she had not thought it would be this lackluster, this painful nothing.

She felt somewhat cheated, *like pikin wey dem give coin wey no dey shine at all at all.* She remembered nothing but a wish that it would not last too long and that the pain between her legs would be very well compensated. The man who held her buttocks tight and swayed and moaned and was responsible for all that pain was forty-five. He was old. Experienced. But, most important, he had money that was rumored to be endless. *Money wey full everywhere like san' san'.* He had promised Efe new clothes. New shoes. Heaven. Earth. And everything else she fancied between the two as long as she let him have his way. "Jus' tell me wetin you wan', I go give you. I swear! You don' turn my head, dey make me like man wey don drink too much *kai kai*. I go do anytin' for you. Anytin'!"

The moaning in the backyard was a culmination of two and a half weeks of laying the groundwork since setting eyes on Efe as she admired a tricolored handbag in a stall close to his Everything For Your Hair supermarket: waylaying the girl as she came back from the market loaded with foodstuffs for the week. Offering her a ride in his car.

Buying her a bottle of chilled Coca-Cola when they got stuck in traffic. Smuggling a crisp thousand-naira note into her shy fist as he dropped her off at her home. It was the last act that swayed her. It was not just the money, it was the crispness of it, the smell of the Central Bank still on it, the fact that he had drawn it out of a huge bundle of like notes, so that she believed all the stories she had heard of his enormous wealth. The smell was enough to make anyone giddy.

Efe shut her eyes and thought of the blue jeans she had seen the week before at the secondhand market: with a metallic V emblazoned like something glorious on the left back pocket. Maybe she should ask for a blouse as well. Titus had money, he could afford it. "De money wey I get no go finish for dis my life," he frequently told her, encouraging her to ask for whatever she desired. His shop did very well. He had no competition when it came to good-quality hair extensions. He was known to have the best weaves. "Straight from India. Not the *yeye* horsehair you see all over this city. I get a hundred percent human hair!" he often boasted, eyes bulging with pride. He said women from all over Lagos stormed his shop for their hair. "Every gal wey you see wit beta weave on, na me." He thumped his chest three times. "Na me, Titus wey supply am."

Perhaps she ought to get a blue T-shirt, Efe thought. She had seen a light blue one that would go very well with the jeans. And the shoes to go with the jeans, of course, without saying. Maybe something high-heeled and sleek. Definitely something high-heeled and sleek. Something to make her look like a real Lagos chick, a veritable *sisi Eko*. She would have to get him to bring her some packets of hair extensions from his shop. How long should she make her hair? She imagined herself strutting down the road, going *koi koi koi* in her new shoes, her extensions stretching her hair all the way to her shoulders. She would be a senior chick, one of the big girls Lagos had in abundance: young women who had money enough to burn, theirs or somebody else's. Maybe she could convince Titus to teach her to drive and eventually buy her a car. Why not? She could be a car owner, too, a small car with a little teddy bear hanging behind the windshield like in Titus's car. She saw herself driving the car, *voom voom voom*, one hand on the steering wheel, the other hand on the gearshift, as she always saw Titus do. Her lips would be bright and beautiful and a shiny mauve. She loved mauve lipstick but had never owned it. Not yet. But things were about to change, were they not? Titus brought his face down to hers and breathed into her nose. She could smell the mint on his breath. It was not an unpleasant smell, even though at the edges of the breath was the smell of food that had been eaten long ago. Rice? Yam? Beans? Fufu? She tried not to think about the staleness of the breath and concentrated instead on the mintiness. He kissed her on the mouth and wriggled against her. He brought out his tongue and licked the side of her face. His saliva on her face was stale, but she tried not to mind, even thought she ought to enjoy it. Her back, bare on the brick wall, itched. His stomach pressed on hers, and she wished she could push it out of the way. *De man stomach dey like water pot.* There was nothing at all in this whole exercise that made her want a repeat performance. Why did women do it over and over again? Why did the girls at school giggle and glow when they talked about meeting boys behind the school's pit latrines to do *it*? When it was finally over, she thought of Titus's wife. She tried to ignore the pain between her legs, which burned with the sting of an open sore (with fresh ground pepper rubbed into it). Did Titus's wife have to endure this night after night? Efe had heard that it hurt only the first time, but how could one be sure? Grown-ups did not always tell the truth. Adults were not to be entirely trusted. Look at her mother. Up until the moment she took her last breath, she had promised Efe that she would never leave them.

"Where am I leaving you to go to? Who am I leaving you for? Wipe your eyes. Don't cry, my daughter. How can I leave you, eh? How can I leave my children? Tell me, how can I? I will get out of this hospital and walk home. Just you wait and see. How can I leave my children? Who will I be leaving them for, eh? It won't be long now and I can come home. I am already feeling better. Soon. Very soon I'll be back home."

She had been so convincing that when the nurse on night duty at the Bishop Shanahan Memorial Hospital tried to pull Efe away from her mother's stiffening body on that Tuesday morning, telling her in the reverential tone reserved for families of deceased patients, "She's dead. Sorry. I'm sorry, my dear, but she is gone. Sorry. Come. Come," Efe had resisted and shouted that her mother was not dead. She would not leave them. She had promised. Up until that day, nobody had suggested to her that her mother might have been lying. Not the doctor with her stethoscope around her neck, who came in twice or so a day to check on the woman. Not her father, who came in after work to relieve Efe so she could go home and look after her younger sister and brothers. Not their neighbors, who sometimes came with food "because we know what hospital food can be like. If the illness does not get you, the food will. It's that bad."

"Wait, she'll soon get up from this bed and walk home!" Efe cried at the nurse.

The nurse had to drag her away from the body. At her mother's burial a few weeks later, Efe had tried to jump into the grave, shouting, "You can't leave me, you promised. Come back. You promised. Come back, Mama. Remember your promise? Remember, Mama?"

But the promise meant nothing to her mother. She stayed still in the coffin, her features set, and allowed herself to be covered with sand and to be gone forever and ever. *Ashes to ashes. Dust to dust.* Efe would never forget the priest's voice as he prayed over the corpse. It had a tone to it that signaled finality, the end of the woman she had believed would not give in to an illness that had sneaked up on her one Sunday morning when she complained of a headache, a tightness in her temple, and a pain that would not go away with two tablets of paracetamol taken with a tall glass of water, not even after she rested all day in bed.

Everything Efe knew about Titus's wife, Titus had told her. She was tucked away in their Ikeja duplex with five bedrooms and three sitting rooms. She was old. Almost as old as Titus. He also said her bones were creaky, *krak krak*, and he needed someone with young bones to make him happy. He told Efe she made him the happiest man in Lagos, the happiest man in Nigeria, even.

"I go to bed with a smile and wake up with a smile because of you, my Efe."

Efe was flattered to hear that she could please such a big man. Titus was big. And not just figuratively. He was tall and broad and looked rooted to the ground. When he wore shorts, his calves looked like they belonged to three men. Sometimes she thought that had her father had half Titus's strength, her mother's death would not have changed him. He would have remained the sober, sound man whom she remembered from before.

He would have remained strong enough for them, and Efe would not have had to quit school to look after the family. She missed her classmates, whom she no longer saw because other responsibilities had taken over and made her a lot older than they were, so that on those occasions when she did bump into them she felt embarrassed for reasons she could not explain. She missed the smell of new books at the beginning of every new term. She missed the smells of ink and chalk. She even missed the school bag, heavy with the weight of dead batteries for blackening the blackboard.

After the wriggling and the moaning had ended but the pain was still raw between her thighs, Titus gave Efe the money she needed for the jeans and the blue T-shirt. Efe wondered what the neighbors would think of this big man with his Jeep parked in front of the house, especially the Alawos, who lived in the flat right above theirs. *Mrs. Alawo wey dey put nose for everybody business. Like rat, she dey sniff out person. Amebo! Tafia!* Efe was convinced that Mrs. Alawo had seen her come out of Titus's car, had seen them both enter the house, and had probably stood at the zinc door that secluded their backyard from the rest of the compound and listened to the moaning and groaning of Titus. The thought almost made Efe laugh. She put the money Titus gave her into her brassiere and went inside for a bath. She hoped the bath would relieve the pain.

The very next day Efe went shopping. She bought the jeans. And the T-shirt. And she still had money left over. Even after she bought the shoes—blue leather with high platform heels—there was still quite a tidy bit of cash nestling in her purse: crisp notes that made her nearly delirious with happiness. Efe hid the money under her pillow and every night ruminated on how best to spend it, siphoning it out in bits to buy this and that which caught her fancy: hair baubles for her youngest sister. Biscuits. Nail polish. Lipstick. A red handbag. Sweets for the little ones. Chewing gum in varying colors and flavors. She traipsed through Lagos markets and upscale boutiques in Ikeja, buying bits of happiness.

Every night for the next four months, Efe saw Titus at his insistence. He said she had taken possession of him, that he had never wanted a woman as much as he wanted her. She had never had any man before him, so she did not know if wanting him less than he wanted her was normal or an aberration on her part. But it did not matter, because his wanting her was enough. His need was buying her stuff. For the first time in her life, she felt that other girls might be envious of her, that they must want the things she had: the jeans with the glorious metallic V and the handbags that went with all colors and the high-heeled shoes that were so glamorous they could have belonged to the governor's wife. Her mother had had such shoes, too. Fancy shoes with slim straps and heels that raised her feet off the ground (and which Efe used to wear and pretend to be flying), but her father had everything burned soon after she died. Her clothes and her shoes and her bags and her lingerie. Everything in a huge bonfire, a big ball of orange that reached up to heaven and roared, "God, why did you take my wife? Why? Isn't heaven full enough? What am I to do with four children who still need a mother?" Efe would remember that bonfire for as long as she lived. She would see the brightness of the fire in the dark, dark night, and the clouds of smoke rising from it to join their mates in the skies. After the why-oh-why fire had burned and died, bringing no answer in its wake, no phoenix rising from its ashes, it was discovered that the clasp of one bag had survived the massacre, and the father, holding the clasp in his right hand, had hurtled out a laughter and said, "Even this lived through the fire, and yet my wife was taken." He had collected the ash and smeared it on himself like a madman. That sight of her father, his face and hands smeared with the ash from her dead mother's clothes and bags and lingerie and shoes, their neighbors gathered outside to watch, some of the children sniggering, would haunt Efe for a very long time. Long after she thought she had forgotten it.

Sex with Titus did not get better, but it certainly got easier. It no longer hurt so much to have him between her legs. It got more frequent, and Efe got bolder and the compensation increased. She asked for bigger things—a suitcase; a red vanity case like her mother used to have and which had been destroyed in her father's fire; a musical jewelry case with a magnetic lock—and she got more money, even saving enough to buy a radio with a cassette player with dots of light that twinkled when it was switched on so that it was a wonder to behold in the dark and sent her youngest brother into a rendition of "Twinkul Twinkul Little Staa Hawai Wonda Wot Youya." The bundle under her pillow grew, and she treated her excited siblings to new clothes. New sandals. New water bottles for school.

Sometimes she and Titus met in hotels far away from their part of Lagos, where he rented a room for a day and the receptionists ignored Efe's greeting, occasionally looking at her with the same disdain they did the bugs that infested the hotels. The rooms were almost always small and the carpets threadbare. At other times it was a quick grope in the dark behind her house, leaning against a wall, trying to block the smell that came from the gutter running the entire length of the wall.

It was easy to escape her father, a man who, never having contemplated living without his wife, had fallen apart completely upon her death two years before. He regularly drowned his grief in glass after glass of *ogogoro* at the local beer parlor, run by Mariam, who was rumored to be a teetotaler and the mistress of half her male customers. *De gin color his eyes sotey him no even fit see him feet.* He left it up to Efe to look after the house and her three siblings, all younger than she was. The money he provided her every month was just enough for food, and Efe yearned for luxuries. If Titus was what she had to endure to get those luxuries, then so be it. *Dat one na small price to pay.*

Even before she missed her period, even before she felt her saliva turn rusty and metallic, Efe suspected that she was pregnant. So when her breasts enlarged and the morning sickness came, and the food cravings came, and the constant tiredness came, and she could not sleep well at night, she was prepared.

The night she told Titus she was sure she was pregnant was the last time, day or night, that he turned up for their daily appointment. He had been lying in bed, stroking her shoulders. "I am pregnant, Titus." That was all it took to get him out of that bed, get him dressed, first the black trousers with the cord pulled tightly under his stomach and then the caftan reaching to his knees. Then he got up, turned his broad back to her, picked up his car key from the bedside table, and walked out of the hotel room, closing the door so gently that it made no noise.

For a long time after he left, after the blackness of his back had faded, Efe lay in the bed pretending to be asleep, welcoming the quiet. She was still naked. She preferred it when they met behind the house, because then their lovemaking did not last long. When they went to a hotel, Titus liked to take his time. He would drag her into the bed, which usually smelled of disinfectant, undress her, and then have her parade around the room naked before jumping on her and dragging her back into bed again. He would make love to her, sleep, wake up, and start again. Everything happened in silence save for Titus's moans of pleasure. They would stay in the bed until Titus decided it was time to go home. In the car, he would give her some money and make an appointment for their next meeting. The day Efe told him of their baby, they had stayed in bed until the streetlights opposite the room they were renting came on, casting a faint glow of orange light into the room, making the peeling blue walls almost beautiful, like a blue sky with patches of white clouds showing and rays of sunshine scattered over it. Efe had commented on it at some point in the evening, but Titus had seen nothing remarkable in it. "Na just streetlight, Efe. Wey de sunshine in dat one?"

While Efe lay down, eyes closed, pretending to be asleep, her greatest worry was not the pregnancy, which Titus obviously was not interested in. Her greatest worry was how on earth she would get home. She cursed Titus for choosing this out-of-the-way hotel in the middle of nowhere. The fried rice she had eaten and enjoyed earlier soured in her stomach and caused it to rumble, so that she had to rush to the bathroom. *What a waste of good food,* she thought as she sat on the toilet, evacuating the rice and the shrimp and the cubed meat that Titus had ordered for her at the beginning of the evening. If she could have, she would have kept them all in; having no idea where she was, she did not know how long it would take her to get home.

Done with the toilet, Efe decided it was time to go. She dressed in slow motion, wondering how long it would take for her stomach to grow and already feeling that it was no longer a part of her. *Like say an alien don invade am.* When she pulled up her skirt, she ran her hands over her stomach, still flat and firm, and could not believe that there was a baby growing inside her, gnawing her insides, feeding off her in a symbiotic relationship she was not entirely sure she appreciated. She hung her head when she walked out into the lobby, not wanting to look into the eyes of the receptionist, who was at that moment, she was sure, staring at her with a smirk. It was not the pregnancy that made her ashamed, for no one could see it. It was the fact that she had been abandoned in this Royal Hotel. She felt cheap, for it was only the cheapest sort of girl who was brought to a hotel and left on her own to find her way home. It was a good thing she had some money in her purse. Although she never had to pay for anything while she was with Titus, she had stuck to her habit of always making sure she never left the house without some money. Her mother had instilled that in her. "You never know what might happen. Always be prepared." *Well, you were right, Mama,* she said to herself, and sent a quick prayer of gratitude to her. What would she have done if she had been empty-handed? Who would she have asked for money?

Abortion never crossed her mind, not that day and not in the days and weeks that followed, when she started to feel really pregnant and her face puffed up and she could no longer stand the smell of okra soup. She had heard enough horror stories of abortions gone wrong. Nkiru, two houses away from theirs, knew of a girl who had died from a cold that got into her stomach when the doctor who performed an abortion on her did not close the stomach properly. Nkiru said the cold went from the stomach and spiraled into the throat, finally blocking the nostrils, so that the girl could no longer breathe. Somebody else knew of someone who had tried to do it with a clothes hanger and had bled to death. What Efe would try, three months gone and horribly sick, would be to punch herself several times in the stomach. She had heard from Nkiru's older sister that this was a sure but harmless way to get the baby to expel itself. "A surer bet than the abortion belt.

It'll just be a clot of blood and you'll be okay." But it had not worked for Efe, and after two different attempts she would resign herself to fate and a baby who was determined to be born.

It took Efe over three hours, a cab, and a bus drive to get home that night. Her father was in the sitting room, snoring off twelve bottles of lager and fifteen shots of *ogogoro*. Efe touched her stomach for the second time that day and, without meaning to, she began to cry for want of her mother.

She wondered how to tell her father about the pregnancy. She could not remember the last time they'd had a proper conversation. Mostly he yelled at them. "How long does it take for breakfast to be ready in this houseful of women? What does a man have to do to get food in his own house?" A normally loquacious man, given to long-winded talk, he became egregious after he had drunk a bit, picking fights on the way until he got home, bruised and battered. The children saw him some mornings when he got up for breakfast and work, and some nights, if they stayed up long enough, they heard him sing meaningless songs about soldiers and women. And about death and how he would conquer it, live forever, because he had death in his pouch. He sang disconsolately of how death had married his wife and taken her to his home. Twice a month, sometimes more, an irate neighbor would walk down to their ground-floor flat and ask him to shut up, his family could not sleep with all the ruckus he was creating. *Some of us have to work in the morning, let us sleep abeg!* Sometimes the neighbor would manage to get him to calm down. Other times, the plea for quiet would seem to inspire more songs in him, louder and more senseless:

I saw a madman weaving a basket and he wove me a trap to catch you in. He said, catch that man with the devil in him, catch him and roast him on a big big big fire.
Lagos dey burn burn burn, you dey here dey chase rat rat rat.

Rat go burn, you go burn
And your bones go scatter over the sea.

In the end Efe would not tell him, leaving it up to him to notice and initiate a discussion, drunk or not. But she would tell her sister. Not that night but in the morning, after they had eaten and the younger ones had been fed and sent off to school. Some things were better discussed on a full stomach and in a quiet house. Rita would not have the words to articulate the fear that gripped her when she heard. What would they do with a baby in the house without their mother to teach them what to do? With a father who stumbled over his own feet after he'd had a drink? But Efe did not need her words because an identical fear had taken ahold of her the moment she suspected she was with child, and the fear refused to let go. But she knew her baby's father. That in itself was a blessing. Rita agreed with her. And from all indications, Titus had the wherewithal to take care of their offspring. Some babies entered the world with far worse prospects. There were babies born with fathers unknown or with fathers who did not have anything to their names. Not even two coins to rub together. *At least my baby will never want for anything,* Efe consoled herself, trying hard not to think about the baby extending her stomach and making it difficult for her to sleep at night in any position. She spent many nights on her back, swearing that she would never as long as she lived go through another pregnancy, wondering how her mother had done it. How had she coped with four pregnancies? And the women who went on to have twelve children? How had they done it, knowing the pain that came with the pregnancy?

If her father noticed that her body was changing, he said nothing of it. He maintained an air of stolidity that Efe found mildly irritating. Surely he could see her stomach. At the beginning of every month, he faithfully gave her money from the wages he earned as a laborer renting himself out to building contractors, and guzzled the rest up at Mariam's, as was his custom. Even when he was in a screaming mood, he never mentioned the stomach that was starting to bulge not just forward but sideways. "Making me look like a pregnant goat," Efe complained to Rita. It was as if the stomach were invisible to him. If his daughter's growing stomach was indeed invisible to him, it was not to the neighbors, the women especially, who pointed at Efe and laughed out loud whenever they passed her, clapping their hands and baring mocking teeth. Their daughters, girls who had played with Efe or gone to school with her, either avoided her or were called away as soon as they stopped to talk to her. *Collectrose! Go and get me matches from the store! Evbu, you need to do your homework!* Efe's laughter became muted. Her steps slower. And it was not just the stomach that hindered her laughter or slowed her steps.

"People look at me as if I am dirt," she complained to Rita.

"Don't mind them, Efe," her sister consoled. "Once the baby is out and the father starts taking care of him, they will know that you're not one of those useless girls who just sleep around with any man."

Efe smiled at her sister, grateful for her support. "I hope it's a boy. If it's a boy, his father will definitely want him."

"Don't worry, Efe. God is not asleep. It will be a boy."

"Amen." Efe sealed her sister's prayer.

When she became too big and developed a waddle like an overfed pigeon's, she handed over the reins of power to Rita, eleven months younger. Their father did not ask Rita why it was she and not Efe who came to him for money. He just counted out the notes, mainly crumpled notes that had gone soft from too much touching, permeated with the musky odor of *utaba*, snuff, the way poor people's money smelled. Rita proved as capable as her predecessor, shopping, cooking, and organizing the younger ones to help with the cleaning so that Efe could get on with the time-consuming business of being pregnant. Efe would think much later, when her life was more settled and she had lost the weight she gained in pregnancy and had regained a normal appetite, that she never would have gotten through it without Rita.

When her water broke and she feared that birth was imminent—she remembered her mother telling stories of when she, Efe, was born, how her water had broken while she was making lunch and how she had barely made it to the hospital before Efe came—it was Rita she woke up and begged to get her to the hospital because the pain was sawing her in two, separating her torso from the rest of her. She held on to Rita all the way to the hospital, pinching her when the pain became too much for her to bear, and Rita bit her tongue and shared her sister's pain, urging the taxi driver to take it easy, go *jeje*, when he drove into a pothole and Efe cried out in agony. The driver snapped at Rita that he was not responsible for the bad roads in Lagos.

"If you wan' complain about potholes, go talk to the gov'ment. Na just driver I be. If you no as I dey drive, I go stop make you comot."

The man had had a rough day, and the last thing he needed was to be told how to drive by two young girls who could have been his children, one of whom was pregnant. He had not noticed a wedding band on the pregnant one's finger. *Lagos girls*, he fumed silently, *they have no morals at all*. When he got home later that night and told his wife about his day, he would tell her that the pregnant girl looked fourteen. "Right about to have her bastard in my car, I swear."

Efe was relieved to see the reassuring creaminess of the All Saints Maternity, and Rita was relieved to hand her sister over to a matronly nurse whose very walk as she guided Efe to a bed was a lesson in efficiency. The *klop klop klop* of her black shoes, the cadenced accompaniment to her hands, which searched around for a hospital gown and gloves. Efe was undressed and hooked up to a machine that bleeped intermittently and then stopped. The nurse unhooked her and said, "Sorry, the machine's stopped working. We have run out of paper. But some hospitals don't even have this. We have three here.

Donation. It shows the progress of labor. It draws it on a paper and we can see how bad the pain is, if it is real labor or not." She tapped the machine in awe.

A doctor with too many teeth came in, a stethoscope around his neck like an oversize metal necklace. Rita worried that he looked tired, that he would not be able to look after Efe well. She wondered if she should voice her worry, ask for maybe a different doctor, say that this doctor needed a bed and hours of sleep. She looked at Efe and smiled, hoping her sister would not see the worry on her face. He sat at the foot of Efe's bed and asked the nurse questions. She gave her answers in the confident tone of one who was competent and knew it. "*Four centimeters dilation. Water broken. Baby not distressed.*" None of what the nurse told the doctor made sense to either Rita or Efe.

The pain in Efe's stomach came and went in waves, peaking and dipping at irregular intervals. She said no to pain relief. She wanted to feel it all, as if in expiation of this pregnancy that had marred her life, marked her out as a loose girl. She wished she could insert her hand inside the womb and drag out this baby who was causing her to writhe so much in agony. Rita sat by her on the bed as soon as the doctor left and cried along with her sister when the pain became too much for Efe to bear. When Efe cussed the "evil child" who was the cause of all her pain, Rita told her to stop, for everyone knew it was taboo to cuss a baby who had its head half into the world. It was bad luck.

"Just try and bear, Efe, you hear? Just try. It'll soon be over. You're doing great. It'll soon be over. You hear?"

Thirteen hours later, when Efe shrieked her son into the world, it was Rita who stood beside her, holding her hand and crying softly as the slimy baby with a headful of hair was laid on Efe's chest. Exhausted beyond words, she left it up to Rita to name her son. Rita, uninspired and emotional, named him Lucky. Perhaps in light of the fact that her sister was lucky she was there for her. Or that the child was lucky to be born. Or perhaps it was simply her wish for her new nephew that he be lucky in life. Afterward, when Efe had recovered and was in better spirits, she would rename him Ikponwosa, Titus's middle name.

The baby was shriveled and small, with scaly dry skin that made her think uncharitably of a reptile. He was about the ugliest thing she had ever set eyes on, and she could not believe she had birthed him. Still, he was her responsibility and needed looking after. Efe did not like the thought of it much, but she was ready to face up to her responsibilities with a maturity that she felt motherhood required. She would look after him, but she thought she would need help from Titus. Babies required things; they needed food and diapers and clothing and medicine. Her father's housekeeping money could not stretch to cover those.

The day she left the hospital, she resolved to get Titus involved in the upkeep of his son. After all, men wanted sons no matter how many they had. Sons were trophies they collected to carry on the family name. Efe knew that Titus had children—he had mentioned them a few times, complaining good-humoredly of how much sending them to a good school cost, how well they were doing in their good school where fees were not paid in the local currency. "Only dollars and pound sterling accepted!" He had money, so one more child should not make a difference.

He could send their baby to a good school, give him everything Efe could never imagine giving him. And so it was that three weeks after she had Ikponwosa, she dressed him up in blue pajamas that covered his toes, wrapped a cream shawl around him, and went to Titus's house on the other side of town. She planned her arrival for the time of day when Titus was likely to be home. She had not seen him since she told him she was pregnant. She wanted to talk to him, to present his son to him. A Titus in miniature, for even at three weeks there was no denying that father and son bore a resemblance that would only get more striking with time. She did not want much: just enough to look after this baby, who ate a lot and was the spitting image of his father. She wanted him to grow, away from the slum she was raised in. Titus had enough money to ensure that.

When Efe was shown in by a maid, husband and wife were eating a supper of *eba* and *egusi* soup. The not-so-old wife had just dunked a lump of *eba* into the communal soup bowl when the maid said, "Somebody to see *oga*." The wife brought out the lump, raising her head at the same time to see the somebody. She took a look at the bundle of cream and blue asleep in Efe's arms and gave a half smile. Titus said nothing, and neither invited Efe to sit. She sat anyway, sinking into the nearest couch. Now she was here, faced with a Titus who gave no sign of recognition, her throat dried up and she felt the urge to cough. The baby woke up and started to cry, and she shushed him. "Hush, hush. Don't cry." She cradled the baby into quietness and said, before she lost her courage, "I brought your baby, Titus."

Titus concentrated on his *eba*, extracting a fish bone that had attached itself to the lump he was about to throw down his throat. It was as if he had not heard her, as if she were not even there. It was his wife who washed her hands in the basin of water beside her, dried her hands on her wrapper, and stood up without her bones creaking, *krak krak*. She walked over to Efe and planted herself before the younger girl. "You." She pointed a finger at the girl. "You come into my house and accuse my husband of fathering your baby. How dare you? Eh? How. Dare. You?" Her voice was soft, and the half smile of before stayed on her lips, so that Efe thought perhaps it was no smile at all but something else. A sneer. Or something worse.

"Useless girl. *Ashawo*. May a thousand fleas invade your pubic hair. Useless goat. Shameless whore, *ashawo*. Just take a look at yourself. Small girl like you, what were you doing with man? At your age, what were you doing spreading your legs for a man, eh? Which girl from a good home goes around sleeping with a man who is old enough to be her father, eh? Answer me, you useless idiot. I see you can't talk anymore. You have gone dumb, *abi*? And you have the guts to show your face. You were not afraid to come into my home with that *thing* in your hands, eh? You were not scared to ring my doorbell and show your face, eh? Now I am going to shut my eyes, and before I open them, I want both you and that bastard of yours out of my home."

Even without looking at Titus, Efe knew that he was still eating. She could hear him smacking his lips as he sucked bone marrow. She got up and slowly walked out.

Lucky Ikponwosa would never see his father again.

What Efe had not known, for who would tell her, was that she was the sixth woman in as many years to come to Titus with an offspring from an affair. And all six the wife had dismissed in more or less the same way, marching them to the door with orders never to return, asking the house help to bolt the door behind them.

From the day she married Titus and caught him looking at her chief bridesmaid with a glint in his eye, she had known that he had a roving eye. As long as women swayed their hips at him, he would go to them, a drooling dog in heat. It was not his fault; it was just the way he was created. She could live with it. He could have his women. Have their children, even. She had no problem with that. What she had a problem with, though, was the women turning up with their children and expecting him to take care of them.

Titus, this is your baby. I'm not looking for marriage, just for you to help with upkeep.

Titus, here is your son. He needs to know his father.

Titus, this. Titus, that. Well, she was having none of that.

When she met Titus, he was just finishing his apprenticeship to a car parts salesman with a shop in Ladipo, but his heart was not in spare parts. He complained that there was no joy in it, but the parts man was one of the wealthiest men from his village, and to have made the money he made, he must have business knowledge enough to spare. It was that—the knowledge of how to make money—Titus wanted to milk, so he had jumped at the chance of living with the man for five years, working in his shop and learning the secret of his success firsthand.

In his first year of marriage, his apprenticeship was done, and even though his former master gave him some money, as was customary, to start his own business in car parts, he had thrown his lot in with a man—another just-graduated apprentice with big ideas—and they pooled resources. They brainstormed and agreed that money was in women; their logic was that even a man who would not spend money on himself would spend it on a woman. They started by importing wigs—shiny, glossy wigs they hoped to sell to all the Lagos women dying for good hair without the trouble of going to a salon. It had not done as well as they had hoped. They had huge competition from Aba and Onitsha traders who imported wigs from Korea and sold them at much cheaper rates than they sold theirs. So they invested a huge chunk of what was left of their capital into skin-lightening creams. Lagos men loved light-skinned women; this was sure to be a winner. But their shipment of *Yellow Skin toning lotion*, with its promise of "noticeably lighter skin in fourteen days guaranteed or your money back," arrived with half its contents broken and the unbroken half sullied by lotion. They spent five days and three thousand naira on cleaning the dirtied jars. Titus's business partner would see this as a warning sign that worse was in store for them if they stayed together, and he would pull out, preferring to cut his losses. But Titus was the sort of man who persevered, especially if he was convinced he was right. That was one of the lessons he picked up from his former master: "Never give up if your heart and your head tell you that you are right. People can disappoint you, but your heart and your head never will. Make them your best friends."

Titus was still certain he could become rich by concentrating on women. There was nothing flawed in the logic that had attracted him to a business that targeted women in the first place. He was also certain that his partner was a fool for pulling out before they had struck gold. He only had to find something that pandered enough to women's vanity to make him wealthy. His wife remained patient, counting pennies while he dreamed up one unsuccessful scheme after another, rubbing his tense muscles at night, telling him, "It'll be okay. It'll be okay, don't worry about it, eh. Just don't worry about it."

He discovered the lacuna in the human-hair business quite by accident in his bed. He said it came to him in a dream, a sort of vision. A deep biblical voice instructed him to go to India and import the finest hair Lagos had ever seen. Not even his wife knew if this was true, if the vision was a tale he had made up. But he had gone to India and returned after eleven weeks, gaunt and hungry for some *proper* food. Close on his feet, a container full of hair extensions followed. "The rest, as they say, is history" was how his wife always concluded the narration of their rags-to-riches story. She was beside him when they bought their first car. She went with him when he consulted an architect to draw up plans for their house, saying how many rooms she wanted, where she wanted the kitchen, the playroom. She stood beside him when the foundation of their new home was laid. And when the house was finally ready, she bought the furniture and curtains. She was not about to let any other woman lay claim to the fruit of her patience. None would share the money she had waited so patiently and so good-humoredly for Titus to make. It was her right and her children's legacy, so she guarded it jealously. He could have his women—honey always attracted bees—but the bees had to remain in their hives and keep their young with them. The honey jar was hers to keep, and she intended to do so, encircling it with two hands to keep it close to her heart.

Titus, for his part, let his wife get away with chasing his out-of-wedlock children out of the house. He was grateful to her for staying with him when he'd had nothing, steeped deep in a penury that he could only fantasize about escaping. Many women would have left for less. Besides, he appreciated having a wife who did not nag him about where he had been, whom he had been with. What man wanted to come home to a nagging woman? She accepted him for who he was, and he knew well enough to be thankful for that.

So when the seeds of his trysts sprouted and were collected by their mothers who came knocking at his door, he let his wife handle them. She had earned that right. And if sometimes his mind wandered to those children he would never get to know, he showed no signs of it.

EFE FELT SHE OUGHT TO HATE HER BABY; AFTER ALL, SHE'D NEVER asked for him. He kept her at home and was a visible sign that she was damaged goods. Now there was very little hope of marriage to a rich man rescuing her from the pit she lived in. *Which kin' man go marry woman wey don get pikin already?* If the man who got you pregnant did not want you, there was no chance of any other person doing so. Her mother would be disappointed. Her mother, who always said she would make a good wife. "You were born a wife," she told this daughter of hers who did not think anything of getting up early to help her mother with breakfast. "Some women, they enter marriages half-formed. They need to be honed. But you are perfect. You will enter marriage already finished." There was no way that would happen now. She would never be the perfect wife her mother had hoped for her. She could not be revirgined. Could never be unpregnant. She was chipped.

At the beginning, Efe had good days and bad days. On the bad days, she woke to a dreary blankness that did not clear no matter how bright the sun shone. On those days, her baby wailed constantly and she wished she had never met Titus. Her head screamed at her to hate their baby. On the good days, her baby gurgled and smiled and the world was right. As the weeks wore on, the good days became more and the bad days receded. It was not long before she realized that, try as she might, she could not hate her baby. She forgot the pain of delivering him. Forgot that she had not planned to have him. Forgot the humiliation at Titus's house. She forged new memories with the baby that had nothing to do with before he was born. When he cried, she rushed to soothe him, cooing to him, "Don't cry, my child, don't cry, your mommy is here," until he stopped. She let him drool all over her and waited with excitement for the first tooth to cut through at five months. When he got ill from cutting the tooth, she held his hands and talked to him until she ran out of what to say, and then she fell quiet and prayed for his fever to break. She cried when her milk thinned and she could no longer breast-feed him at six months. She loved him, astounding herself with the force of her love. She thought she now knew why women went on to have more and more children. It was easy to forget the pain associated with the de-livery. She delighted in the solidity of this child whom she had brought into the world and often would pick him up just to convince herself that he was there, that he had not gone up in smoke. *Jus' to be sure him never disappear like money-doubler trick.*

Efe was still determined to provide her son with the kind of life she had dreamed for him when she thought she would be able to get Titus's help. Every morning before she went to her cleaning job at an office in GRA, she whispered in her son's ear so that only he could hear, "I promise you, I shall get you out of here. I don't care how I do it." She had never been more serious about anything else in her en-tire life.

Everybody called the baby L.I., the initials of his name, because his grandfather, in one of his clearer moments, had come out of his drunken stupor to announce that was what he was to be known as. "All this business of two names will only lead to trouble. Giving a child a mouthful of a name is incurring the wrath of the gods. It is a big name that kills a dog."

And although neither Efe nor Rita understood his speech, they never referred to the baby as Lucky Ikponwosa again.

Renaming the baby was about the only time Efe's father showed an interest in the plump baby who was always crying at night. The only other time had been the day Efe came back from the hospital with him. Her father had slurred that had their mother been alive, she never would have let Efe bring a bastard child into their home and that not a penny of his was to go toward the boy. "I cannot be raising my children and be raising another man's child, too, you hear that? There is only so much trial a man can bear in this world."

L.I. grew and his mother worked to provide for him, cleaning first one office and then a second. She left early, before her son woke up, and by the time she came back he had worn himself out from playing and was winding down, ready to end his day. Left in the care of her sister, Efe did not see enough of him, and it pained her, so she took to praying. She prayed for longer hours in a day. And then she prayed for more work so she could save enough, soon enough, to take a break. It was only the second prayer that got answered.

She was going home at the end of a working day, seated at the back of an *okada*, weaving through Lagos traffic, her arms around the cyclist, when she spotted an advertisement for a cleaning woman for an office on Randle Avenue. Randle Avenue was close to the location of her second job, and she was sure she could juggle all three. Three jobs meant more money, more bonuses, which equaled a better life for L.I. A better life for L.I. totaled a happier life for her.

She begged the cyclist to take her to Randle Avenue instead. If he hurried, she might still be able to make it to Dele and Sons Limited: Import-Export Specialists before the closing time of 6:30 P.M. The bearded cyclist with the bandanna said she had to pay more money.

"No problem," she answered. "Just get me there as quick as you can."

He asked her to hold him lower around his waist, as getting to Randle Avenue before 6:30 required his "James Bond moves." She moved her hands to the area around his belly button, but he asked her to move lower and to hold him tighter to ensure she did not fall off the bike. Efe did not argue, willing him on to her third job. She held him tight, hid her face from the wind by placing her head in the small of his back, and tried to stay on while he swerved and revved, meandering through traffic, avoiding potholes and almost knocking down a bread hawker.

She was glad to make it to Randle Avenue in one piece, though slightly shaken. The man's James Bond moves had involved riding at top speed and with total disregard for other road users, especially pedestrians. Many times during the ride, Efe was sure she was going to be thrown off the back of the bike or that they would ride under a moving truck and that would be the end of her, a mass of bones and flesh flattened under the wheels of a truck carrying crates of soft drink. She could not decide which was the worse prospect of the two. Which would mean a more merciful death? At some point she had begged, "Softly, softly, *oga*. Don't go too fast, please." But either her words had gotten lost in the medley of honking and hawkers calling and people raining abuse from open windows, or the cyclist had chosen to ignore her. In any case, he rode just as hard until he had deposited her in front of her destination.

"Shall I wait for you?" he asked Efe, his engine still running. He had one leg resting on the ground, the other foot on the pedal, but she'd had enough of him. Besides, she had no idea how long she would be there for, and *okada* fare mounted if a cyclist had to wait. So she dismissed him and said a quick prayer before walking into the building.

The office was still open, and Efe was interviewed on the spot by a man three times the size of Titus, who would become her new employer, and who, despite the "and Sons" attached to the name of his company, seemed to be the only one working there.

"Do you know how to use a vacuum cleaner?" the man wheezed, to which Efe said, "Yes, sir."

It was the default answer she gave to all his other wheezed questions. "Can you be here every Thursday?" "Can you get here before seven A.M.?" "Do you live close by?" "Are you a hard worker?" Had he asked her if she could fly, she would have replied just as enthusiastically as she did to the other questions, "Yes, sir! Of course I can fly."

Dele would also turn out to be the most generous of her three bosses, giving her huge bonuses at holidays.

He often complimented her, noticing when she had her hair done, when she looked worn out, or when she had a new outfit on. When she mentioned that she had a nine-month-old son, he exclaimed that she did not look like a mother, telling her she must be one of the lucky women whose stomachs were like rubber bands: No matter how hard they were stretched, they snapped back into shape. He inquired cautiously if she had a husband. Or a boyfriend. Anybody waiting for her at home?

"No. The papa of my son no wan' sabi him. We no sabi him, too." She dismissed Titus and any claims he might lay on the boy later, had he been interested. "I no get anyone," she added, head bent, eyes down. She hoped she had given enough hints that she was available but not loose, the sort of girl he could have an affair with but treat with respect at the same time. And, if she played her cards right, even marry. She did not have anything left over from what she'd saved while she was with Titus. And the money she made working just about paid for L.I.'s necessities. She did not want to be reduced to the sort of girl who went around with just any man for money. The sort of girl, like so many she knew, who went with carpenters and car mechanics for a bit of cash. She might have had a baby outside wedlock, but it did not mean she was cheap. She could still pick, and Dele seemed the type of guy to give his girlfriend a munificent allowance. The type to give L.I. everything she hoped for him and more. The sort of man to see that she got a break from the scrimping and the cleaning and the tiredness that were taking over her life.

But try as she might, Dele never asked her out, and it was not until seven months later, when she started to complain about finding a good nursery school for L.I. so that Rita could go back to school, that Dele asked if she would like to go abroad. "Belgium. A country wey dey Europe. Next door to London."

He made it sound as if you could walk from Belgium to London. From one door to the next.

Had he not started talking seriously about payment, an installment plan to repay the debt, of her sharing a house with other "Nigerian women" being looked after by a friend of his, she would not have believed that he had not asked her the question in jest, that he had not dangled the idea in front of her like a wicked adult might dangle food in front of a hungry child, keeping it always out of reach but close enough to be seen and smelled.

"If I wan' go abroad, Oga Dele? Anybody dey ask pikin if de pikin wan' sweet?"

Who did not want to go abroad? People were born with the ambition, and people died trying to fulfill that ambition. Was it not just the week before that the cyclist whose *okada* she had boarded told her of the Nigerian man who died at the airport in some abroad country he could not pronounce because the bags of cocaine he swallowed had burst in his stomach? "Sister, dem say the man face come swell like dis and he jus' fall dead!" the cyclist said, demonstrating with his hands how the head had swelled, so that Efe had to ask him to please keep his hands on the bike, she still had a long life ahead of her. "If you are tired of life, take only yourself out of it. Leave innocent people alone, *abeg*," she pleaded.

People knew the risks and people took them, because the destination was worth it. What was it the song said? *Nigeria jaga jaga. Everytin' scatter scatter*. Nobody wanted to stay back unless they had pots of money to survive the country. People like Titus and Dele.

She had agreed to Dele's terms before she asked what she was expected to do abroad. "Clean?" To which Dele laughed and said, "No. Sales." It was the way he sized her up, his eyes going from her face to her breasts to her calves under her knee-length skirt, that told her what sort of sales she was going to be involved in. She would be Dele and Sons Limited's export. L.I. would get a better life. Go to good schools, become a big shot, and look after her when she was old and tired. L.I. was a worthy enough investment to encourage her to accept Dele's offer. And even though leaving him would be the hardest thing she would ever do, she would endure it for his sake.

When she got home that night, Rita was already in bed but not yet asleep. Efe called her into the kitchen. "I have something to tell you," she said as she went ahead of her sister and drew a kitchen stool to sit on. Her dinner was still in the pot on the table from under which the stool came. She ignored it. There would be time enough for food. Cleaning three offices always tired her legs. She sat gratefully, with her back to the gas cooker, and Rita stood in front of her, blocking the door.

"Rita," she began, her voice already acquiring a tone that was at once distant but warm, the way it would sound on the telephone when she would call home to ask about L.I., "I am leaving Lagos." She stopped and started again, as if searching for lost words, mindful of not saying the wrong thing. "I am going abroad." The word "abroad" brought a smile that stretched her lips from one end to the other and a sweet taste to her tongue, a taste not unlike that of very ripe plantain. "I'm going to Europe. Belgium."

Before Rita had a chance to ask her how and where, Efe preempted her and said, "Close to London. Next door to London." She repeated Dele's phrase, seeing in her mind's eye two big doors one beside the other, with BELGIUM marked on one and LONDON marked on the other. Belgium's proximity to London suggested that it was like London. Everybody knew London. Had sung London in rhymes while playing in dust-covered front yards, clapping to its tune:

London Bridge is falling down
Falling down
Falling down
London Bridge is falling down
My fair laaaaaaaadddyyyyyyy
Pussycat, Pussycat
Where have you been?
I have been to London to see the queen.

"A man has promised me a job in Belgium."

The sound of it thrilled her. Belgium. *Bell. Jyom.* Something that tinkled and ushered in dawn, clear as glass.

"My boss. *Oga* Dele. The kind one. You remember him, *abi?* The one who gave me extra five hundred naira at Christmas. He'll get me a job. In Belgium." Her voice fell. "He says a woman can earn easy money there. They like black women there." A pause. She did not look at Rita. "He says before I know it, before one year even, I'll be rich. I'll buy a Mercedes-Benz!"

Dele had not exactly told her that, but sitting on the bike on her way home, Efe had dreamed up the riches she would amass and had calculated that she would be able to afford a Mercedes by the time she had spent a year working. As for liking black women, Dele had told her they were in great demand by white men tired of their women and wanting a bit of color and spice. She would not tell her other siblings; they were too young to deal with the truth. They were still at the age when the world was either black or white. They would be told that Efe was going abroad to live with a rich family and work as kitchen help. She would make lots of money and send them to school. And for a very long time, they believed it and told anybody who cared to listen that they had a sister living in London—for nobody had heard of Belgium—cleaning homes and making pots of money for them.

To her father, she would say simply that she was going abroad to live for a few years. It would have been impossible to tell him the truth, even if he had been a different sort of father, even if he had been the sort of father to insist on knowing how his teenage daughter was getting the money to travel abroad and, once there, how she was going to live. Rita, practically a woman herself and blossoming in more ways than one, would understand. She would not judge Efe. And if there was one human being into whose care she could entrust L.I., it was Rita, who had always been there for him, from the very beginning. She knew she was right when Rita's response was a hug and a whispered, "Get me a Mercedes, too."

In fact, in the thirteen years Efe would be abroad, Rita would become such a mother to L.I. that whatever memories he had of Efe would be replaced by those of the rounder Rita. Rita would let him sit beside her as she cooked. She would take him along with her when she went to the market. When he got taunted by the neighborhood children who called him a bastard, it was Rita who comforted him and told him he was no bastard, he was a child whose father was dead. When he asked what sort of man his father had been, Rita would tell him that he was a rich, strong man, better than the fathers of the boys who laughed at him and called him the bastard son of an unmarried woman. It was Rita who explained to him that sometimes his grandfather came back loud and angry because he had been given a cross huger than he was able to carry, and he, L.I., was not to pay any attention to the man. And when L.I. started school and his teachers asked for his mother, Rita would be the one to go, asking how he was doing at school, was he well behaved? If there was any scolding to be done, Rita would be the one to dish it out, telling him, "Your mother is working hard to pay your fees, and this is how you repay her?"

L.I. would call Rita Mommy. And the first time he would see his real mother again, in a crowded Lagos airport, he would look to Rita for confirmation that indeed Efe, and not she, was the woman who had brought him into this world. It would be Rita who would nudge him forward, a boy on the cusp of manhood with a headful of dark oiled hair, and whisper in his ear that his mother would appreciate a smile, a hug, some recognition.

Efe was the last to leave the plane. She had flown Iberia through Barcelona. Dele told her that before, she could have taken Sabena straight to Brussels, direct, but Sabena had gone out of business. Iberia was the one everyone used these days, he said, because it was cheaper and gave more luggage allowance. Air France was the one to avoid, he advised, as if Efe were thinking of going home the very next day and the information was pertinent. Air France was very strict with its luggage allowance. "Dem no go let you carry even one kilo extra," Dele said. KLM, apparently, was the one you wanted if you did not get Iberia. "You fit beg for excess luggage." It did not make any difference to Efe. All the worldly belongings that she was interested in taking along could be contained in a plastic bag, leaving just enough room for the sadness she felt at having to leave L.I. behind. But the baggage allowance mattered to Dele, obviously, because on the day Efe was to leave, he brought two big suitcases packed full of food he said Efe had to deliver to the woman who would be looking after her: smoked fish and peanuts and palm oil sealed in a tin to avoid detection. "Dem no dey like make we dey bring palm oil, but you no go get good palm oil from there. She dey miss Nigerian food. Very soon you go begin miss am, too." Efe was certain she would not.

The only luggage of worth she carried was in her head. A strong memory of L.I. holding on to Rita, crying as Efe walked through security at the Lagos airport. Rita had said not to bring him to the airport, it would be better to leave him at home, but Efe had insisted. She wanted her son with her for as long as possible. She wanted to soak in the smell of his skin after he'd had a shower. And right up until she had to hand him over to Rita, she'd had her nose buried in his hair, where the scent was the strongest. She wanted to take the smell and store it where she could have easy access to it. She believed she would never forget that smell, but before she had been in Belgium three weeks, life would take over and she would struggle to remember the smell amid all the other ones suffusing the space around her. But on the plane, still far away from Antwerp and her customers, Efe remembered the smell and saw her child before her eyes and cried in a way she believed she never would again. Losing her mother had been hard; losing her son, even if temporarily, was worse. She hoped she would never have to cry like that again for as long as she lived. She was wrong. In the sixty-eight years she lived, she would find out that there were things far worse than leaving behind a child whom you hoped to see again.

Efe got off the plane feeling older than she was. Her knees hurt and her ears ached. The flight had not been as pleasant as she had thought it would be. She had always imagined that being on a plane, flying high above God's own earth, would feel a bit like flying with your own wings. She'd always imagined that people in planes felt free, like gods who claimed the skies. But the experience for her had been anything but. She felt trapped in her seat beside a window that was so small it did not qualify to be called as such. It was a night flight, so she had been unable to see anything but the taillights of the plane whenever she looked out the window. The air was cold and felt used up, like secondhand air, and it made Efe slightly nauseated. The times she went to relieve herself, she felt claustrophobic in the toilet. And unlike in the buses back home, there was no one to chat with. The man beside her slept right through the dinner of potatoes and salad. *And de dinner sef, na wahala.* White people might be good at a lot of things, but their culinary skills left a lot to be desired: *No pepper. No salt. No oil. How can they call this food? It's like eating sandpaper,* she thought, leveling the mashed potato on her plastic airline fork with a knife.

It was a long walk to the baggage claim, where she had to go for the Samsonite suitcases, but the floors were shiny and the air was purer, so she skipped, skipped, skipped, and took in the first sights of her new world. Belgium. *Bell. Jyum.* Next door to London. Tinkling like a bell.

SISI

THE DAY SISI LEFT LAGOS, IT RAINED. IT WAS NOT AN AUSPICIOUS DAY for traveling ("Rain, rain, go away, come again another day!" a mother and her three young children sang as they waited to board the plane), but the rain had not bothered Sisi at all. She stood at a window and watched the rain tripping the light fantastic, glistening on the tarmac with a phosphorescence that seemed to be for her alone: a glowlike halo that reminded her of the vision that had been seen for her. Assuring her that she was doing the right thing. The only thing she could. It was to her Prophecy that she was headed. A Prophecy she now believed in, not with the wounded faith of her father but with a faith that was so total it left no room for doubt, not even a hairline crack. If she stayed back, if she let this chance slip, she would only be giving life the go-ahead to treat her dreams with derision, the same as it had done with her parents'.

There was her father. He worked in the Ministry of Works. A civil servant, he had imagined that one day he would be able to buy a car, a secondhand Peugeot 504, but apart from a pay raise in his first year, his salary had remained static even as the prices of everything else rose. He could never afford a car. Especially now that President Obasanjo had put an import embargo on cars older than five years. (Hot on the heels of his wife banning a certain type of lace she wanted exclusively for herself. "That president *sef*! While people are busy killing each other in senseless riots, he is busy banning the importation of everything. Toothpaste. Chloroquine for malaria. Soaps. Detergents. Envelopes. How am I ever supposed to buy a car? We thought we were suffering under Abacha. This is worse! At least a military dictatorship did not hide under the cover of democracy. This is worse." He could never buy a car. He could never buy a decent house. He could never earn enough to fulfill his dreams.) His predicament weighed on his shoulders and resulted in a stoop that belied his fortysomething years. He walked like a man in his eighties, shuffling, head bent, perpetually searching for the dot on the ground that would either signal a change in his fortune or widen and eat him up whole, obliterating him from the earth. He never looked people in the face when he spoke, raising his head only a few inches, so that mostly people had to ask him to repeat himself.

Her mother had had her own dream of being a landlady, of owning a house in Ikoyi, a Lagos suburb she had eyed ever since she set foot in the city that her new groom had told her had towers that grazed the skies. (She, with the brazenness of a new bride, had squealed, "How can? There can never be houses that high! I don't believe you." But it turned out to be true. Her new husband had taken her around Lagos, hopping on and off *danfo* buses to gaze at the high wonders that Lagos had in abundance. The truth of the high towers had solidified her trust in her husband, and her certainty that he would fulfill the promise of getting her into a better house in Ikoyi.) She had in her head the plan of the house she was going to own. A duplex with a wide garage and a fenced lawn. Behind, there would be a boys' quarters with two rooms for her maids. She dreamed of being rescued from the Ogba flat from which they eked out their daily existence, sandwiched between Mama Iyabo with the rolls of flesh under her chin and the brood of six children to their left and the white-wearing, churchgoing young couple to their right. She had cosseted dreams of having her own bathroom, her own kitchen, her own toilet, and three rooms since the day Godwin married her and brought her from her village, Oba, to Lagos. He had promised her that the flat was a temporary arrangement until he got a promotion. "I shall whisk you off to become a landlady. We cannot have a family here. We cannot raise children here. We need a house of our own. A big house, with separate bedrooms for each of the children. We cannot have a baby here."

But a year later, their daughter had come. And twenty-four years later, they were still there, their daughter having to sleep in the sitting room. Mama Chisom had nurtured the dreams through the years, nursing them and drawing them out to comfort her on days when she felt tears spring to her eyes for no reason at all, finally watching them flail and plunge weightless onto the cement floor of their flat. "No leave, no transfer," she often told her husband these days, laughing at the dreams she had dared to have. These days when she laughed, her laughter sounded like it was being dredged from behind her throat rather than from the stomach, which is where laughter comes from. And as for children, after Chisom no more babies had agreed to take root. It was as if something within her expelled them, and month after month she suffered the low-waist pain of menstruation. "It is just as well," she said when her husband was not within earshot. He missed not having a son and would say whenever they had a quarrel that every man had a right to a son, as if it were due to a shortcoming on her part that he had failed to have one. On days when his temper was up, he would tell her that if he could afford it he would have married a second wife, someone whose womb was more receptive to sons. Sons might have changed his fortune.

He would be quieted only by Chisom's mother reminding him of the Prophecy. "Do not forget the Prophecy!" By 2005 even that was no longer enough to soothe his apoplectic rant. His faith in the Prophecy had become wounded, his belief in it tried by time.

The memory of her mother's behind-the-throat laughter and her father's anger at life's unfairness would accompany Sisi on the days she went walking and her housemates wondered where she'd got to, why she would not let anyone go with her. And when she would receive her first epiphany, it would be of her parents that she would think. Of their dreams, so intertwined with hers that there was no separating them.

ZWART

ZWARTEZUSTERSTRAAT

NONE OF THEM CAN SAY HOW LONG THEY HAVE BEEN SITTING THERE, huddled together on the couch as if seeking the heat of one another's bodies, listening to Efe's story usurp the silence. Their arms touch, and the fight of before is all but forgotten. Joyce's rag is balled up in her fist.

Efe says she wishes she could see L.I. She says that when she talks to him on the phone it's like talking to a stranger, and that bothers her. "He's polite and all, but I always feel like he wants to get off the phone, that he'd much rather be somewhere else." She says that she is worried that L.I. does not see her as his mother, even though Rita once told her on the phone that he carries her picture to school, the picture of her in snow boots that she had sent home her first winter in Belgium. "But in that photo, I'm all covered up and you can't even make out my face. All you see is snow," she complains to the women. "Maybe he just wants the photo for the snow. I sure say na de snow wey dey sweet am." She laughs, emitting a sound like the engine of a car spluttering to life and then spluttering out.

Joyce says she never would have guessed Efe had a child. "Your stomach is still very flat!"

"Oh, but I do," Efe answers. She opens up her wallet and fishes out a tattered passport-size picture of a boy whose face is half covered by a cap. "I'm his mother," she says, passing the picture to Joyce. Joyce says, "Wow. Good-looking boy!" Efe smiles her gratitude and concurrence. Joyce takes the picture from Efe and holds it out to Ama.

"Having a child, that's a big thing. It's a big deal. How could you even think of having that baby when neither you nor the father wanted him?" Ama asks. "Why would you want to fuck up a kid's life?"

"I didn't want to *fuck* up anyone's life, Ama!" Efe responds. "I was a kid. And let me tell you, I don't for one second, not for a single second, regret having L.I. He gives my life meaning." She hastily pushes the picture back into her purse.

"Some meaning he gives it!"

"Ladies, please. Not today." Joyce tries to restore peace. She wrings the duster in her hands.

"Fuck off, all of you," Ama says, and lights another cigarette. She gets up and starts pacing the room, the tip of her cigarette glowing an angry cherry.

Efe hisses.

And Ama hisses.

And Joyce hisses.

Then silence.

Inhale. Exhale. The neon cherry of the cigarette dims. Ama stops pacing. "You really don't regret your son?"

"No. Never. Everything I do is for him." The love in Efe's voice is palpable; they can almost see it in the room. A soft, glowing love with angel wings and a cherub face.

Ama's jealousy is so visceral that it claws at her chest. She rubs a thumb against her cross. Says, "He's a lucky child." She lights another cigarette and takes a long drag. Efe and Joyce look at Ama. "What the fuck are you looking at me like that for?" She shuts her eyes. Brings the cigarette to her lips. When she pulls it away, she blows a delicate ring that glides across the room. No one says a word.

The silence is lugubrious. Time moves slowly. By and by the women get hungry. However, no one wants to suggest food at a time like this, even though it is probably gone midday and they have not even had breakfast. They hadn't had the time to go to the bakery before the news of Sisi's murder came and soured the day that the weather forecast had said would be dry and sunny. Not a day for dying.

It is not appropriate that they should talk about food when they are supposed to be grieving. The sorrow is supposed to take away your appetite, take precedence over food. It would be unseemly for one of them to go to the kitchen and start cooking. Even Madam seems to understand this, so she did not bother to ask any of them to cook before she left, her cigarette held tightly between her fingers as though she wanted to snap it in two. She left incense burning on a stand in the middle of the room, smoke fluttering weakly from it.

"Back home in Nigeria," it occurs to Efe, and she says this out loud, "neighbors would have gathered to cry with us. Nobody will let you cry alone!"

Here their grief has to be contained within the four walls of their flat. No matter how large it becomes for them, they must not let it swell and crack the walls. Efe recalls when her mother died. Neighbors had come to cry with them. Their mother's sister had come to live with them for two weeks, helping with the cooking and the cleaning. After she went back to Warri, where she lived, the neighbors had taken over, cooking and looking after the family, even helping with the laundry and shopping, until her father's drink made him obnoxious and difficult to help. He took umbrage at the neighbors' help, sometimes shouting at them that he did not need their pity, his dead wife was three times the women they were. He screamed at them, "Get away from my family. Get out of my home. I don't want you near my children. Witches."

The women shut their ears to him, saying, "Poor man, he can't handle his wife's death. Her death has broken him into pieces, he is not who he used to be. Poor Papa Efe."

So they ignored him and kept coming with their offerings of food and companionship, which the children were grateful for, having been left with a father who was drinking more and more. Efe tells the women now of how the father broke a neighbor's plate, flinging across the wall the rice and chicken stew the woman had brought, laughing all the while, the *caw caw caw* of a deranged hyena. The neighbor had picked up her plate, broken neatly into two equal halves as if by design, complaining while she did that not even the loss of a wife gave a man the right to throw kindness back into his neighbor's face. That plate had been one of the woman's favorites: expensive china edged in silver. "Go to Tejuosho and ask how much a plate like this costs," she yelled above the manic laughter of Efe's father. Efe had gotten the task of wiping the rich stew off the wall, tears of red and green flowing down the cream walls. There was spinach in the stew. The green came off easily, but the red stayed. "And is still there even as I speak."

The neighbors had stayed away after that. "But it was all my father's fault. Nobody will ever let you mourn alone back home."

Ama and Joyce say it's true. Nobody cries alone back home.

"Me, I dey feel for her family, *sha*," Efe says. "To lose a pikin go hard!"

Joyce unfurls her rag and, leaning forward, starts rubbing at a spot on the table in front of her.

SISI

WHEN SHE GOT OFF THE PLANE IN BRUSSELS, THE REMNANTS OF HER old life folded away in her carry-on luggage, and saw her new life stretching out like a multicolored vista before her eyes, full of colors and promise, she knew she would make it here. She left the pumpkin her mother had insisted she carry at the airport in Lagos. Dumped it, together with any misgivings she had about her trip, in one of the huge dustbins outside the washrooms. Lagos was a city of death, and she was escaping it. She should not carry a pumpkin the size of the moon along with her. Or doubts that could make her back down. True, she liked pumpkin, and it crossed her mind that she might not find any in this place she was moving to. ("White people eat only bread. Drink only tea. *Eiya!* You are going to die of starvation." The neighbor had sounded almost happy at the thought of Chisom's demise from hunger in the white man's land.) But she would learn to like other things, find substitutes for the things that would no longer be easily available to her. She would shed her skin like a snake and emerge completely new. It would all be worth it.

The flight landed at night, so she saw nothing of Belgium but lights (working streetlights at the sides of roads!) as the reticent man who met her at the airport drove her to Antwerp and deposited her in a house on a narrow gloomy street. She had thought at first that its

gloominess was attributable to the darkness, but in the morning she
found out how wrong she was. The Zwartezusterstraat wore the look
of a much-maligned childless wife in a polygamous home. No
amount of light could lift it from the gloom into which it had settled,
gloom that would only deepen with time, given the events that would
happen there.

The house itself was not much to look at. Truth be told, it was
quite a disappointment, really. A ground-floor flat with a grubby front
door and, as she would find out later, five bedrooms not much bigger
than telephone booths. The sitting room was a cliché. An all-red affair except for the long sofa, which was black and against the wall
right beside the door; a single thin mirror ran from the ceiling to the
rug. Sisi often thought that had she been asked to draw that room, she
would have drawn exactly that, down to the mirror. The only thing
she would have left out would have been the incense, which Madam
burned nonstop, believing totally in its ability to rid the world of all
evil.

Sisi was shown into a sardonic room with a single bed dressed up
in impossibly white sheets. The whiteness shone bright, astonishing
her. She ran her hands over the sheets, feeling the softness of the cotton, reveling in the richness of the texture. The walls were red, the
same blood red of the sitting room. And on them hung two pictures:
a white girl lying on her back, naked with legs splayed in a tanned V.
She sucked on a lollipop. The other picture was of an enormous pair
of brown buttocks jutting out at the camera. Buttocks with no face,
two meticulously molded clay pots. Sisi wondered for a minute whose
they were, those firm, wide buttocks, unmarked by stretch marks. She
wondered if her buttocks looked like that. And for a moment she felt
slightly self-conscious.

The man who had driven her from the airport—Segun, she now
knew was his name—had not said much since they got in. He had
just uttered his name haltingly, like a sacrifice being dragged out of

him, and ushered her into the room. "Some . . . some . . . bo . . . bo . . . somebody, I mean, somebody wi . . . ll be with you soon." Sisi noticed that when he stammered, he tapped his left foot on the tile floor and clasped and unclasped his hands as if the words he could not articulate were in there, hiding from him. *Busy hands*, she thought. She remembered her mother telling a newly married niece that she had made a good choice marrying a man who could not keep his hands still, a man who, even as he sat at the high table on his wedding day, kept *tap-tap-tapping* on the table in front of him, his nervous fingers refusing to be restrained. "Men who cannot keep their hands still certainly make the best husbands, the best providers, because they always have the urge to work. Those hands have to find something to do," her mother had said. But this Segun man walked with very lazy, very peculiar steps. He flung one long leg in front of him, drew a wide arc with it, let the foot fall, paused, and then the other leg was put through the same tortuous ritual. As far as Sisi could see, there was nothing, no discernible disability, that would inhibit him (should inhibit him) from walking properly. He did not look like he was the sort to want to keep busy. He had not even offered to help her carry her luggage when he met her; he had simply walked ahead of her to the parking lot, displaying the walk that made her think of puppets and hernias. It did not matter that the suitcase was small and not at all heavy. A man who was not lazy and had proper manners would have offered to help.

Sisi wondered if it was the stammering that made him reluctant to talk, or just plain bad manners. Beyond confirming that she was Sisi, he did not say a word to her from the airport to the house in Antwerp, letting the silence between them mount and mount and mount until she wanted to scream at him. Was he not Nigerian? Did he not know it was bad manners to just keep quiet like that? No word of welcome. No curiosity about home. No "So how's Nigeria? I hope you brought some home food? How are the people back in Naija?

What was that I heard about a bomb exploding in the military cantonment in Ikeja?"

She had cleared her throat in the car—a classic prelude to a conversation or, if the other party was smart, an indication that it was expected to initiate conversation—but he had not caught the hint. Lips sealed. Eyes on the road. Hands with long, beautiful fingers turning the steering wheel. Sisi fumed at this blatant show of bad upbringing. She sat on her hands (badly bitten nails, palms rough from a habitual forgetfulness to rub hand cream in them) and fumed at the beautiful hands wasted on a man. Months later, after what would happen, Sisi would think of this moment, of Segun's hands, looking soft and feminine. And of a momentary envy.

Sisi was tired. She yawned, kicked off her shoes, and stretched.

Sisi. Funny how she had started to call herself the name even in her thoughts. It was as if Chisom never even existed. Chisom was dead. Snuffed out. A nobody swallowed up by the night.

Hunger rumbled her stomach, the chugging of an old goods train. A cursory look around the room failed to reveal any food. She had not eaten since she'd left Lagos. The food on the plane had tried her resolve not to miss anything she was leaving behind and made her think, almost with regret, of the pumpkin she had thrown away, its orange pulp cooked and dipped in palm oil. Rice and steamed vegetable, so bland that it seemed like a joke without a punch line. How could anyone eat that? *I wish I had shut my eyes and eaten that rice.* She thought of her mother's favorite riddle:

Question: Who beats a child, even on its mother's lap?
Answer: Hunger.

She wondered if she could ask the Segun man for food. As unbearable as he was, he was the only person she knew in this country. She would not know where to find him. Why could he not look her in the eye? Was he shy? Embarrassed for her? Did he know why she had come into the country? *Not like I care, anyway. There are worse ways to put my punani to use.* There was no room for shame. Or for embarrassment. Or for pride. She would toss them away with the same careless ease she had dumped the pumpkin and the nagging misgivings. She could not afford to lug them around in her new world; they would either slow her down or shackle and kill her. She would work for a few years, keep her eyes on the prize, earn enough to pay back what she owed Dele, and then open up her own business. She would resurrect as Chisom, buy a house in Victoria Garden City. Marry a man who would give her beautiful children. And her beautiful children would go to a private school. She would have three house girls, a gardener, a driver, a cook. Her life would be nothing compared to what it was now. And nothing compared to her parents'. The thought filled her with an airiness that made her feel all she had to do was raise her hands and she would fly.

There was a knock on the door. Sisi looked around her and for a second wondered where she was. She had not flown. The airiness had lured her instead into a deep sleep.

"Come in," she said, yawning and sitting up.

A woman of indeterminate age walked in, one masculine leg after the other. She had on white tennis shoes, tight gym trousers that accentuated firm calves, and a purple pullover. Sisi could barely make out her face, hidden behind a massive blond wig. From the little she could see, the face was a dotting of black spots on a yellow surface.

"Hello. Efe." The woman smiled. She looked between twenty-five and thirty when she smiled.

Sisi looked at her in confusion.

"I'm Efe. That's my name."

"Ah, sorry. I'm Sisi," she answered, relishing the name, the entrance into her new world.

"I brought you food," Efe said, pushing some hair away from her face. Sisi had not noticed that she was carrying a paper bag. She saw it now. A big blue-and-white bag with ALDI written across it. She wondered what Aldi was. A supermarket? Or perhaps a brand. *Soon I shall know this and more. I shall part my legs to this country, and it, in return, will welcome me and begin to unlock its secrets to me.*

Efe's paper bag contained a package of six rolls, a jar of jam, a box of orange juice, and a bunch of firm synthetic-looking bananas.

"Ah, I forgot a knife. Let me go and get a knife from the kitchen. I'll be back immediately."

She went out but returned promptly with a table knife, a glass, a chipped white plate, and a low kitchen stool. She set out the food on the stool, and the rest she put on the floor beside the stool. She settled herself on the bed beside Sisi, causing it to creak and dip even though she did not look that much heavier than Sisi. She waved a hand over the bounty and told Sisi, "*Oya,* chop. The food's ready. Eat. Eat." She sounded like a mother calling a child to dinner, urging the child to eat the food placed before it.

Her fingers sparkled with the glitter of rings. She wore a ring even on her thumb: a thick coil of metal with a broad tip that rested on her nail. Sisi wondered if they were gold or gold-plated. She had never owned gold and could not tell the difference. *But this is another thing Europe will teach me. To spot real gold.* Antwerp would provide her with the ability to sift the real thing from the chaff, to adorn her own fingers with real shiny gold. Every single finger like the woman's before her. And like this woman, she would wear them with an air of someone who was used to the good things of life, so used to them, in fact, that she no longer noticed them.

"Won't you eat, too?" she asked the woman, her eyes gobbling the rings. They hypnotized her, making her dream loud dreams. *One day I shall own these, too. I shall. I shall. I shall.*

"Ah. No. I ate already."

"But the food, it's too much for one person," Sisi responded, all the while calculating in her head how much the food would have cost her in Nigeria. How it was enough to feed her family.

Efe laughed. "You just eat what you can and leave the rest. You no need to finish am." A warm voice. Massaging Sisi's aching limbs.

They fell into the sort of awkward silence that befalls people on first meeting.

"So, how was Naija when you left?" Efe asked at last.

"Same as always," Sisi said, thinking that for her, nothing would be the same again. She had watched her dreams and those of people around her scatter every which way. Like having a jar of marbles, glossy with promise, tip and scatter, hiding them from sight, under chairs and under cupboards. Antwerp was where she would tease out those marbles, gather them and have them fulfill their promise. It was the place to be when your dreams died, the place of miracles: a place where dead dreams resurrected and soared and allowed you to catch them and live them. She was ready, finally, to embrace the prediction of an enviable future that had dogged her every day since she was born, its omniscient presence like an eye, always following her. She was eager to begin.

"The man who brought me, he lives here, too?"

"Ah. Segun? Yes."

"He didn't even help me with my luggage."

Efe let out a snort. "Dat man na only himself he sabi. He no dey talk to anyone. No dey do anyting. But him dey good with a hammer. Na him dey fix everytin' around here!"

"With those hands?" It was out before she could stop it. Segun's hands did not look manly enough, strong enough, to lift a hammer.

"You should see de tables wey him make!"

Sisi would see the tables and proclaim that indeed Segun's hands were deceptive. She would watch him saw off the legs of a gawky table that Madam bought and marvel that his palms did not callous, that his fingers did not become thicker, stumpier.

The two women fell silent. Strangers with no words between them. Sisi slathered jam on the bread. *When was the last time I had jam?* The magenta-colored spread delighted her taste buds. She could get used to this, to living like this. The life of the rich and the arrived. If she had any misgivings left about leaving home, they were chomped into bits with each mouthful of food and pushed down into the pit of her stomach.

ZWARTEZUSTERSTRAAT

SEGUN IS IN HIS ROOM. EVEN AFTER ALL THESE YEARS, THEY ARE NOT sure what his job is, exactly. He hardly talks to them. Sometimes he acts as Madam's driver, chauffeuring her to business meetings that they know nothing about. Sometimes he goes out on his own, dragging his lazy feet across the hallway so they heard the *sheesheesh* of it, as if he were bent on erasing the prints on the carpet. Once he came back with Sisi in his car. She would never talk about it.

"Maybe," Ama suggested then, "they meet in secret, Segun and Sisi. Maybe they're secret lovers. Why would he carry her in his car, eh? And they both had boxes of chips!"

While they cannot prove that Segun and Sisi are lovers, or determine the exact nature of his job, one thing about him is not in doubt: When there is a job to be done in the house—lights that need changing, a cupboard handle that needs fixing, nails to be hammered into the wall for Madam's paintings, a table to be made—he is the man for it. Always working in silence. Not even humming to himself as he unplugs lights or tightens screws or hammers in nails. Beyond his name, nothing else is known about him. Sisi once joked that he was a spy, drawing laughter from the rest because Segun, with his habitual look of buffoonish imbecility, mouth constantly hanging open, hands flailing, does not look smart enough to be a spy. Somebody else said that he was maybe Madam's bodyguard. This drew more laughter than Sisi's suggestion because, as Joyce said, Segun looked like he could not even guard himself. Bodyguards were supposed to be huge and muscular and with fists of steel. Segun's frame suggests a pusillanimity that would shrink from danger, no matter how small. "How would he guard Madam? With his screwdriver and hammer?" Sisi had asked, breathless with laughter. "Screwdriver in one hand, hammer in the other, shadowing Madam!" The image had made them laugh so much, they had to hold on to one another so as not to fall over from laughter. They settled on Joyce's suggestion that he was either Madam's or Dele's relative. They would never know, because Segun would never volunteer to tell them. And of course they could not ask Madam.

Ama sits down and picks up a cushion and hugs it to her body. "Just yesterday, just yesterday, Sisi was telling me about the bag she was saving up to buy," she says, all the while rocking herself forward and backward, thinking about the bag that will now never be bought by Sisi. She finds something inconsolable in the fact, and the tears that come down are furious. "Fuck it!" she says, and hurriedly wipes away the tears with a tissue that she has discovered in her pocket.

"*Shebi*, it was only last week she borrowed my eyeliner," Joyce adds, her palms cupping her face. It looks like she is crying. But she is not. Joyce is not one to cry easily, explaining when pressed that she has done all the crying she will ever do. "Who would have known that she would be dead a week later?"

Joyce details how Sisi had come to her to ask for her eyeliner because she could not find her own and could not begin work without her trademark lined eyes. Joyce speaks into the room, remembering how she told Sisi, even as she gave her the eyeliner, that not lining her eyes would not kill her. "Maybe that was a premonition," she suggests, but no one answers her.

They all have their memories of Sisi. Little meetings become poignant, as they often do when someone dies. A remark, a look that would otherwise have gone unremembered, takes on a monumental meaning. Sisi's earrings, forgotten on the pane of the bathroom window, become "her way of leaving a bit of her behind," Ama says.

Two days later, Madam will bin the earrings because "leaving a dead woman's property around the house is inviting her spirit to visit." And a spirit, good or bad, has no dealings with humans. Their visits can never forebode well. For that reason, she will also bin all of Sisi's clothes and shoes, her scarves and bags. She will tie them up in thick black garbage bags—even the Hermès scarf that Sisi bought from a wandering salesman and that Madam envied—and throw them down the throat of the green metal receptor opposite the house, which is emptied once a week for charity. She will also walk with incense through the house, a warning to Sisi's ghost to keep at bay. Sisi's ghost will listen, for she did not even haunt her former housemates in dreams the way some ghosts do. Madam believes in the power of incense to keep spirits away, and not just the spirits that belonged to humans. None of the other women believe in the efficacy of her incense, but Madam is not one to be contradicted.

Three days ago, Ama reminds them, Madam had walked around with her incense stick, purging the house of the spirit of jealousy. Madam said the evil spirit of jealousy lived in their house, and the incense was supposed to exorcise it. "You are sisters. You are all the family you have here, and yet you cannot live in peace."

She was talking to the four women, yet her speech had been directed mainly at Sisi and Ama. The two women had been in a fight over who was supposed to clean the communal bathroom. There had been a roisterous party the night before, and bottles had been left upturned and drinks spilled on the leather chairs. Even though Sisi had been on the roster to do the cleaning, she had refused to, claiming that Ama's guests had made the mess. Ama refused to take responsibility for her guests, and fists flew. It took Madam's intervention to tear the girls away from each other.

Ama's voice is soft. "If I had known she was going to die, I'd never have fought with her, I swear." The scratch marks Ama got from Sisi are still visible on her chin. She tries not to think about them.

"None of us knew," Efe responds. "Who would have thought that Sisi would be dead today? Murdered for no reason at all?"

"Who would want to kill Sisi?" Joyce asks, not for the first time since they got the news.

"Nothing was stolen," the police said. "At least not that we could see."

Joyce's question is rhetorical, but she continues nevertheless. "What did she ever do to deserve a death like this?"

The death of the Malian nanny and her ward is still on their minds, but they skirt around it, refusing to speak of it. Not now. Not when they are all feeling very vulnerable. But they think it all the same. The Thursday morning they woke up to hear that, with a machine gun, eighteen-year-old Hans Van Themsche had *pop-pop-popp*ed and killed two people on their street. They had all watched the news on TV, gorging themselves on the re-creation of the crime, remembering when they themselves had walked down that same spot without any thought of being in danger, thinking it might have been them. "Antwerp is becoming America, with all these shootings. First that boy that was killed at the Central Station for his MP3 player, and now this. What is happening to Antwerp?" Sisi had queried that day. And when Ama reminded her that the MP3 murder had occurred in Brussels, not in Antwerp, Sisi had said that it did not matter. It could so easily have been Antwerp.

Antwerp is changing on them, but they will not think about it. Not with Sisi murdered, too. The police told Madam they were investigating the case as a possible racist attack.

"Which kin' possibly be dat?" Efe fumed when they were told. "They know say na racist attack. Who else go wan' kill Sisi?"

"Fucking shitheads, that's what they are," Ama said.

Joyce gets up, sighs, and switches off the TV. She has had enough of the soap, she says, even though she has not been watching it. She starts to wipe the top of the TV. "Leave that alone, Joyce. You don wipe am a hundred times today!" Efe shouts.

Joyce stops.

One second.

Then she starts again. *Swish swish swish*, wiping like a woman possessed. Efe throws her hands up in exasperation.

"Fuck! Just stop!" Ama stands up, then sits again.

Joyce ignores her. *Swish. Swish. Swish.* She breathes on a spot and wipes.

Suddenly, she stops. Smiles. She has had a brainwave. She suggests that maybe they should have some sort of a service for Sisi. Something to send her soul on the way. "We just can't let her die like that. We have to see her off. Have a pastor come here and pray and send her soul off properly. We can't do much, but we can do that, at least. See it off on its way." She seems pleased with her suggestion. "It is the least we can do for her. Invite some people we know. Have a small get-together for her. But first a church service to send her on her way." She is getting animated. She wants to talk about how many people they can invite, what they can cook, but Ama interrupts her.

"On the way to where?" It sounds as if she is about to laugh. Joyce ignores her, as does Efe. She repeats her question, this time standing up, as if for emphasis. Her eyes are blazing. No one answers her. Efe tries to pull her down. Ama hisses but lets herself be pulled into the chair. They know that she has a dislike for all things spiritual. Once she was invited to church by Efe but turned her down rudely, saying that her stomach had had about as much church as it could ever hold. "I had a bellyful of church growing up. I don't like pastors.

Never trusted them. I am not about to start now." She will repeat these words again many years later, when she is ninety-three, a tiresome old woman on her way to death. By then her voice will be weaker and the fire in her eyes gone. "I don't like pastors. Never trusted them. I am not about to start now." She would die listening to young boy bands croon about love and lust and life in the fast lane.

While she is sitting there in the room, surrounded by the news of Sisi's death, and the smell of Madam's incense that is still strong, and Efe's story still in her head, she closes her eyes. She feels an obligation to tell them her story. Her true story, like Efe has just done. She opens her eyes and begins. "I grew up in Enugu. We lived in a house with pink walls."

She draws out an ashtray in the shape of a chimpanzee hand from under the sofa, stubs out her almost finished cigarette, and fishes in her bag for another one. She flips open a pack of cigarettes and passes it around. Both Joyce and Efe shake their heads and say no thank you.

Ama thinks about the Udi Hills surrounding Enugu, rolling and folding into one another like an enormous piece of green cloth, and smiles.

"How did you meet Dele?" Efe asks.

Dele is the common denominator in their lives.

"At my auntie's canteen. He used to come there to eat sometimes."

"Why would he want to eat outside?" Joyce asks. "That man has a cook and a wife, what would drive him to a canteen?"

"I don't know oo," Ama answers. "Perhaps he does his scouting there."

"I met him in his house," Joyce says. "A man called Polycarp took me there." She winces when she says the name, as if it gives her a toothache. "I hated that Dele as soon as I saw him. Bastard."

Ama smiles and says softly, "Oga Dele just wanted to help. What choices did we have back home, eh? Oga Dele is trying to give us happiness."

"And are we really happy?" Joyce challenges. Now she is sitting beside the table, on the floor, wiping smudges from the table legs.

"Me, I try not to think about happiness. L.I. is getting a good education. Dat one suppose dey enough for me." Efe draws out her words with the hesitancy of a participant in a political debate, careful not to say the wrong thing. Parameters of happiness change, she thinks, but does not articulate it. "Sometimes I think my life is like a set of false teeth. The world sees what you show it: clean teet' wey white like Colgate. But you know for inside dat your real teet' don rot finish!"

The women laugh at Efe's analogy, but the mood turns serious almost immediately.

"And as for me," Ama starts, "I don't know if I'm happy or not. I don't like Madam. She's a snobby bitch. I meet interesting people at work. In what other job do you earn money just for lying on your back? Heaven knows there is no way I can be any of the other alternatives open to us here. No way I am fucking ruining my manicure cleaning up after snotty women too busy or too lazy to clean up after themselves. I can't braid hair. Even if I could, I don't know that I want to stand for hours on end doing that for peanuts. Remove Madam from the equation, and I might be doing fucking cartwheels." She laughs. *Ha-ha.* Then stops. An abrupt laugh.

"You know what, Joyce? I made this choice. At least I was asked to choose. I came here with my eyes wide open." Ama cracks her knuckles and continues, "I get food, I have a roof over my head, I have a life. I can't be greedy. Sisi is dead. Is she happy? We think our stories are sad, do we even know what hers is? Where did she always slink off to?"

Her voice rises as if in sudden anger, as if in a realization of that anger. "You're asking me about happiness. You want to know how the fuck I ended up here?" She takes a puff on her cigarette and exhales, curlicues of smoke escaping her nostrils and her pursed lips. She taps ash into the ashtray. "Let me tell you about my life, Joyce. Let me tell you about my fucking life." She tugs at the crucifix around her neck.

SISI

MADAM LOOKED EXACTLY LIKE SISI HAD IMAGINED SHE WOULD: LIGHT-skinned, round, and short. Very much like something that was meant to be spun. She did not walk, she barreled. She rolled into Sisi's room early the next morning, her arms barely covered by the cropped sleeves of the baby-blue blouse she was wearing on top of black bell-bottom trousers. On her chin, tufts of hair curled comfortably into one another, and when she spoke she rolled the hairs between her fingers as if trying to draw attention to them, to get you to notice them and comment on how well maintained they were. "I am your Madam," she said by way of introduction, walking over to the window and opening Sisi's blinds. "I heard you arrived well. I trust you have rested well. Today you start work. We haven't got any time to lose." Every sentence came out like an order. She caressed the hair on her chin. Sisi thought: *How confident. How totally self-assured.* She would envy that self-confidence and would try to imitate it in her bearing on the days she went walking alone.

Sisi was shocked that Madam spoke good English. She had imagined that Madam would be like Dele, unable to string together an entire sentence in proper English. It went with the image she had of her before meeting her. She would learn later that Madam had a master's in business administration from the University of Lagos. Not only did she speak perfect English, she spoke perfect Dutch, too. And was at this moment taking lessons in French.

Madam's accent was sophisticated. Her words well enunciated, filed around the edges so that there was not a trace of roughness. The closest thing to the queen's English Sisi had ever heard. It thrilled her to listen to it.

Madam opened the black leather bag she had slung across her left shoulder and brought out a pack of cigarettes. "You smoke?" she asked Sisi, holding out the pack to her.

"No. I don't."

"I didn't before I came here. But this is a different world. This place changes you. You learn to eat cornflakes with cold milk. Can you imagine?"

Sisi could not imagine but said nothing.

"They clear the head, cigarettes. Just be sure to steer clear of dope. I have seen it mess with people's minds. Antwerp is full of them: people who've been made mad by dope. This is not the right place to go crazy. Europe is for living, and living in full. I always think that our people who come here and run mad are a waste of space."

She pulled out a cigarette and threw the pack back into her bag. Sisi watched her short hand disappear almost completely into the bag and come out with a slim black lighter, elegant in its compactness. Madam clicked the lighter and lit the cigarette. She inhaled, blew a cloud of smoke, and smiled at a memory she was not sharing. She took another draw, looked around, sat down beside Sisi on the bed, and tapped ash onto the table beside the bed. Then she spoke.

"Dele was right about you. Ah, that man knows his stuff. He never disappoints. He has the best girls on the show, you know? To see the girls some of these jokers bring in! Shitty faces, bodies that need serious panel beating, and breasts hanging like scrotums." She laughed.

Sisi kept quiet. She did not know how to respond to what was obviously a compliment. Instead, she gazed at Madam, wondering if her body weighed heavy on her, trying not to laugh at the idea of breasts hanging like scrotums. Her silence was instinctive: Laughter might have been looked at as insolence.

Madam inhaled and exhaled another cloud of smoke, suffusing the room with the smell of the cigarette. Sisi wondered if it would be rude of her to move, to stand up and maybe go to the other end of the room. The smoke irritated her. Her thoughts wandered to her parents, and she asked herself how they were, what they were doing. She thought of Peter, almost wishing that things had been different. He would have made a good husband, a considerate one, the sort who would wash his wife's clothes if she were indisposed, maybe even cook for her. She chased away thoughts of him. She had had no choice but to leave. *Peter had nothing to offer me.* Maybe after she had made her money, if Peter was still available, she would marry him. If he was no longer available, there would be other men. *There are always other men.* One could buy anything, an attentive husband included. You just had to have enough disposable income. *And I'll make it. Even if it kills me.* She shifted on her buttocks, and Madam looked at her.

"Not nervous, are we? You can't afford to be. Not in our business." She tapped some more ash on the table. "Ah, hand over your passport. From now until your debt is paid, I am in charge of your passport."

Handing over her passport would be tantamount to putting her life into someone else's hands, would it not? What if she changed her mind? What if she decided she was not cut out for this after all and that she wanted to go home? She looked at Madam, sized up the gold necklace hanging around the thick neck, and imagined it around her own neck. Who was she kidding? There was no way she could go back to the life she knew before. She would stay here and make it, so what did it matter who had her passport? She got up, knelt, and dragged her suitcase out from under the bed. She unzipped an inner pocket and brought out the envelope with her passport. She handed the brown envelope to Madam.

"Once you've eaten breakfast, you have to go and register at the Ministry of Foreign Affairs."

"Why?"

The question was out before Sisi could stop it. She did not really want to know. Answers were irrelevant to her. The only thing that was of substance, that really had meaning to her at this point, was survival. And the revelation that she would do everything required of her until she achieved her dream was not an abrupt one. It did not come upon her like an unexpected rain shower, catching her unawares. It was more like a shadow, comfortable enough to follow her around.

"Why?" Madam echoed, her voice mocking and lilted by a laugh. "My dear . . . what's your name?"

"Sisi."

"My dear Sisi, it's not your place to ask questions here. You just do as you are told, and you'll have an easy ride. I talk, you listen. You understand? Three days ago I gave Joyce the same instruction. She did not ask me questions. She just listened and did as she was told. I expect the same of you. Silence and total obedience. That's the rule of the house. Be seen, not heard. *Capisce?*"

Yes. She understood. Voice as still as the night.

Sisi had met Joyce briefly the night before. She had come to introduce herself in an accent Sisi could not place as Nigerian. Sisi thought she looked young. Still a girl, really. And even though she said she was from Benin City, she did not look very Bini. She looked more Fulani than anything else, what with her cheeks that looked chiseled out of something pure. *None of my business. We all come with our stories, and who cares which version is the truth. Everyone lives with their secrets. Everyone lives their secrets. We are all secrets to each other.*

Sisi detested Madam's tone, the way she spoke as if Sisi were a child. Back in Lagos, nobody would have dared talk to her in that manner. But this was not Lagos. And she needed this woman's help in this city that was full of strangers.

"I shall get you a cab that will stop you in front of the center. Tell them there that you are from Liberia. Are you listening to me? Tell them that your father was a local Mandingo chief, and soldiers loyal to Charles Taylor came at night to your house and killed your entire family: father, mother, sisters, and brothers. You escaped because you hid yourself in a kitchen cupboard. You dared to come out only after the massacre ended and the soldiers had gone. Tell them you heard a soldier shout that one family member was missing, that they were under obligation to kill you all, and that they would be back to do just that. Look sad. Cry. Wail. Tear your hair out. White people enjoy sob stories. They love to hear about us killing each other, about us hacking off each other's heads in senseless ethnic conflicts. The more macabre the story, the better."

She paused to take a long drag on her cigarette, blew a ring of blue smoke in the room, and continued. "Talk about seeing the corpses of your dead family. About stepping on the corpses as you made your way out of the house. Tell them that you couldn't trust your neighbors, most of them were pro-Taylor and would have killed you themselves if they had caught you. Don't forget, cry. Make sure tears come out. Real tears, eh? The cab will come back for you. You wait outside the building until you see him, okay? Don't go with anybody else. He'll bring you straight back to this house. Remember, you are Mandingo. You have no passport. You escaped Liberia with only your head and the clothes on your back. A white man took pity on you and helped you escape. He saw you outside a church begging for money. You understand?"

"Yes." It was the only possible response. Not only would Sisi be Liberian, in the next months she would be other things. Other people. A constant yearning to escape herself would take over her life, so that being Sisi would no longer suffice. It would take Luc to put a stop to that. Briefly. And then she would be gone.

ZWARTEZUSTERSTRAAT | AMA

THE WALLS OF THE SITTING ROOM WERE PINK. SHE COULD NOT REMEM-ber if they had ever been another color or if they had always been that chewing-gum pink she recalled so vividly, the pinkness rising up to meet her whenever she needed a friend, enfolding her in an embrace that was as warm, as comforting, as it was familiar. *Fucking bloody pink. Can you imagine?*

The girl liked to run her hands on the walls. When she got older and wiser, she would think of it as making love to the walls with her hands, feeling their silky smoothness, letting her hands glide, a lover's hands, over silky-smooth skin. Those bloody walls were her best friends.

Silent, constant friends whom she could trust. They were not like her sandals, which she sometimes played with, but which had gaping mouths that reminded her of Christie from across the road, who her mother said had to be the biggest gossip alive. Radio Without Battery, her mother called Christie. "She never runs out of steam, broadcasting news from one set of ears to another." Ama could never trust those horrible sandals that were never entirely comfortable (too tight, too loose, too wide, too narrow), and when she played school with them, she lashed them hard until she was sure she heard them cry.

Ama learned from childhood to keep secrets. It was like having a boil inside you waiting to burst and thinking that once it did, it would kill you. She had to share the secrets with someone. And her pink friends were the ones whose ears she filled with the stories she did not dare tell anyone else.

She was grateful for those walls, who were all the friends she needed. And, most times, all the friends she had. Her father did not encourage her friends to visit because he said friends sometimes led one astray. When they did come, he told them Ama had to study. From the window of her room, Ama would watch young girls from the neighborhood shouting out to one another as they played *oga*, their feet raising dust as they stamped on the ground. She wished she could crumple up her father and hurl him off the balcony. Fling him so far that his face would smash into the hills. She told the walls this.

She had not always spoken to the walls, but the day after her birthday, when it started, there was nobody else she could tell what she told the walls. The walls kept quiet and listened and did not push her out. They did not say, "Not now, go and play, that's a good girl," and so a satisfying friendship that was to span many years had begun.

It was 1987 and she was turning eight. Her father was throwing a party for her, a big birthday party with a clown hired to entertain her guests and a cameraman to capture the laughter on her face and the love of a father who would lay all these out. She had been top of the class for the third time that year, and this was her reward. A big party. A big cake with eight candles. And ribbons in her hair. The house smelled of jollof rice and *moi-moi* and fried beef. Her mother and two of her mother's friends sat on low stools in the sweaty kitchen, sipping Maltina and supervising the housemaids' cooking. Ama was in the sitting room, watching TV. She had been asked to keep out of the kitchen. "Go and watch something on TV, don't disturb us here, be a good girl and run along," her mother had said, shooing her out of the busy kitchen. Once in a while a face peeked out of the kitchen and called to her: "Ama, come and taste this. Is this rice to your liking, *nne*? Not too hot? Is the meat tender enough? Not too dry?" "No." She shook her head. Everything was *sam-sam* perfect. Nothing could go wrong today. Ijeoma, the housemaid one of her mother's friends had lent her for the day, had sweat running into her eyes. She wiped it off with the back of her hand and screamed that she had gotten pepper, *ose, ose*, in her eyes. "That girl is very foolish. *Atulu*. She's a sheep," her mother's friend who had lent her out said. "Who forgets that she is cooking with pepper and rubs her eyes with her hands?"

The three women laughed as she ran around shouting, "Water, water, my eyes are on fire." One of the other maids got her water and helped her wash the sting of the pepper out. After her pain had calmed and the women had stopped laughing, the woman she lived with told her, "Let that be a lesson to you. If this little pepper makes you shout 'Fire, fire' like a madwoman, think of how bad the fire of hell must be, and keep away from evil. Yesterday two naira disappeared from the table where I left it. Two days ago a fifty-kobo coin went missing from my room. Even if I have not caught you red-handed, the devil is keeping stock and shall come for you." *Bloody advice!*

"Don't even try to deny it. I know it. And you know it. Money does not have legs. We both know who has been doing the pilfering, and God help you the day I have my proof. That day you shall suffer more than Job. *I ga atakalia* Job *n'afufu*," the woman said.

Ama's mother said it was a shame that these days one could no longer trust one's domestic help. When were the days when a woman could trust her maid with her life? She remembered her mother once telling her about a servant who had risked her life during the war of 1966 to get food for her employers' children. "The girl risked enemy bullets, *mgbo*, to dig out yams and cassava for the children. And she dug them out with her bare hands. True! These days," she continued, "the devil has taken ahold of house help, turning them into thieving scoundrels. To find a good one is like squeezing water from a stone."

The women played Ping-Pong with their stories of thieving-snoopingstickyfingered domestic help.

The house girl who stole perfume from her mistress. "Wonders shall never cease. A common house girl. What gave her the guts?"

"The devil!"

Then the one who seduced and slept with the husband of the woman who had employed her.

"How could she?"

"The devil."

"Sometimes I wonder if I should not get male help," Ama's mother said, prompting a heated discussion on the pros and cons of houseboys.

They were stronger than girls and therefore better workers.

They got clothes cleaner.

Fetched more buckets of water.

But.

Wait.

What if they turned against you and raped you?

Or raped your daughters? It had been known to happen.

You could get a small boy, but small boys were generally less disposed to housework than small girls.

But.

Wait.

Ama was not listening anymore. She was too excited to stay focused on the multiple merits of a houseboy, which one of the women had started expounding on, her hands flailing every which way as if she were a conductor guiding the choir through Sunday-service music, do re mi fa so laaaaa, houseboys are definitely better!

Everything was perfect. *Today was a perfect, perfect day,* Ama thought, not paying much attention to the cartoon playing on Channel 8, either. It was a day from one of her picture books, in which the sky was always clear and blue, an even watercolor-blue blanket without any tears in it. She got up and went to the bathroom. She stood on the tips of her toes and looked into the mirror hanging above the sink. She touched her hair. Her mother had straightened it with a hot comb. That was agony! The comb coming off the gas cooker and digging deep into her hair to unravel the knots, her mother grumbling all the while that there was absolutely no difference between Ama's hair and sisal. *Now,* she thought as she touched her hair, parted in the middle and held in two by pink ribbons, *I have proper* oyibo *hair!* The hair would go very well with her party dress, which was laid out on her bed. A pink dress with a satin bow in the front. "Cinderella dress," her father had told her when he gave it to her. "A dress for my princess." It was the most beautiful dress Ama had ever seen, and she was sure she would want to wear it every day. But after what would happen that night, she would never wear it again. Her mother had instructed that she was to wear the dress only when the guests started to arrive and not a minute before. Ama wondered how much longer it would take. Oh, why did time not go nearly fast enough when she wanted it to? Later, she would want to go back to this moment, when the sky was blue and her dress was new and her life was *sam-sam* perfect.

Her father always called her his princess, drawing out the I; Priiiincess! His lips tight, so that it seemed like he was not the one talking. When Ama learned the word "ventriloquist," it made her think of her father, of the way he spoke with his lips set in a thin tight line, a pencil drawing, hardly opening to let sounds out.

There was music playing on the turntable beside the TV. The two men from Voices of the Cross whined out melancholic tunes about sin and hellfire and a perpetual gnashing of teeth. God and Satan tussling for souls. God with a big book with names of the saved. The devil with a pitchfork pricking evil souls. Deliverance and flying into heaven for the righteous. Ama thought the two men looked lithe enough to fly, but not so her father—whom everybody called Brother Cyril because he was a Christian and belonged to a church where everyone was Sister and Brother. He could hardly climb the stairs to their second-story flat without losing his breath, already panting by the time he got to the twelfth step, twenty steps from the front door. He would go to heaven because he was righteous, but Ama supposed he would have to be carried there. Strong, muscled angels would have to carry him, and when Ama dreamed of it she saw a huge piece of reclining flesh being heaved into the skies. Ama did not really like the voices of the men who made up the Voices of the Cross band. She preferred to listen to something else. And her desire for another kind of music sharpened her hearing so finely that music from the record store across the street blared into the house. Loud, happy voices that trembled the house, making her want to tap and dance. But her father would have none of those. "They are the devil's music," he said. "They do not edify the things of our Lord. They are the devil's music. The devil shakes his waist and sways his horns when he hears music like that. He claps his hands and stokes his fire for the many souls that he's winning." He was an assistant pastor of the Church of the Twelve Apostles of the Almighty Yahweh, Jehovah El Shaddai, Jehovah Jireh, one of the biggest churches in the city. The devil did not belong anywhere near the house of which he was the head. So instead of the kind of music she heard from across the street, Ama's house was infused with music from Voices of the Cross, the Calvary Sisters, Jesus Is Savior Band, *Ndi Umuazi Jesu*. Voices that grated on her nerves. She never thought of telling her father that the voices irritated her. She knew what would happen if she did. The things of the Lord were not to be abused. Nor slighted. Nor ridiculed. She knew that her father would put her across his knees and, with her mother watching in a corner, tear into her with a treated *koboko*, the cow-hide cane that he nicknamed Discipline. There was nothing Ama feared more than Discipline cutting a rawness into her skin that hurt for many days after. Discipline also always showed its face when Ama disobeyed her parents, because her father was a great believer in "Sparing the rod spoils the child." He even had a wooden tablet with the Bible passages alluding to that inscribed in a flourish on it and hung up on the door of Ama's room. "So that you'll never forget."

Thou shalt beat him with the rod, and shalt deliver his soul from hell. —Proverbs 23:14

He who spareth the rod hateth his son: but he that loveth him correcteth him betimes. —Proverbs 13:24

The music of the world was to be kept in the world, away from the confines of the house. As were alcoholic drinks. And cigarettes. And magazines with lewd pictures. And bad language. Their house was a house of holiness. And if Brother Cyril had his way, he would have had the entire house painted white for its sanctity. But the harmattan wind that graced Enugu from November to around August made such an undertaking impossible. Not only did it carry debris from one part of the town to the other, it turned grass to rust and sprayed dust over houses so that a white house was entirely out of the question. "If we had faith as small as a mustard seed," Brother Cyril often lamented, "we could tell the harmattan wind to pass over our houses, and it would." To which Pastor Ishmael, if within earshot, was sure to reply with a determined "We have faith enough. But God still has to do His work, Brother Cyril. The harmattan wind is the hand of God passing by. We cannot stall it! We are, after all, but His servants. And nothing more." Every word of the pastor's had the authority of a pronouncement. And Brother Cyril would nod in agreement. But the regret on his face, that he could not paint his green house white, remained. *He also probably regretted that he wasn't the pastor. That he didn't fucking have the last word.*

Everyone in sleepy Enugu knew Brother Cyril. Two years after he joined the church, he had risen in rank to assistant pastor, only one set of ears away from God. This was due mainly to his moral uprightness and the holiness that shone off his stiff white collar. The sins of the world curdled on his forehead, causing furrows, five or six lines that lay like lax S's, one on top of the other. The furrows got worse— little brown worms squeezing together—whenever he saw a female in clothes that did not cover her knees. The sight always threw Brother Cyril into a righteous coughing fit, coughing out curses on "the daughters of Eve who destroy the reputation of women," and always ended with him calling for his wife, "a woman fit for Christian eyes," to soothe him and get him a glass of water.

His wife was tall, nearly as tall as he was. Everyone said his holiness had rubbed off on her, giving a sheen to her face as if she had just rubbed on Vaseline. Her cheeks shone, reflecting the light of purity trapped in them. Brother Cyril always introduced her as "my Rose whom I married a virgin." And many of the male members of the Church of the Twelve Apostles of the Almighty Yahweh, Jehovah El Shaddai, Jehovah Jireh, said to Brother Cyril that if every woman were as Christian as his Rose whom he had married a virgin, God would never destroy the earth. Brother Cyril would always smile at this, accepting it as his due that "God always provides for His people." He had been given Rose, a Christian wife, "to ease my journey in this world." It was expected that Ama would follow in her mother's footsteps and become a model wife for a good Christian man someday.

Brother Cyril, in standing with his status, wore a white robe to church. White for holiness. His whiteness rivaled the pastor's, and when they stood together at the altar, the congregation was hard-pressed to decide whose robe was purer.

Brother Cyril wore white at home, too. White safari suits and white dashikis that did not tolerate stains, and which his wife had to boil in a huge pot of water before washing to ensure that the whiteness glowed in holiness. She would not entrust its care to the housemaid. "You have to be prepared to meet the Lord at any given moment," Brother Cyril always said, so that Ama used to wonder if the Lord did not permit Himself to be met in any other color. For Ama's big party, her father, predictably, wore one of his white safari suits. After Ama had blown out the candles on the cake and the cake had been eaten and the clown had made the children laugh and the cameraman had captured all the joy and laughter on video, after the guests had gone and Ama had been sent to bed certain that this was the happiest day of her entire life, her father floated into her dark room in his white safari suit. Ama thought he was a ghost and would have screamed if he had not preempted her by covering her mouth with one broad palm and smothering the scream in her throat. With the other hand, he fumbled under her nightdress, a cotton lavender gown with the print of a huge grinning bear.

That was the first time it happened. The next morning, unsure whether she had dreamed it or not, Ama spoke to the pink walls.

The next night he floated into her room again. Ama told the walls how he held her nipple between his fingers and squeezed. She told the walls of the pain of the squeezing and the coldness of her father's hands.

Over the next days the walls heard how he ignored her when she said that he was hurting her inside. They heard of how she tried to push him away when he lay on top of her, but he was a mountain and she did not have the strength in her to move a mountain. She told of the grunting and the sticky whiteness like pap that gushed out of him. "It's warm and yucky," she complained to her walls. "I'll never eat pap again!"

The walls could sketch her stories. They could tell how she wished she could melt into the bed. Become one with it. She would hold her body stiff, muscles tense, as if that would make her wish come true. When she did this, her father would demand, "What's the Fifth Commandment?" "Honor thy father and thy mother," she would reply, her voice muffled by the collar of her nightgown in her mouth. And then she would relax her muscles, let him in, and imagine that she was flying high above the room. Sometimes she saw herself on the ceiling, looking down at a man who looked like her father and a girl who looked like her. When the pain made this difficult, she bit on her lower lip until it became numb.

Afterward she always fell asleep sitting up in her bed, her back to the door and her face to the window, waiting for something, someone, to come and rescue her. To take her away, far away, from her father and his grunts. She did that last night, and when she woke up she was sure she had been crying, even though her eyes were dry and she could not remember crying.

Her eyes hurt, and when her mother looked at her in the morning and worried that she had Apollo because her eyes were so red, she did not say otherwise. She even let her mother put some eyedrops into her eyes. She knew without being told that she must never share what her father did to her with anyone else. Not even her mother. The walls were different. They did not count.

Every night her father came, and as time passed she came to expect it, her palms clammy and her mouth dry. Sometimes she tried to get out of it. She told her mother she did not want to sleep alone, she was afraid of the darkness, but her mother would always tell her not to be silly, she was eight years old, old enough to sleep alone, and did she not know how lucky she was to have her own room? How many children her age had their own bedrooms? "*Eeh nne?* A beautiful bedroom all to yourself, and you want to sleep in my bed!"

When Ama got older and wiser, she would think that her mother walked around in a deliberate state of blindness. Otherwise she would have seen into her heart and asked her, "*Nwa m*, my daughter, what is the matter?" She wished her mother would ask her so that she could tell her, but she never asked, choosing instead to complain about Ama's hair being as tough as sisal. And of children not being as obedient as they were in her youth. And of *otapiapia* not being as effective as it used to be in killing mice. And of their housemaid stealing cups of rice from the huge sack in the kitchen. And of NEPA doing a shoddy job of providing electricity. And of Ama being ungrateful because she would not eat her pap, and did she know how many children there were who had no food to eat? And since when did she stop eating pap, anyway? When did this nonsense start?

Ama told the walls she wanted to go abroad. When she slept, she saw herself, hair long and silky, in a city very far away, where her father's whiteness did not stifle her. No one she knew had been abroad, but every night when she prayed she asked God for a miracle, whispering her prayer furiously, hoping it bypassed her father's ears and the pastor's ears, that it pierced heaven to land gently beside God's right ear.

She wanted to go to London. She had seen pictures of London Bridge on TV. Her other choices were Las Vegas. Or Monaco. She heard the names once in a song playing from the music store across the road:

So I must leave, I'll have to go
To Las Vegas or Monaco

The names sounded elegant, like places where people walked around all day well dressed and doing nothing more strenuous than carrying a handbag. She imagined telling people she lived in Las Vegas. She imagined Las Vegas air blowing her hair across her face and tickling her nose. She imagined being in Monaco, all rich and

grown up, without the huge menacing presence of her father, drinking and smoking in defiance of her father's rules, shaking and twisting to the devil's music.

When Ama did leave home, thirteen years later, it was neither to
Las Vegas nor to Monaco. It was to Lagos. Bigger and wider than
Enugu. It was a good place to start from.

The events that led to her leaving home had nothing to do with
her long-harbored wish to escape. She'd had no hand in the events
that set the wheels of her freedom in motion. At least not intentionally.

AMA WAS TIRED AND HOPED TO BE ABLE TO SLEEP ON THE BUS. SHE HAD
to be at the Ekene Dili Chukwu bus stop at five in the morning in
order to catch the earliest bus to Lagos. At that time of the morning
even Enugu was chilly, temperatures dipping almost as low as sixty-
two degrees. Ama buttoned up her cardigan, raising the collar up to
her ears, where the cold bit her the worst. Her stomach let out angry
grumbles from being empty. There had been no time for breakfast,
even if she had been offered one. She had managed to take a bath
only because she had stayed awake all night, rushing into the bathroom at the first hint of dawn, daring the cold water, which gave her
goose pimples as huge as chicken pox bumps.

She tried to steer her mind away from the hunger that was starting
to make her feel a bit weak. She could pretend she was fasting, one
of the numerous mortifications her father often imposed on the family to purge them of their sins. *My father,* she thought. *But he's not my
father. He's just the useless man my mother married. I'm well rid of
him. I'm well rid of both of them.* This was what she had always
wanted. So why did she not feel as elated as she had always imagined
she would be? She could not be sorry to be leaving her mother. *What
has she ever done for me? She let that man rule her, let him ruin my*

life. She did nothing. Nothing to help me. What sort of a mother is that? Yet when she thought of her mother, she felt miserable and cold. She kept her eyes away from the many hawkers filling the depot. A little girl carrying on her head a wide tray piled with loaves of bread wrapped in see-through plastic walked up to her. "Sister, *gote* bread." Ama waved the barefoot hawker away, watching almost sadly as the girl went up to another waiting passenger. "Sweet sweet bread, sah. Buy my bread." She watched as the man helped the girl — she could not be more than eight years old — off-load the tray from her head, watched as the man chose a loaf, and turned her head resolutely away from him as he began to tear into it. Ama was hungry but did not dare to buy food, as she did not want to start spending the little money she had. Eight hours was a long time to be on the road, and she wanted to be sure she had money in case there was nobody to meet her at the bus depot in Lagos. After everything she had heard about the city, it would be unwise to enter it completely penniless. Lagos was not a place to rely completely on the kindness of strangers. All the songs about Lagos said so:

Lagos na no man's land, Lagos na waya.
For Lagos, man pikin no get sista or broda.
For Lagos, na orphan I be. Lagos na waya aaa.

She was relieved when the bus doors yawned open and the call was made for passengers bound for Lagos to enter. The driver, chewing gum in mouth, seemed eager to leave. Ama was pleased. She wanted to be as far away from Enugu as possible. The conductor, a thickset man who looked better suited to work on a farm than on a luxury bus, shepherded the passengers in, turning back a man who had a he-goat tethered around his wrist. *Mba.* "No goats allowed on the bus," the conductor shouted, halting the man's progress onto the bus with a palm on his chest. The would-be passenger's red cap faltered on his head and he held it in place with his free hand, extending his hand upward to ensure that the feather stuck in it was still in place. The goat bleated as if in anger. The man croaked, "I'm a chief. How dare you lay your hands on me? Even if you have no respect for age, show some respect for royalty. See my eagle feather?"

"Royalty, my foot," the conductor spat out, pushing the man firmly out of the way so that Ama, who was behind him, could enter. "You are the chief of your shitty buttocks. *Eze ike nsi.* That feather on your cap is a vulture's!" He guffawed as the man complained that he had paid for a seat, the conductor had no right to turn him back. "This is not one of those nonsense buses where you can come in with your goats and your rams. Bushman. This is *eggzecutive* bus. *Eggzecutive.* We don't want goats and rams shitting all over the place. Does this look like a *gwongworo*? This is *eggzecutive.* We'll give you your money back. Bushman." There was scattered laughter, and someone made a joke about chieftaincy titles being for sale; even a dog could have one as long as it had an owner willing to pay. Ama felt sorry for the chief, but what could she do? She got in and sat down on the first free seat she saw, grateful to be out of the cold. The conductor stood at the door and shouted that there was still room on the bus. "Lagos. One more *nyash*! Lagos, one more *nyash*!" He waited for a minute or two to see if there were any takers. There weren't. He shut the door and hit the side of the bus, and the driver started to ease out slowly onto the road. Hawkers had milled around the bus as it filled, and when it started to move they chased it, urging customers to buy their wares. *Sweetbread. Moi-moi. Special moi-moi. Banana. Buy banana. Peanut. Orange. Honey orange.* Most of them were young girls. One or two were women about Ama's mother's age. The woman beside Ama stretched her hand out of the open window to take possession of a wrap of *akara* she had just bought. Her bangles rattled. She smelled of clothes that had stayed too long in a box. It was a mixture of staleness and camphor. The smell irritated Ama, and she began to wish she had a window seat. The bus gained speed, and the depot in Uwani and the hawkers and the people who had come to see friends and relatives off disappeared from view as it rounded a bend and joined the long, slow traffic out of Enugu. Outside the cathedral, the beggars were already up. A woman with a scarf that was going awry on her head held a melancholic baby on her hip with one hand and with the other extended a metal begging bowl toward the bus. "*Nyenu m ego.* Give me money, please. God go bless you. *Chukwu gozie gi.*" The conductor screamed at her to get away from the *eggzec- utive* bus. "*Ga,* go and tell the man that got you pregnant to look after you. *Anu ofia.* Wild animal. If you spread easily like butter, you get what you deserve."

The woman beside Ama shouted at the conductor that did he not know it was men like him, men with jobs and homes, who got such women pregnant and left them to their lot? Some dissenting voices rose, and a loud one said that everybody knew men could not control themselves, it was not in their nature. "*Umu nwoke bu nkita.* Dogs! That's what men are!" It was up to women to make sure they did not put themselves in a position where they would be used. A woman with a broad face and a huge pimple on her chin, across the aisle from Ama, told of her neighbor's daughter who was raped. "When they said she was raped, me, I was not surprised. 'Why would she not be raped?' I asked the mother. The things she allowed the girl to wear. *Tufia!* Dresses that showed her thighs. Blouses that stuck to her, hugging her everywhere so you could see her breasts standing at at- tention, saluting everything that passed by. Why would she not be raped? *Biko,* let me hear word."

Voices rose in support. The woman beside Ama tried to shout above the din. Sensing that she was losing ground, she turned des- perately to Ama for support. "*Oro eziokwu?* Is what I'm saying not true? Men cannot keep those things between their legs still. And it is men from homes who do this. You think it's their fellow beggars who are busy trying to survive that sleep with them? *Mbanu*. No."

Ama made some noncommittal murmurs that she hoped would satisfy the woman and at the same time stop her from trying to engage Ama in conversation. She had no inclination to be drawn into the argument. She did not want to think of men. Or of rape. Or of her father who was not really her father. As if to signal her withdrawal from the discussion that had taken over the bus, the woman unwrapped her parcel of *akara*, spreading out the crumpled newspaper wrapping on her lap, smoothing it so that the six bean-cake balls lay displayed, balls of molded gold. Its aroma hit Ama straightaway, intensifying her hunger. "*Welu ofu.*" The woman offered her a ball. Ama smiled politely and said no, thank you. The woman urged her: "It's too much for me. *O rika. Welu.*" Ama kept her smile while protesting that she had no hunger, she'd had a heavy meal before leaving her house. "Rice. You know how rice sits in the stomach for hours."

"True," the woman agreed. She prodded the balls with a finger, chose one, and raised it to her mouth. She bit into it, exposing a creamy white inside. "Hmm. *O soka.* Delicious," she announced through a mouthful. Ama's stomach rumbled and she closed her eyes, anticipating sleep to overwhelm the hunger now that the bus had become still again. Sleep did not come, but she resolutely kept her eyes closed. It was a shame that she could not pinch her nostrils shut, too. She heard the woman wrap up her food, and then she asked Ama, "Are you sleeping?" Ama nodded, determinedly keeping her eyes shut still. "You are lucky. I can't sleep in a moving car. I wish I could. I haven't slept all night."

That makes two of us, Ama thought, willing the woman to let her be. She figured that if she kept quiet the woman would stop talking and allow her to sleep in peace.

"I'm going to America. I mean, I'm going to the embassy for my visa interview," the woman announced.

Ama said nothing, hoping she would catch the hint. The woman did not, for she continued, "But I'll get the visa. My son says this is just a formality. He knows these things. He knows the Americans. He has been living in America for eighteen years. Eighteen years. He is American now. Even when he talks to us on the phone, I can hardly understand him. *Supri supri*, that's how he talks now. Wanna. Gonna. Momma." She laughed and continued. "Next month I leave for America."

Her voice rose at "America," and the passenger in front of her turned back to give her a quick look. America was coveted. It was the promised land that many heard of but only the chosen few got to see. Ama gave up and opened her eyes. She realized that there was no hope of getting any sleep unless the woman fell asleep herself, but the way she was going there was very little hope of that happening. She was one of those who would carry on a monologue with the dead.

As the bus entered Awka and joined the highway to Onitsha, the woman began to talk about her family: her children in America and her husband in the village. She was afraid of going to America. Of the flight. Of going to a foreign country. Of having to stay with her only son and his white wife. What would she eat? What would they talk about? Why had he married a woman whose background they knew nothing about? Whose background they could not check? Nobody knew her parents, what sort of people they were. What if they had been criminals? Lepers? *Osu*, outcasts, even? Her husband had been heartbroken when the son sent them news of his impending marriage three years ago, enclosing a picture of a woman with hollow eyes who was so skinny that it was impossible to imagine her ever being able to carry a pregnancy. What had attracted their son to this woman when he could have had any woman he wanted? How could those skinny hips keep a baby? But she had, much to the woman's amazement, carried pregnancies full-term and delivered healthy babies. She had given her son children. As an only son, he had the duty to perpetuate the family line, to live up to his name, Afamefuna: *May my name never be lost.* It was his obligation to enrich the lineage with children, but not children from a white woman. In any case, she was looking forward to meeting her grandchildren. It had been difficult for her to accept, but *nwa bu nwa.* A child is a child. She was going to see all her grandchildren. Her son's two, Harry and Jimmy. What sort of names were those for boys who would grow into men? And the other eight scattered all over the States. Her three daughters had done well, marrying men from their town, men whose families they knew. If only the son had done the same, she and her husband would have had nothing to worry about. "It's bad advice," she said. "Someone advised my son wrongly, and I curse that person, whoever he is. May his eyes never see good. May his stomach bloat until it bursts. May he shit fat worms until he enters the grave." Her son had always been sensible, right from a very young age, she said, and could not have made such a wrong choice if not for the wrong sort of people around him. "The road is far, *uzo eteka,*" she added wearily, "or I would have seen to it that the wedding never took place." Her breath hit Ama in the nose, filling her nostrils with the smell of *akara.* She could not decide which of the two was worse: the smell of *akara* or of stale clothes.

The woman was still talking two and a half hours later when the bus stopped in Onitsha to pick up some more passengers. Ama wondered where the three women who had entered would sit, as all the seats seemed occupied. She watched as the conductor hauled three squat stools from somewhere under the bus and set them at the back in the aisle. She had not thought that Ekene Dili Chukwu did *attach,* too: Passengers paid a fraction of the full fare for the privilege of sitting on those stools, earning the driver and the conductor some extra money. Ama wondered if the stools were not uncomfortable. As if in response to Ama's unasked question, one of the three attach passengers stretched her legs out in front of her and was scolded by the conductor, who told her that she was not in her kitchen or in her bedroom. "This is *eggzecutive* bus!"

When the bus stopped at its Benin depot, the woman beside Ama finally ceased talking. Ama was grateful for the quiet. Perhaps now she could squeeze in some sleep before they drove into Lagos. But a young bald man joined the bus. He stood in front beside the driver, a traveler's bag hanging from his shoulders, and began to preach. He reached into the bag and brought out a leather-bound King James Bible. His voice, even without a microphone, carried into the crevices of the bus so that it was difficult to escape. "If you love Jesus, raise your hands." A few people raised their hands; the rest ignored him.

"I said, if you are not ashamed of Jesus, raise your hands. Hallelujah!" He got a stronger response this time. Ama's neighbor woke up and raised up both hands, keen to show how extreme her love was. Ama shut her eyes. She had had enough of preachers and pastors. By the time the man opened his Bible and started to read a passage, he had lost Ama.

Yesterday still seemed surreal in the way that dreams sometimes did. But it happened. If it did not, she would not be in this bus, on her way to her mother's cousin in Lagos, beside this woman who smelled of *akara* and stale clothes and camphor.

Ama still could not tell what had possessed her to talk to her father the way she did. Maybe it was her frustration at not passing her JAMB, the university entrance examination that would have enabled her to leave Enugu, to seek her future at the Nnamdi Azikiwe University, Awka, where she had applied to study laboratory science. All her life she had dreamed of going to university, somewhere outside Enugu but not too far that she could not see her mother often. And then getting a job and cutting herself completely off from her father's whiteness. She would still come home to visit her mother, no matter where she lived. She sometimes felt sorry for her mother, the way she had to boil the clothes the assistant pastor on his way to becoming pastor had to wear so that his purity glowed, the way she walked with her back hunched when the clothes did not come out clean enough and Brother Cyril, who did not tolerate shortcomings and wanted them all "to make it to heaven," expiated her sin with a beating. Ama wished there was a way she could free her mother and herself from the house in Enugu with the thirty-two steps leading up to heaven. Even though it had been years since he stole into her room, searching in the dark for her breasts that were not yet fully formed, the image still tormented her. He had stopped coming when she started her period at eleven. Although she hated the bloody discharge every month and the accompanying ache in her back, she was grateful for the respite from her father. It made the pain of her period worth it.

She had sat and passed her SSCEs two years ago, but two years in a row she had failed to score high enough on the JAMB examination to get a place at the university of her choice. If she had the money to pay someone to take the examination for her, she would have. Everyone was doing that. She knew people less deserving of a place at the university who had either bought examination papers from corrupt JAMB officials and practiced at home, or who had paid others to sit the examination for them. Ogonna, the dullest girl in her class, entered the university straight out of secondary school. Yet everyone knew that Ogonna could not even write her own name without misspelling it. It was not fair at all. Not after all the studying and the praying Ama had done. She had spent the entire morning locked up in her room, crying and cursing the world for its unfairness. In the afternoon her mother had persuaded her to eat some lunch, reminding her that she could always try again next year. "It's not the end of the world." But as her mother spoke, all Ama saw ahead of her was a one-way tunnel and her, stuck in the middle of it, going nowhere. It was the end of the world.

When her father came home from work to be confronted with the JAMB result, he had accused her of not studying hard enough. "If you had spent some time studying for your exams instead of floating around the house like a ghost, you'd have passed! You are just lazy. Plain lazy. Period!" He had thrown the white officious-looking paper at Ama and asked for his food. "Get out of my face, you lazybones, and help your mother in the kitchen. Idiot. You crawl around like a lizard, *ngwerre*, how do you expect to pass JAMB? You think passing JAMB is drinking *akamu*? Get out of my sight, *ka m fu uzo*, let me see the road." He hissed and half pushed her away from where she stood, in front of him, as if there were really something behind her she was blocking from his sight.

Ama staggered back but found her balance almost immediately. Anger spasmed through her body and exploded from her mouth. "You call yourself my father?" Later, she would think it was the reference to her floating like a ghost that tipped her and spilled the words. "You call yourself my father? You call yourself a pastor? You disgust me! *I na-aso m oyi.*"

Her mother ran into the sitting room where they were. "Shut up, Ama! Shut up. *Mechie onu.*" She tried to drag Ama out of the room. The daughter resisted, pulling her wrist away from her mother's hand. She was stronger and had no problem disengaging herself from the older woman.

"*Mba.* No. I will not shut up. Mama, do you know what he did to me when I was little? He raped me. Night after night. He would come into my room and force me to spread my legs for him. Remember when you always thought I had Apollo?"

Ama's mother lifted a hand and slapped her on her mouth. "How dare you talk about your father like that? What has taken possession of you? *I fe o na-eme gi n'isi?* Have you gone mad?"

Brother Cyril's voice cut into her mother's, slashing off her words meant to be placating him, words meant to be asking him not to listen to Ama, to ignore her. "No. Let her talk. *Ya kwube*. Let her spew her venom. See the kind of child you brought into my house? See? *I fugo ya nu?* In fact, open the windows so that our neighbors will hear. Let our *agbataobi* come and hear your child's nonsense."

"Mother, you have to believe me," Ama begged. "I'm not lying. He raped me. *Eziokwu*, Papa raped me."

"Do not call me that. Do not call me Papa. I am not your father, you stupid lying girl." Each word, carefully enunciated, rolled out in claps of thunder.

"Not now, Brother Cyril. Please?" Ama's mother was on the floor, kneeling, hands stretched out in front of her, palms outward: the same position she assumed when she prayed and called on her God to forgive her, a poor sinner. There was something deeply shaming in her posture, and Ama wanted to drag her up.

Brother Cyril laughed and unfolded himself from the chair he had been sitting on, waiting for his supper. He planted himself in front of Ama, his toes big and masculine, sneering at her from his leather sandals. "I am not your father. You hear that? I took in your mother, and this is all the thanks I get. All the thanks I get for saving you from being a bastard. All the years I raised you, fed you, this is all the thanks I get. You know what happens to children without fathers? Children who are born at home? Father unknown. *Ime mkpuke*. I want you out of my house. I want you out. *Tata*. Today! As God is my witness, you shall leave my house today!"

"Whatever your problems are, bring them to the Lord today. Hallelujah!"

"Amen," the bus chorused.

Ama, lost in thought, was momentarily dragged back to her present. She had never been to Lagos. How would she survive there? It was the only place her mother had thought of sending her. It was far enough away from Enugu and the people they knew. Ama wondered how they would explain her absence to everyone. Would her mother tell them she had gotten a job in a different city? Gained admission into a university? What? She could not believe that the circumstances surrounding her birth had been kept a secret from her all these years. How could they have done that? She had a father she knew nothing about. Last night she had felt relieved that Brother Cyril was not her real father. When she thought of it now, she felt gratitude, a thankful relief that her father was a better man than Brother Cyril. He had to be. She willed it. But the relief was short-lived. It was soon replaced by the nagging question of who her real father was. What did he look like? Where was he? What was his name? How tall was he? How short? Did he have a beard? A mustache? Did she have another family? Brothers? Sisters? What did they look like? Did they know about her? Questions grew wings and flew around in her head, knocking against her skull so that she soon developed a headache. She rubbed her temple. In an instant her life had crumbled. Her solid life had disintegrated, and she no longer knew who she was. It was like being thrown out of a cage only to land on a bed of thorns. She could not decide which was better, the claustrophobic cage or the scratchy thorns. At least, she thought after a while, she could get up from the thorns and walk away. Her thoughts returned often to her father, her biological father. It was impossible for her to imagine that her mother had ever been with someone else. That her mother, quiet and obedient, a Christian man's wife, had actually had sex outside of marriage!

Back in her room, which had remained the same since she was a child, she had demanded that her mother tell her who her real father was, but her demand had been met with a lamentation that she was an ungrateful child. A wicked child whose sole aim in life was to ruin her mother's life.

"I made a mistake. One mistake that could have destroyed me completely. Yet Brother Cyril took me in and married me. He saved me from a terrible life. How many men would marry a woman who was carrying a child for another man? Tell me, Ama, tell me. And you throw all that in his face. What have I done to deserve this? Tell me, Ama, what have I ever done to deserve this? He could have sent both of us out tonight. Many men would. You know that. Yet, out of the goodness of his heart, he didn't."

Ama tried to tell her mother about the year she was eight. On the tip of her tongue, she tasted the fear of the nights he came into her room and yearned to spit it out. She started, but her mother cut her short.

"Just shut up. Shut up, Ama, before I am thrown out of my husband's house because of you. *Mechie onu kita.*" There was a strange hardness to her voice that silenced Ama. "Just pack your things. Pack your things. First thing tomorrow morning, *ututu echi*, you shall be on the bus to Lagos. I have called Mama Eko. She knows to expect you." Her mother threw some crumpled naira notes on the bed. "That's for your fare and for food on the road. You will not have time for breakfast in the morning."

Ama did not pick up the money until her mother, shoulders drooped, backed out of her room with the incongruous dignity of a disgraced masquerade.

The next morning she let herself out of the house in which she had grown up. Neither Brother Cyril nor her mother had come out to see her off.

MAMA EKO WAS AMA'S MOTHER'S COUSIN. SHE RAN A BUKA IN IKEJA, VERY close to the Diamond Bank on Ezekiel Avenue. She had the sort of face that many people would describe as jolly: dimpled and full. Before coming to Lagos, Ama had seen her only once, when she came to Enugu on a two-day visit. Ama remembered that Mama Eko complained about Enugu. She said it was too small. Too dead. Too quiet. She said, "People here walk as if they are on their way to their graves."

Even Lagos at Christmas, when everybody went to their villages, was not as deserted, she said.

"Lagos is the place to be! Lagos *bu ebe ano.* The happening city." This was at breakfast the next morning, her bangled wrists waving over the plates of fried eggs and toast, so that they produced a sound like the clang of a distant gong, prompting Brother Cyril to mutter loud enough for her to hear that perhaps those to whom Lagos was the beginning and the end of their world should not bother to leave it. Ama was not sure if it was that comment that made Mama Eko leave the next morning or if she had planned all along to spend only two days.

Mama Eko was one of the first faces Ama saw as soon as the bus drove into its depot in Lagos. Her dimpled smile when she spied Ama in the bus relieved the latter. It was an open smile that Ama knew was at once genuine and pleased. Ama half ran into her outstretched arms, gratefully letting herself into the space between for a hug. "Good afternoon, Mama Eko. Thank you for coming."

To which the woman simply replied, "Your father is a difficult man to live with. *Nno.* Welcome to Lagos."

Mama Eko's house was smaller than Ama had imagined. Somehow she had thought that a woman as large and as flamboyant as Mama Eko would live in more opulent surroundings. Mama Eko lived in the ground-floor flat of a three-story building.

"This is my mansion." She chuckled as she turned the key in the lock of a grimy leaf-green door that led directly to a living room choking on furniture. Mama Eko's bulk filled the room. There was a huge beige sofa running down one side of the room's mud-brown wall, behind it a dining table. A blue velvet love seat and two rattan dining chairs faced the sofa. And, in the middle, a wide, low table with a glass top and massive marble legs shaped like a man's. On the table was a brown vase, the same shade as the walls, filled with yellow, purple, and red artificial flowers. The flowers were clean, as if they had been recently dusted and cleaned with a damp cloth. To the left of the table, on the side of the love seat, was a three-tiered oak-paneled TV stand with a twenty-one-inch Samsung color TV, and below it a stereo set, and under that a video player. Squeezed in between the TV stand and the glass-topped table was a narrow vitrine containing a large selection of CDs. The most Ama had ever seen in any one person's collection. She scanned the names on the CD covers, muttering them to herself: Marvin Gaye. ABBA. Victor Uwaifo. Peter Tosh. Onyeka Onwenu. Dora Ifudu. Nina Simone. Barry White. She picked up one and turned it over and stared, entranced, at the titles of the tracks. "My Baby Just Cares for Me," "Love's Been Good to Me," "I Loves You Porgy," "Falling in Love Again," "Alone Again." All irreverent titles that stood out in luscious contrast to the pious titles of those by the Voices of the Cross. And when Mama Eko let out a swear word when she switched on the fan and the blades did not turn, Ama knew that she would make this place home. She smiled a long blissful smile. She could never use a swear word at home. She repeated the word Mama Eko had just let loose to herself and enjoyed its impiety on her tongue, relishing its very profanity, which tasted like nothing she had ever had. She felt treacherously happy. The happiest she had been in as long as she could remember. She had a feeling that her whole life before now had been spent waiting for this moment, that every other time she had felt she was happy was in preparation for today. "Nice collection," she said to Mama Eko, who had just come out of a room, rubber slippers on her feet.

"Oh. Yes. Sorry, *ndo*, I didn't even ask you to sit down. You've come a long way. *Nodu ani.* Sit. Biko, don't mind me. Those shoes I was wearing always pinch my feet, but they go well with this *boubou*." She wriggled her toes in the slippers. "Ahhh. My poor toes. What we do for fashion, eh?"

Mama Eko gathered the sides of her multicolored *boubou* between her legs, complained of the heat, and sank into a chair. She invited Ama to do the same. Ama chose one of the rattan chairs. It was surprisingly uncomfortable, propping her up as if it had anticipated a slump, as if it were her school principal scolding her: "Sit up, girl!" Its back was hard and hurt her. She eyed the sofa and wondered if she should change chairs. The sofa looked more welcoming than the rattan chair. She weighed it for a minute in her mind and decided against it.

Someone shouted "NEPA!" from across the street. There was a squeak. And then the blades of the fan began to turn. First, laboriously, the *groom groom* of a tired lawn mower on its way to retirement. And then it gathered speed and the *groom groom* became an almost noiseless whirr that transformed the fan into an efficient machine for cooling the skin and spreading enormous goodwill. "The power is back on," Mama Eko announced, happy, smiling. "This heat was getting to me. NEPA doles out electricity like it is doling out charity. We have to be grateful for whatever little we get. We are at their mercy." She hissed. Mama Eko did not look like she could endure being at the mercy of anyone. "Uju will soon be back, and then you can have something to eat. Should I play some music? There is nobody who can sing like Nina Simone. I had never heard of her until I bought one of her CDs from a hawker in a *go slow*. I liked the look of the woman. Ugly. *Ojoka*, but in a very attractive way. I started playing the CD in the car and there, in the traffic jam, I felt as if I had won the lottery. *Eziokwu.*"

She got up and inserted a CD in a player. Presently, the room was filled with a voice that stunned Ama with its tragic beauty. It felt to Ama like she was being delved into the depths of her darkness, but she was certain she would come out clutching something beautiful — the tail of a rainbow, perhaps. A lusty, heartbreaking crooning. Of sadness and joy. And of a father who was already a ghost.

• • •

UJU, A GIRL WHO LOOKED ABOUT TEN, CAME IN JUST AS THE MUSIC WAS winding down. She called Ama "Auntie" and said "*Nno*" to her, kneeling on one knee to show respect. "Should I get food now, Mama?" she asked Mama Eko. Mama Eko nodded, and Uju slunk away into a corridor that ran adjacent to the living room.

"That girl is heaven-sent. She is the best house girl anyone could have ever wished for. She is small but mighty. That's what I call her," Mama Eko eulogized the little girl. "Small but mighty. *Obele nsi na-emebi ike*. She is the small shit that causes a grown-up to strain and groan. Lagos is a hard place. I'm busy all day in my canteen, but Uju manages the house and does a good job of it. Girls twice her age would have been overwhelmed, but no, not Uju. And her food is excellent. *O na-esi nni ofuma ofuma*."

As if on cue, Uju wafted into the room on the aroma of bitter-leaf soup. She set the tray of food on the dining table and went back into the kitchen for a bowl of water. She put the yellow plastic bowl in the middle of the table and disappeared as furtively as she had appeared. The women washed their hands and fell to. Ama licked soup off her fingers and declared that Mama Eko had not exaggerated the gastronomic qualities of her help.

"I have never had anyone make bitter-leaf soup this tasty before," Ama said, grateful for the food, her first meal that day. She picked up a piece of stockfish and licked it clean of soup before popping it into her mouth. "*Okproko aa amaka*. Good stockfish. The food is just divine."

Mama Eko rolled a ball of *gari*, dipped it in soup, and announced that the soup was not Uju's best. "I tell you, the girl is a genius in the kitchen. The man who marries that girl will never stray. She is a diamond. A treasure. *O site*. She can make even palm fronds tasty. *Eziokwu ka m na-agwa gi*. I'm telling you the truth. Uju can cook first-class jollof rice with just palm oil and crayfish. I swear." Soup dribbled down her chin, and she wiped it off with the back of her hand. She called to Uju and asked her to bring two bottles of Guinness from the fridge. Ama had never had Guinness. Alcohol was banned in Brother Cyril's holy household. "You'll have one, won't you?" Mama Eko asked.

"Yes. Guinness is good," Ama said. She eyed the bottle covered in mist. Mama Eko tilted a glass and expertly filled it for her, a layer of white foam on top, dark ruby liquid at the bottom. Ama took a sip. Tentative at first, then she swallowed. Another sip. She tried not to pull a face. It was bitter. It tasted like *dogonyaro* leaves, boiled and strained and then drunk to cure malaria. Her mother had to force it down her throat, telling her it was for her own good, did she want to stay in bed weeks on end, down with malaria? "Drink it up, *nne*, drink. Be a good girl." She would shut her eyes, hold her nose, and let her mother pour it down her throat. But now she did not shut her eyes. She swirled the glass, looked into the drink, and saw flecks of light at the bottom. Ama gave the glass another swirl, brought it to her lips, and drank. It went down her throat and released something wondrous on the way. She looked at Mama Eko and was grateful for her; she wanted to hug this woman, who was warm and irreverent and cheery and full of promises. Everything that Enugu had failed to provide her.

Mama Eko had neither husband nor child. Ama wondered if that was why she had been sent here. Or had her mother known that Mama Eko would be the one to ask the least questions about the whys and wherefores of Ama's being sent out of the house? Perhaps she already knew. Maybe she also knew that Brother Cyril was not her real father, Ama thought, and wondered how many people knew. Was she the only one in the dark? Did the rest of her parents' family know who her biological father was? Most likely Mama Eko knew, but Ama dared not ask her. If she did not know, Ama did not want to risk having to be the one to expose a family secret. Yet it gnawed at her.

On the other hand, she was glad that Mama Eko did not mind her reticence. It was almost as if Mama Eko had no desire to know what had happened and was simply pleased with the company. "For a city that's so full of people, Lagos can get very lonely once you are indoors." She winked at Ama in the car as they drove to her house from the bus depot, making Ama wonder if her words masked something deeper.

Ama was sent off to her room after lunch to unpack and get some rest from her trip. She was tired but had protested that she was not. After all, she said, she did not walk all the way from Enugu. Mama Eko would have none of it. "Go and rest, my sister's daughter. You have had a long trip. *Ga zue ike.*"

With some food in her stomach and a comfortable bed to lie in, Ama was glad of the opportunity to sleep. Lagos was an adventure she was eager to embark on, but it required energy. Lots of it. She could sense it in the air and in the noise that filtered into her room from the other flats close to theirs. She could not wait for the next day to start her journey of discoveries. She would go with Mama Eko to her canteen, where she would help in the kitchen, cooking and serving customers. That was all Mama Eko required of her in return for a home and peace of mind.

The *buka* was a small building, ambitiously named Mama Eko's Cooking Empire. The billboard bearing its name also carried weighty promises inscribed in cursive gold: DELECTABLE FINGER-LICKING DISHES. AN ORGASMIC EXPERIENCE. ONE TRIAL WILL CONVINCE YOU! Beside the promises, the face of a man with his tongue hanging out lusted after a bowl of pounded yams. Lining the front of the Empire, cruel-looking cacti. Mama Eko said they brightened the building better than flowers, which needed watering and love, caring for like a child. "These don't mind whether you remember them or not. They just keep growing!"

In the ten months Ama stayed in Lagos, her life followed a routine that began to bore her in its insistent constancy. Every morning from Monday to Friday, she would get up at half past five, have a quick shower, dress up, and take the *molue* to the Empire.

She would arrive just before seven. Jangling keys, she would open first the burglary-proof door, a blue construction of security grille, and then she would open the wooden door, draw the curtains, dust the chairs, and start slicing bread for the breakfast customers. Mama Eko would come about an hour later, and Uju would be there in time for the lunch rush. On Saturdays Ama went food shopping with Mama Eko and Uju. And on Sundays they rested. There was no frantic *hurryuporwe'llbelateforchurch*. Just a stretching out on the bed with the ease of a pampered cat, yawning at leisure and watching TV while Uju whipped up delectable dishes in the tiny kitchen, sending Mama Eko into realms of culinary pleasure where she *haahed* and *ahhhed* and said Uju could not but marry a good man. Any girl who cooked the way she did was sure to end up with a good man. That was how the world worked.

It was a better life than Ama had in Enugu, she could not contest that, but its predictability, its circular motion that took her from the small flat to the tiny Empire and back to the flat, nibbled at her soul, which still yearned to see the world.

During the week, the breakfast run was fairly easy; it was slow, and many people asked for buttered bread and tea. Ama could butter bread with her eyes closed, and mixing tea and milk was a child's chore. The afternoons were hectic. The food got more complicated, and customers were more exacting, having spent the morning shut in their offices, chasing deadlines, listening to impatient bosses tell them what to do. They came to the canteen for a world far removed from their offices. They wanted their *fufu* to be the right consistency, the soup to be just right, and would complain if it was not.

"Ah, Mama Eko, this *fufu* dey like water oo."

"Sister Ama, na so *fufu* dey dey for where you come? Dis one na for to drink?"

"Na small child cook dis food? I no go come here again if na like dis your food dey!"

"Dis food no sweet today at all at all. Na so so salt full am."

"Dis na soup abi na water?"

"Wey de meat wey suppose dey dis soup? Na ant you give me make I chop?"

Ama and Mama Eko would apologize, promising better food; blaming inclement weather or the time of the month for the fall in standard of the food; offering an extra piece of meat, a bottle of something to drink. Any incentive to keep the customer happy.

Ama looked forward to the customers, for sometimes they came with bits of her dream. Reminding her of what she might otherwise have forgotten, keeping her on her toes, so that she could never be complacent: young women slinging expensive handbags, coming in from the bank on their lunch break. Sometimes they came accompanied by eager young men in suits and ties. But mostly they came alone, bringing into the *buka* the sweet-smelling fragrances of perfume and freedom. And the elegance of perfectly groomed nails and expensive hair extensions. Ama spoke to them. She always spoke to them. They had a charm that pulled her, so that after she had taken their order, noting it in meticulous handwriting on a sheet of paper, she hovered around.

"Sister, your hair is very well done. Where did you have it fixed?"

"Oh, thank you. Headmaster's. I always go to Headmaster's."

Ama could see the smugness in their eyes as they announced the salon, lifting hands with painted nails to the hair, touching it as if in reassurance that it was indeed well done. Ama could not afford the exorbitant rates charged by the hairdressers at Headmaster's. She always got her extensions fixed at small salons, cubicles with one hairdresser or two, who charged her sixty naira for their labor. These young women made it sound so easy. Doling out thousands of naira for their hair. Ama knew for a fact that Headmaster's charged about three thousand.

Ama served them, and if their hands inadvertently touched hers when they took the tray of food from her, she saw it as a sign that their luck would rub off on her, that one day she could afford to patronize a salon like Headmaster's, ask for a pedicure and a manicure while a professional hairdresser wove expensive extensions into her hair.

She saw the life she could live (she had a right to it as much as these women did, didn't she?) fluttering about the room long after the women had eaten and gone. They left a trail of longing like footsteps in the mud, and Ama knew that she had to leave. But how? How could she break a circle, a line that connected to itself, looping itself around her, manacling her so she could hardly move?

She had become somewhat friends with the regulars, interspersing the food and drinks with tidbits about the day and with questions about their families and work. "Is your son better now? Poor boy. Typhoid fever is a hard illness for even an adult to handle." "Did you get the promotion? Ah, we have to celebrate it oo. We go wash am oo!" She was especially friendly with a man called Dele. He always wore rich lace suits and left her huge tips. The other regulars knew him, as he would sometimes offer to pay for their food and drinks, shouting across the tables so that his voice tripped, tripped, tripped along them and found its way to the counter, where Mama Eko stood watching over her customers. "Mama, I dey declare today! For everybody. Even you! Eat! Drink! Senghor Dele is paying." Face beaming, he would accept with a bow the applause and the thanks of the other customers as they ordered extra pieces of meat, another piece of fish, another bottle of beer. Senghor Dele is paying!

One day he came in the morning, rather uncharacteristic of him. He was the only customer, and Ama came out to greet him and take his order. "Today I just wan' talk to you," he said, dragging her down to sit beside him on a wooden chair. "You been working here now for how long? Seven months? Eight months? Almost a pregnancy! You na fine woman. You deserve better. You wan' better?"

Ama had smiled in response, at a loss. Of course she wanted better. Did she deserve it? Why not? She did not want to spend the rest of her life cooking and dishing food. Not knowing where Oga Dele's speech was going, she kept mum and waited for him to land. He had mentioned his wife often enough for her to know that he was married, so he could not be asking her to be his wife. Plus, he often spoke about his daughters. "Fine fine gals so," he would say of the girls he said were eleven and twelve. "Any man wey mess with dem in future I go finish am. I go kill de man. I go squash am like ordinary mosquito, I swear!" He would touch the tip of his tongue with his index finger and point to the ceiling to show that he would make good his threat. Nobody who heard him doubted him. Could he be looking for a mistress? Ama hoped not. The last thing she needed was a valued customer, whom she did not fancy, making a pass at her. She would not know how to deal with it.

But Oga Dele was not walking that road. "If you wan' make easy money, if you wan' go abroad, come my office for Randle make we talk. But only if you dey serious o. If you no dey serious make you no waste my time and yours. You hear me so?" He rubbed his knees and raised his bulk from the chair.

Ama nodded. "I hear you, Oga Dele."

"I no wan' food today. Na jus talk I wan' talk," he repeated solemnly.

He gave Ama his complimentary card and asked her to come and meet him at the office the following day, once the canteen was closed. Most people ate at home on Fridays, so the canteen traffic would not be great. Ama guessed, rightly as it turned out, that she could be at his office by eight.

Dele's office was as wide as the man himself. It was huge and made Ama wonder how big his house must be. Its size reassured her—somewhat—that in coming to see him she was making the right decision. There was a comforting elegance in the depth of the rug on the floor, in the wall clock that showed the time in different zones, and in the three slim mobile phones on his executive table. Dele sat behind the table, swiveling on his chair like an excited child.

"I dey happy say you come." He swiveled as soon as she walked through the door. His smile rumpled up the three wide marks etched into each cheek.

When she had told Mama Eko she would be late coming home because she had an appointment with Dele, Mama Eko had not told her not to go, but she had not minced words in telling Ama she was unhappy about the meeting. "Ama," said she, "what are you going to him for? Why would he want to send you abroad? Does he not have relatives who need his help? Lagos is full of men with money, full of *big* men with heavy wallets. They are like sand in Lagos. *Fa dika aja. A di acho fa acho.* But the problem is that nobody knows how they make their wealth. What does Dele do? Who does he work for? He has the time to come to the canteen at least once a day, five days a week, yet he drives expensive cars and wears the latest lace. You know how many ritual killings are carried out here every day?"

Mama Eko piled gory stories one on top of the other. Severed heads found under the bridge in Ojuelegba. The policeman who apprehended a driver with a busload of little children he was ferrying to a secret location in Benin City to be killed for a moneymaking ritual. The passenger in a bus who was discovered to be carrying a little boy's head in his travel bag. He was beaten to a pulp by an irate mob, and then a car tire was thrown around him and set on fire to kill him. The mob applauded as he died.

"People disappear every day, and men without obvious means suddenly become rich. I'm not saying Dele is a ritualist oo. Look at my armpit, I have no hair there, *nekwa abu m n'aji adiro ya*. I'm not calling anyone a ritualist. I'm just saying look before you leap. I've spoken. Count your teeth with your tongue, *welu ile gi guo eze gi onu,* and tell me what you come up with. He comes to the *buka* when other men are at work. Wears gold, gold, everywhere. You are a grown woman. You make use of your senses. Me, I've spoken."

"I go straight to the point," Dele told Ama, ushering her into the chair opposite his. "You no be small gal. Na woman you be. Mature woman. I go tell you wetin it be. I need women. Fine, fine women like you make dem go work for abroad for me. For Europe. For Belgium."

"What kind of work?" Ama wanted to know. What sort of job did he need women to go to Europe for? Everybody wanted to leave the country; why should he be wanting people to leave? Ama knew people who would give their right arm for an opportunity to work abroad. People with university degrees. She did not even have that. Mama Eko's words started to drift into the corners of her mind. She was amazed at how much she remembered of the speech to which she had paid scant attention, convinced as she was that Mama Eko was an alarmist, like most women of her generation, and that Dele did not have the haunted look of men who chanted strange rituals over lobbed-off heads.

Dele laughed a deep laughter that invited Ama to join in, but she did not.

"What kin' job I go dey wan' fine fine women to do for me? Na for to wash clothes? Ugly woman fit wash clothes, too! I no need fine woman for dat. I tink say you na mature woman. Why you wan' disappoint me?" He laughed loud, exposing incongruously small teeth with silver fillings. Black gums.

Ama looked at him. "Stupid fucking man. What do you think I am? I look like *ashawo* to you?"

Dele laughed. And laughed. "I wan' help you you begin abuse

me. You get life! Plenty fire for your voice. Any man wey get youna real pepper soup him get, I swear!"

Ama watched him laugh and heard Brother Cyril call her a lazy good-for-nothing and she pooled saliva in her mouth and released it, aimed at Dele. It missed its target and landed with a *plop* on a sheet of paper in front of him. Dele hit the table with a massive palm, stood up, eyes blazing, stomach wobbling. "Make you never, ever try dat again. You no know me oo. Make you never try dat kin' behavior again. I don warn you!"

Ama hissed, turned, and walked out. What did he take her for? She wanted a better life, but not that badly.

But.

Wait.

Maybe.

What if.

So?

At night when she tried to sleep, mosquitoes buzzed in her ear and kept her awake, and being unable to sleep, she thought. But. Wait. Maybe. What if. So? And one night she thought, and thought and then she laughed. Maybe she was going crazy.

Brother Cyril had taken what he wanted, no questions asked. No "please" and "may I" or "could I." And a discarding of her when she no longer sufficed. And strange men taking and paying for her services. And it would not even be in Lagos. But overseas. Which earned you respect just for being there. It was not like she would be standing outside nightclubs in Lagos Island, hoping that she would not run into someone who might recognize her. So. Why not? Mama Eko's was nice. Mama Eko herself felt almost like a mother. A proper working mother. But Mama Eko could not give her the kind of life she dreamed of. She could never save enough from working in the *buka* to set up her own business. So why not?

She gave herself two days. *Two bloody days*. And then she went back to see Dele. "I am down with it," she said, relieved by the option of choice.

"Wetin?" Dele shook his head in confusion.

"Yes, I said. I will do it. I go do am."

"You go do wetin? Me, Dele, offer you sometin', you insult me. Who you tin' say you be?" He opened a magazine, and his face disappeared behind it.

"I dey sorry, Oga Dele." Not contrition but fear of a lost opportunity made it a whisper.

A ruffling as he turned pages. Maybe he had not heard. So again: "I dey sorry, Oga Dele."

"Sorry for yourself. No disturb me. Abeg, I no wan' abuse today, so make you just leave my office."

Did he want her to bloody kneel down? She said she was sorry again. Could not tell what had come over her that day. Sorry. Sorry. Sorry. Sorry. She would say it as often as she had to. She would say it until he relented.

But. Wait. Had she no shame? No. Not today. Fuck! So.

"Sorry, Oga Dele."

He put the magazine aside. Did she know how many girls were lining up for the chance he gave her two days ago?

"Sorry, Oga Dele."

Did she know how many girls had come to him, begging to be one of his girls?

"Sorry, Oga Dele. Sorry, sir."

He got up from his chair, toddled out from behind the table, and hugged her. "I forgive you. I like you, I swear! And dat na de reason wey I go forgive you your abuse of last time. You be fire!" He pulled Ama close, and she could feel his penis harden through his trousers. "I shall sample you before you go!" He laughed. A laughter that stretched itself into a square that kept him safe. Lagos was full of such laughter. Laughter that ridiculed the receiver for no reason but kept the giver secure in a cocoon of steel. It was not the sort of laughter that one could learn. It was acquired. Wealth. Power. Fame. They gave birth to that kind of laughter. And then: "I like you. If to say I be Muslim, I for marry you. Make you second wife. But na Christian I be. And I be good Christian. One man, one wife." He sounded regretful. "But I must sample you. I must. I swear! See as little Dele just dey stand. Little Dele like you. I like you, too. You na my kin' woman!"

He smiled at Ama, and Ama smiled back. No more but, wait, maybe. Just a wanting to make money and own a business and show fucking Brother Cyril that she did not need him. Did not need her mother. Did not need their fucking blinding whiteness standing in her way.

MAMA EKO WAS NOT CONVINCED BY HER STORY THAT DELE WAS SENDING her to Europe to work as a nanny to the three-year-old daughter of a rich Jewish family, and she told her so. "Me, I have never been to *obodo oyibo*, but I am sure they have enough nannies for their children there without having to import one from Africa. Count your teeth with your tongue. I've spoken. I've said my own."

"The ones from Africa are cheaper, Mama Eko, they don't charge as much as the *oyibo* ones do," Ama countered, worrying that Mama Eko would discover her lie.

Mama Eko said, "I don't trust that Dele. Not one little bit. I joke with him and laugh with him, he is my customer, but I don't trust him as far as I can throw him. I don't trust that man at all at all. I wish I could make you stay, but I can see that you are determined to go. Since I can't stop you, I want you to promise me that you'll look after yourself."

"I will. I am a big girl, Mama. Don't worry about me."

There were tight hugs and maybe even a few tears, and just before Ama left for the airport Mama Eko sneaked a tiny gold crucifix into her hand. "May God guide you, *nwa m*." Ama was touched. Nobody had ever cared for her in that way, had given her a sense of totally belonging, but even that was not enough to stop her from anticipating with delight the start of her new life.

Antwerp welcomed her the day she arrived, engulfing her in a sunny summer embrace that shocked her, as she had thought Europe was always cold. She would hear later that the summer of 2000 was one of the hottest summers Belgium had ever seen. Her hair itched under the long extensions that came down to her midback, and she regretted the corduroy trousers and matching jacket she had chosen to travel in. They were a parting gift from Dele. He had told her the airplane could get cold and there was nothing like corduroy for keeping warm on a cold plane. It did get cold on the plane, and she was glad for the warmth of the corduroy suit, but no one had warned her that once she got off the plane temperatures could get fevered. In all the stories she had heard about abroad, she had never heard it said that it could be so hot she would wish she had worn a sleeveless dress.

She had nothing loose to change into, having brought along only clothes that would keep her warm in the cold of Europe: sweaters and thick trousers and shawls that she had bought at the secondhand market. She was not at all prepared for this heat that got between the skin and clothes like the heat of Lagos.

"I can lend you something to wear," Efe, the woman who brought her lunch, offered. "We are almost the same size, after all." She rubbed sweat off her forehead. She disappeared and came back later with a dress. "This should be long enough. You're not much taller than I am."

"Thank you," Ama said, accepting the tie-dyed gown Efe had brought her: a riot of colors she could not discern running into one another, and which Ama found, quite frankly, distressingly ugly.

When one of the girls with whom she shared the house asked about her parents, she said that they were long dead. Her mother had died at birth, her father a few years after in a car accident, so that she did not really know them; when she looked at pictures of them it was like looking at pictures of strangers. She was raised by a generous aunt. Later, she wondered if she had, in telling this lie, articulated a wish for her mother and Brother Cyril. In bed, she thought about her real father. She created features for him by peering in the mirror, excluding traits she had inherited from her mother: the eyebrows that were almost joined, the nose that looked almost European, the hirsute legs that needed waxing at least once a month. Those were unquestionably her mother's. Which meant that her father had:

1. Slightly bowed legs
2. Naturally light skin
3. Long eyelashes

This did nothing to stop the wanting, did not stop the peering into strangers' faces for signs of likeness. And when Joyce told her that her father used to let her play with his baton, Ama wished her own father had raised her. Maybe her life would have been different. Maybe it would be different if she found him. But she had no idea how to. Later, after Sisi's death, she would decide that even if she could, even if there was a chance of someone finding him for her, she would not seek him out. Mama Eko loved her with a mother's love. That would do for her. As for Brother Cyril, he could fucking jump off a bridge, her mother holding on to his shirttail. She did not bloody care.

SISI

THE MINISTRY OF EXTERNAL AFFAIRS BUILDING WAS A CASTLE THAT looked as if it had been there since the beginning of time, erected for life. It made Sisi think of chandeliers and heavy drapes and rooms with uniformed servants. Outside it, people stretched out like columns of ants in front of a huge metal gate, the type of gate one would find in the more prosperous suburbs of Lagos, protecting the mansions of the very rich. Many of the people outside the ministry huddled inside jackets, hiding their heads inside the collars as if they were spies. There were a few with suitcases, many more with huge travelers' bags. They could have been at a car park, waiting to go on a trip. She tried to block the voices that came to her head—her mother's, mainly, telling her that she was disappointed. Asking her if she would really sell her body for a chance at making some money. Instead, she tried to crowd her head with visions of a future in which she would have earned enough to buy her father a car, buy her mother a house in Ikoyi, and buy herself a good man who would father her children and give her parents the grandchildren they had always dreamed of before they were too old to appreciate them. With the amount of money she imagined she would earn, there would be no limit to her purchasing power. She would even be able to buy her father a chieftaincy title in their village. Buy him some respect and a posture that belonged to a man his age. *Back home, everything is for sale.*

She joined the line, standing behind a tall black man hugging a brown leather attaché case close to his chest. It looked as if whatever was in the case was something he was prepared to protect with his life. His face looked like worn leather but retained the vestiges of an earlier handsomeness that reminded her of a Hollywood star. Some African-American guy who was in this film she had seen—Poitier. Sidney Poitier! That was who he looked like. She wondered what this man's story was. She wished she could ask him, but she did not know whether he spoke English. And if he did, what would she ask? "Are you genuine? What's your story? You want to hear mine? Would you like to trade stories? Mine for yours?"

She ran her tongue across her teeth and dislodged a strand of ham stuck between two front teeth. It brought back to her the memories of a breakfast so scrumptious, she wished she could parcel it and send it to her mother to eat. White sandwiches so soft they melted in your mouth, jam, ham, two boiled eggs, and tea with milk that was not rationed.

The line moved at a languid pace, and she watched as people disappeared into the mouth of the ministry. Finally, it was her turn. With a smile, the guard directed her to a room with glass sliding doors and wooden benches that reminded her of the church pews at St. Agnes in Lagos. She wondered if the smile was ridiculing her. Mocking her story. She entered the room. There were about twenty people waiting, most with tired faces. She tried to smile at a young white couple as she sidled in next to them. The woman had on her knees a little boy in a checked sweater and black denim trousers. He had a runny nose and was whimpering. The mother said something to the boy, kissed him quickly on the head, and dug in her handbag for a pack of cookies, which she gave him. The toddler smiled and proceeded to hastily tear open the pack. The man whom Sisi presumed was his father stared straight ahead as if in a world of his own, detached from what was going on around him. Sisi wondered what was in his mind, what weight he carried around his neck that stiffened it so that he could not turn and smile at his son when the little boy tugged at the collar of his maroon jacket. Sisi watched the boy stuff his mouth one cookie at a time, dropping little bits onto his mother's thighs. She did not brush off the crumbs but instead left them, as if they were badges of honor, to gather on her gray skirt: specks of cream on a gray polyester cloud.

Sisi let her thoughts be consumed by the boy and his antics, so there was no space in her head to think of her family. Or of Peter. She had thought that leaving him would be easy—after all, they had no future together—but she was starting to realize that she could not have been more wrong. She saw him whenever her eyes were closed. And even in this room, right now, she could swear she smelled him, that she could smell the mentholated powder he always rubbed on his back for pimples and for the heat. She missed their moments of intimacy, and when she let her thoughts stray she wondered if she was wrong to have given him up. She stole a glance at her watch. The leather band was worn and stained in places. She would have to buy herself a new wristwatch as soon as she could afford it. Maybe one with a slim gold band. She was in Europe now, and everything was possible, she told herself. She might even buy an extra one and send it to her mother. She imagined her mother's joy at owning a gold wristwatch.

She would never buy a gold wristwatch. Not for herself. And not for her mother, either. She would enter shops and ask to be shown this gold watch. That other one. She would try them on and put them down, saying they did not suit her. Her wrist looked chunky in that. Too thin in the other. She would wave aside the smiling salesclerk's assurance that the watches fit. But right now she was unaware of this.

Sisi shut her eyes and replayed the events of the past two days in her head. She had to make this work, she told herself. There was no turning back now, no room for regrets. It seemed that the misgivings she had dumped with her pumpkin in Lagos had managed to find their way back to her. She ignored them. She heard her number called and got up. She was directed to a small room. She had to walk through a high door manned by a policeman with steely eyes. He had thick curly hair that came down to his eyes, and he had to flick the hair out of his eyes before he could run a long security stick down her body. His face was impassive, bored. Satisfied, he waved her on.

"Good afternoon, madam."

"Good afternoon."

The man she was standing in front of flashed her a wide smile, as if pleased to see her. "First we have to take a picture of you," he explained as he stood her in front of a camera and took pictures. The front. The side. Then he held her right hand and took fingerprints, each finger, until he had all five fingers smeared with ink like some sort of a welcome ritual. Then he had her stamp her inked fingers on a sheet of paper.

Another man with black hair took her into another office and listened as she poured out her Liberian story. She made sure she did not forget any detail. Yes. She was sure her name was Mary Featherwill. Yes. She was Mandingo. Yes. Her family had been killed and there was a price on her head. Could she have a tissue, please? She was sorry for crying. Yes. Her life was in danger. No. She did not think she would survive a day in Liberia. No. She had no other family alive. No. She knew no one in Belgium. The man bent over his computer and typed as she spoke, stopping occasionally to ask her to verify a fact, a piece of information. His voice was patient. Once their eyes met, and she saw something in his eyes that convinced her he knew she was lying. Yet she did not stop. She stuck to her story. Yes. Yes. She was born in Monrovia. No. She did not have a passport because she had left the house in a hurry and was really scared for her life. No. She did not have any form of identification. No. No driver's license; she did not know how to drive. No. She had no birth certificate. She had taken nothing from the house. She was running for her life. No. No family pictures. She had not thought of taking anything from the house but herself. Her security was the only thing she had thought about. No. No dates. She could not be sure of the exact dates the killings occurred.

At last he looked up from the computer. Ran his fingers through his hair. Printed out the statement, asked her to sign it, and gave her a number. "Wait in the waiting room," he instructed.

ZWART

ZWARTEZUSTERSTRAAT

AMA IS STILL TALKING.

"I am in Europe. I am earning my own money. I'm even managing to put aside some. That should make me happy. I didn't leave any sort of life behind to come here. Mama Eko is the only person I really miss. One day, when I make it, I'll go back and build her a mansion! I don't have a child like you, Efe. Nobody I love without reservations. Or somebody who loved me like that. Mama Eko is the only one who comes close." She tugs at the crucifix again. There is a tenderness to her tugging.

"And I haven't got anyone at all. If I make it here, it's for me," Joyce says.

"We'll make it oo. There is no 'iffing' about it. How can we come to Europe and go back empty-handed? God forbid bad thing!" Efe says. She thinks again of Sisi. "Poor Sisi. She no even stay long enough." The thought subdues them. Nine months is not long enough to realize any of the dreams that have brought them to Europe. Even if they were not privy to Sisi's dreams, they know that they are all bound by the same ambition, the same drive. What grandiose plans did Sisi have that would never be completed?

Madam has not said anything, but the women know that they are not expected to work today.

None of them will go to the Vingerlingstraat today to stand in front of the glass showcase, strutting in sexy lingerie, lacy bras, and racy thongs to attract customers. It is a demanding job, their job, and not one that can be combined with grief. Sisi's death has sapped them of energy and left them floppy, like rag dolls.

They often talk about it: the strutting and waiting to be noticed by the men strolling by, wondering which ones are likely to tip well and which are not. From their glass windows, they often watch the lives outside, especially the men's. It is easy to tell those who have stumbled on the Schipperskwartier by mistake. Tourists with their cameras slung around their necks, mostly Japanese tourists who do not know Antwerp, seduced by the antiquity of the city and deceived by the huge cathedral, they wander off and then suddenly come face-to-face with a lineup of half-dressed women, different colors and different shades of those colors. They look and, disbelieving, take another look. Quickly. And then they walk away with embarrassed steps. Not wishing to be tainted by the lives behind the windows.

Those who know where they are and why they are there walk with an arrogant swagger and a critical twinkle in their eyes. They move from one window to another and, having made up their minds, go in to close a sale. The street starts filling up at around nine o'clock. Young men in their thirties with chins as soft as a baby's buttocks and pictures of their pretty wives in their leather wallets, looking for adventure between the thighs of *een afrikaanse*. Young boys in a frazzled eagerness to grow up, looking for a woman to rid them of their virginity. Bachelors between relationships, seeking a woman's warmth without commitment. Old men with mottled skin and flabby cheeks, looking for something young to help them forget the flaccidity time has heaped on them. Vingerlingstraat bears witness to all kinds of men.

The women often discuss their customers, dissecting the men and heaping them into one of two categories. The good ones. The miserly ones. They lack the patience, or perhaps the inclination or inventiveness, to find any in-between men. The ones who are neither good nor miserly. Etienne is one such good customer. Etienne with the garlic-scented smile and hair slicked back, wet with gel, so that they constantly speculate on the jars and jars of gel he must go through.

Etienne is a generous tipper, but you would not tell just by looking at him. He is proof that looks do not always tell the real story about people. Etienne is small and always wears trousers that are too tight for him. Trousers that look like he has owned them since he was fourteen and which make the women joke about the state of his genitals. Not what you would expect from a man who doles out money left, right, and center as if he is scattering rice grains to his pet chickens. He is one of Joyce's regulars. He calls her "Etienne's Nubian Princess." Joyce cannot stand him, the way he calls her "Mama!" when he comes, digging into her waist with his nails, his breath smelling of garlic. She cannot stand the way his gel leaves stains on her pillowcase so that she always has to wash it once he has been. But she smiles whenever she sees him, a reminder that her life has changed, that her affection is for sale. Etienne is, more than any other customer, the motivation for her to leave the Vingerlingstraat. He makes her fear that she has forgotten the person she used to be and that, if left for too long, she may never find that person again.

Joyce does not like to think about her past, preferring to concentrate on the future, on what her life will be once she leaves Madam's establishment. But the past is never far away. She has discovered that it never leaves us completely, no matter how hard we try. The past is like the juice from a cashew. It sticks. And whatever it stains, it stains for good. It is always breathing over our shoulders, and all it needs is an incident, an event, to make it rear its head. And so it is that today, with Sisi's death still recent and unreal and the other women opening up the lives they always kept under wraps, telling the truth, Joyce finds her mind taking her back to life before Joyce was born. She brings out the rag tucked in the waist of her trousers and starts walking around the room, wiping the walls with a furious agitation. "I was not named Joyce, you know. It's not my real name. And . . . and I am not even Nigerian." She has her back to Efe and Ama. Her rag moving in violent circles. This time Efe does not try to stop her. Like Ama, she just watches her.

"I always thought you did not look very Nigerian," Ama says finally.

Efe laughs and says, "Today na de day for confessions. What are you, Joyce? Who are you? Where are you from? Really?"

Joyce turns away from the wall. She stoops, facing the women, and begins to work on the center table. When she starts talking, her voice does not have the hard edge that her housemates have become used to. Instead, it is a child's voice.

"My real name's Alek."

Alek: It sounds like a homecoming. Like the origin of life.

SISI

"SO, HOW DID IT GO? WHAT DID THEY SAY? DID THEY GIVE YOU ANY-thing?" The questions rolled off, chasing one another heel to heel as soon as Sisi entered the sitting room where Madam sat, cigarette in hand, waiting for her. Madam was a huge yellow sun with green com-bat boots under flared yellow trousers. Her yellowness clashed with the redness of the walls, and Sisi thought the whole effect was rather obscene.

Sisi was tired. Her eyes hurt. She could not tell if they ached from the bright yellows of the woman in front of her or if they ached sim-ply because she was tired. Sleep had never been so desired. She longed for the bed in the room that had been her world since she ar-rived. *I really don't want to do this now,* she thought of telling Madam. She wanted the freedom to allow sleep to woo her, to caress her with its softness, until she succumbed. She tried to avoid the yellows and kept her eyes on Madam's face. It was passive, the face of a woman who was not in a hurry to hear her answer but who nevertheless was not used to being disobeyed. Sisi let her eyes follow the patterns made by the smoke from Madam's cigarette. The smoke made faces that mocked her. First her mother's. Then Peter's.

"They said no. No asylum for me." She fished in her handbag for the paper they had given her and gave that to Madam as she repeated herself. "They said no."

The officer behind the table had told her: "We are not satisfied with your story. This paper here says that you have three days to leave the country." A stamped document had been slid over to her. She gave it to Madam. She wanted to ask why she had gone to the ministry if the paper meant that she had to return to Lagos in three days' time.

The gold bangles on Madam's right wrist jangled and flashed as she took the paper. Without even reading it, she folded it and slid it into her handbag. She looked up at Sisi and, as if she had read Sisi's mind, said, "This paper is no concern of yours. All you need to know is that you're a persona non grata in this country. And you do not exist. Not here." Madam puffed on her cigarette, lifted her face upward, and blew smoke into the room. It sailed up to the ceiling and disappeared.

Sisi would always wonder why Madam went through the process of sending new girls to the castle. Did she really expect them to be granted asylum? And if they were, then what?

Madam half closed her eyes, took another long drag on her cigarette, released flimsy smoke into the room, and slowly opened her eyes. She let them run over Sisi, slowly, thoughtfully. As if she were trying to size her up—a commodity for sale, a piece of choice meat, a slab of meat at the local abattoir. "Now you belong to me. It cost us a lot of money to organize all this for you." She spread her left hand, palm downward, as she spoke, sweeping at the sofas in the room as if to say that "all this" referred to the sofa. Her cigarette lay snuggled between the middle and index fingers on her right hand. "Until you have paid up every single kobo"—she pointed the cigarette at Sisi—"every single cent of what you owe us, you shall not have your passport back. Every month we expect five hundred euros from you. That should be easy to do if you are dedicated. But I understand that sometimes you may not be able to, so we have set a minimum repayment of one hundred euros. Every month you go to the Western Union and transfer the money to Dele. Any month you do not pay up . . ." She let the threat hang, unspoken yet menacing, her left hand plucking at a tuft of hair under her chin. Suddenly, she reached behind her and, from somewhere at the back of the chair she was sitting on, drew out a black rucksack. She threw the bag at Sisi. "Here. Your work clothes. Tonight you start." With a flick of her right hand, Sisi was duly dismissed.

In her room, Sisi dropped the bag on the floor and sagged into her bed. There would be time enough to discover what her work clothes were. Right now tiredness curbed her capacity for curiosity. She hoped she could sleep, but it was always difficult for her to sleep when she wanted to. She tried to command her body to relax.

Rest, legs, she ordered her legs. They twitched.

Rest, hands. Her hands folded themselves under her head.

Rest, eyes. She shut her eyes.

Rest, mind. The amount she was supposed to pay every month echoed in her head. *Five hundred. Five hundred. Five hundred. Five hundred.* She tossed and turned. She lay on her side, her hands between her thighs, her eyes still shut. *Five hundred. Five hundred. Five hundred. Five hundred.*

Five hundred euros was a lot of money. If she converted that to naira, it amounted to more money than she had ever dreamed of making in any single month, even working in her bank of first choice. That was five times her father's salary. Surely, if she was expected to pay back that much, it meant that she was expected to earn a lot more. How much more? She could not get her head around it. Her dreams were within reach of coming true. The gold jewelry, the house for her parents, the posh car. If dedication was all it took, then she had it. Months from now she would discover that dedication was not always enough, that there was a resilience required that she did not have. And she would think that maybe that was what the dream that first night had been about.

ZWARTEZUSTERSTRAAT | ALEK

SHE WAS NAMED FOR HER GRANDMOTHER. TALL. REGAL. A BLACKNESS that shone as if polished. She did not know the woman whose name she bore, the old woman having died of a rabid dog bite before Alek was born. But her memory lived in the pictures of her around the house. In the stories that were told of her (every man wanted her for a wife; her beauty was unrivaled; she could have been a queen: the way she carried herself was simply regal). In the name that her grand-daughter had been given. And in the family's fear of and utter hatred of dogs.

Alek had inherited the shiny blackness. The legendary beauty. The height. The darkened lips. But she was not imperial. Her grand-mother's regality had completely passed her by, leaving her with a tomboyishness that both disappointed and worried her mother. *Do not play football, Alek. It's not ladylike. Do not play 'awet, it's for men only. Do not sit with your legs spread like that, Alek, it's not ladylike. Do not. Do not. Do not. Do not.* Sometimes the *do nots* were screamed at her in frustration. At other times they were whispered to her, fervent pleas of a despairing mother who tried to get her interested in other things. Taking her along to milk cows. Finding chores for her in the kitchen. But Alek had her eyes elsewhere. The udders of the cows distressed her. The kitchen was unbearable.

When her period arrived, at twelve, her mother took her aside. She gave her a list of things boys were never allowed to do to her. "Do not let them touch you."

"But why not? What's wrong with touching, Mama?" She was itching to go out and play; that insufferable Ajak would be showing off on the skipping rope. But she, Alek, had practiced all week and could skip better than Ajak. Oh, she could not wait to show her. To wipe the smirk off her face. She hoped her mother would not see that her *asida* lay unfinished. She had no appetite for it. She did not like the food much.

"Not that kind of touching." Her mother shifted on her stool. How to tell this? How to explain herself? She shifted again. "Touching . . . in a different way."

"How different?"

"Do not let them see you naked. Okay?"

"Never!" Why should she want a boy to see her naked? The idea. How could her mother think that?

The mother smiled, relief washing over her face. "Girls who let boys see them naked are not good girls. Nobody will give any cow to marry them. Save yourself for the man who will marry you. Marriage first. And then the touching. *E yin nyan apath*, be a good girl, my daughter. Promise me."

"I'll be a good girl. I promise," Alek said. She got up, but her mother motioned to her to sit down.

"Your food. Eat it up."

Alek groaned. The lump of porridge on her plate winked in mischief.

IT WAS MARCH. IT WAS DRY. IT WAS DUSTY. *IN THE NIGHT I COULDN'T SLEEP because of the cold. But also because we were leaving Daru for a refugee camp.* Her father, Nyok, hoped they could get resettled somewhere close to Khartoum. And, eventually, a migration to the United Kingdom or America. *I was fifteen. I did not want to leave.*

She had learned to write on the kitchen walls. Ignoring the food on fire, ignoring her mother's admonishment that the kitchen was not a classroom. And that nobody would pay cows for a girl who let her food burn.

The SPLA—the Sudan People's Liberation Army—which had been guarding the predominantly Dinka town, was withdrawing. There was a rumor that the *janjaweed* militia was making its way to Daru. To sniff out the SPLA members. And to cleanse the city of its Dinka population. People were disappearing. They would have to travel light, Nyok said. They might not be able to hitch a ride. Not with four of them: Alek, Ater—her younger brother—Nyok and Apiu, the parents. *I liked going to Khartoum. It was a different world. High-rise buildings. Lots of cars. And women with henna on their feet and hands.* The elaborate designs intrigued her. They seemed to have their own lives. To move. Alek often wondered what it would be like to be hennaed all over. (But she would be careful not to get the henna around her cuticles. Henna around the cuticles spoiled the beauty of it. It made the cuticles look dirty, as if the women had spent hours digging up crops and had not bothered to wash their hands.) But this was not a shopping trip. Or a sightseeing trip to the museum. This was a fleeing from home.

In the morning, breakfast and a bath. And an argument. Apiu did not want Nyok in his white *jalabiya*. "In this weather, your gown will be brown before we have reached the end of our street."

Nyok would not be moved. "I shall wear white." Solidly said. A voice not to be argued with.

A normal day. *I was upset at having to leave.* Then a scream. Aiii-iii! Aiiiiiiii! Loud enough to etch cracks into the walls of the house. Aiiiiiiiii! Aiiiiiii! Paralyzing in its horror. Nobody moved. *I dropped the bundle Ma had given me to carry. Covered my ears with my palms. Too late. Too late,* she thought.

"We'll survive," Nyok said. A promise. A voice not to be argued with. "Everybody into our bedroom!"

The children in the clothes cupboard. Husband and wife at the bedroom door. Locked. A sigh of relief. Maybe the soldiers would pass them by. Alek peeped through the keyhole. Dust. Darkness. The key in the lock stole the light and whatever she might have been able to see. Her father's voice. Talking to his wife. Everything. Will. Be. Fine. Then a *boom, kaboom*. The door knocked off its hinges. A gasp (her mother? probably). Loud footsteps that could belong only to soldiers.

Splintering of glass. The mirror beside the door, the only breakable thing in the room. The soldiers laughed.

"Where are they?" A rough voice. "Where are the rebels? Bring them out!" *Brrgghh*. A kick against the cupboard door. Alek held her breath. Did she dare exhale? She reached out for her brother. His hand, slithery with sweat, slipped.

"There is nobody here, sir, just my wife and me." Polite. Politeness never led anyone astray. Maybe, just maybe, it would sway the minds of the intruders. Alek prayed.

"Nobody here, sir, just my wife and me!" A voice mocking her father's.

Alek felt dread worm its way into every crevice of her being. It filled up the cracks that fear had left exposed. The soldiers wanted to ransack the room. To check every bit of it. Under the bed! The cupboard! The drawers! Between the books! *Pa tried to stop them from checking the cupboard.* "It is just us, sir, honestly. There is no one else here. Just my wife and me." Alek imagined her mother nodding. Hoping that the force of her nods would convince the men. Then her father's voice. Faltering. A leaf blown by the wind. "Please, please, spare us." A voice that did not sound like his.

Alek had never heard her father sound like that: timid. Servile. She felt embarrassed for him, this efficient policeman. Maybe on his knees. "Please, sir . . ." The faltering voice. Begun but not finished. A shot amputating the rest of his sentence. A stillness. Inside the cupboard, the smell of fear. Rising and rising. Then a wail. *Ma sounding bigger, louder.*

"Shut up!" a soldier caterwauled at her. The rest took up the refrain.

Wail.

"Shut up! Shut up!"

Wail.

"Shut up, Tora Bora wife."

Wail. "Are we not people like you? Are we not?" Her grief raising her wails to a crescendo that made Alek's lungs clog up as if she were inhaling dust. Alek wished she could block it out, this sound that was horrific in its peak. *I wished I could just wipe off the day and start again.* The wailing continued. Ripping Alek's heart to bits. If she looked hard, she might see the pieces. Scattered over the floor, bloody and irretrievable. A shot. And then a dreadful nothing. Alek shut her eyes. Maybe, if she shut her eyes, she would wake up from this dream. The dust clogging her lungs would clear. Tips of her fingers against her eyes. She had to keep them shut. Let the still darkness segue her into some other realm where her reality was different. *And then I heard a soldier cough and say something that made the others laugh.* The raucous laughter punched her. Her mother's wails replayed in her head. They raised an anger from deep inside her that took over her fear. And her reason. And she went insane. She scurried out from the cupboard. Her parents' bodies were sprawled on the ground, an island between her and the soldiers. Her father's white *jalabiya* was turning the bright red of a medicine man's. She looked away from the bodies. Quickly. And focused on the men. *All I wanted was to be able to attack these men who had just blown my life away as if it were a handful of dust.*

The soldiers looked at her. A bean pole. Breasts like baby man-goes straining against her flowered dress. One of the soldiers smiled. A lopsided grin that caused her to instinctively cross her arms over her chest. He laughed. A long laughter that held no mirth but took its time in dying down. He slapped her hands away. Grabbed her breasts. Pinched them as if testing some fruit for firmness before buying. Her nipples hurt under his fingers. "Stupid African slave!"

Another joyless laughter. *He tore my dress. I fought, but he tore my dress. And. And. And threw me on the bed.* She tried to bite him. He felt her teeth graze his arm and slapped her. She dug her nails into his arm. Another slap. She aimed for his eyes. He pinned her hands down. *I wanted to gouge his eyes out.* She wanted to inflict on him a darkness that he could never emerge from. A pain in her back. One of the other soldiers had hit her with the butt of a rifle. She could not stop it. A scream. It catapulted her brother from his hiding place. A soldier aimed his gun at him and shot. Lifted him off his feet. Landed him with a *whack* on the floor. He did not make a sound. Not before. And not after. Alek tried to scream but could not. Her voice failed her. And then her body followed suit. A warm trickle from between her legs. Soaking her dress. The soldier on top of her slapped her. "Why are you urinating on the bed?" Another slap. "Stupid bitch!" Slap. Slap. No energy to fight back as he spread her legs. He tore off her underwear. She imagined that she saw her mother cover her face with her hands so that she did not have to watch. When he thrust his manhood inside her, when he touched her, Alek felt a grief so in-comprehensible that she could not articulate it beyond chanting, "This is not happening. This is not happening." A mantra to keep away the layer upon layer of pain that seared through her as he went in and out of her, groaning like a dying man. One by one the other men thrust themselves into her, pulling out to come on her face. Telling her to ingest it; it was protein. Good food. Fit for African slaves.

She concentrated on her mantra. Until she started to descend into a darkness, a void, where she felt nothing.

Alek had no idea how long she was left there. Naked. The pain between her legs, harsh. And in her nose, the smells of raw fish and dust. She remembered waking up with the sense that she was in mourning for something she could not immediately identify. And then her eyes fell on the floor. And she remembered. Alek let out a shout that dried her mouth. She groaned, scratched her hands, and screamed again. *Aiiiiiiiiii. Aiiiiiiii.* A scream that made her hoarse. And heralded a stampede of tears. *I had to get out of there. That was the only thing on my mind.* She dug her hand inside the cupboard and dragged out a dress. It was her mother's. She held it against her nose and smelled a warmth that did not console her. She held it against her body and cried into it. Still sniveling, she pulled it over her body. It covered her and billowed out at her waist like a rainbow-colored parachute. She walked out, refusing to look at the corpses on the floor. *I thought if I did not look at them, it would all be a . . . I don't know . . . a mistake, a dream, you know? Maybe they forgot me and left without me.* She yearned to wash out her nose. To wash out the raw-fish smell of the soldiers' come. She wanted to scrub between her legs until she forgot the cause of the pain.

At the front door, her slippers. She had to be strong. Outside, dead bodies scattered on the street. Women in brightly colored clothes walking in a line, bright flashes of color in the midst of such utter desolation. There was something hopeful in the sight. Perhaps all was not lost. Maybe her family still lived and she was trapped in a nightmare. Some of the women had children strapped on their backs. Some had young children walking alongside them. *I joined the group.* No one asked who she was, and Alek did not volunteer. A collective sadness bound them together. Clamped their lips. Occasionally, a young child would sniff. Ask for food. Or a drink. Apart from these, the group walked on in silence toward the bridge. Stepping around corpses. When they saw a football and a child's sandals at the side of the road, Alek thought of Ater. His love of football. *He wanted to play professionally, you know. A midfielder for Hilal, his favorite team. Or Meriekh. His second favorite.* Alek swallowed hard. She would not cry. Crying would be giving up. Or giving in. She was determined to survive. She owed that much to her parents. And to her brother. They had sacrificed themselves for her. She could not let them down. That would be worse than what she had gone through.

She lifted one heavy foot after the other, swallowing her tears so that her stomach filled up with them. Made her so bloated that she was certain she would never need to eat again. It was not until they reached the bridge that Alek looked back. A silent goodbye to her city. She did not know when she would be back. Or if she would ever return. She let memories of the past play in her head. She edited the past. Clipped the horror. Kept only the laughter and the smiles. Her memories were black-and-white reels of evenings spent bantering and eating dinner and good-humored family teasing. But then she remembered. She was alone. She looked down at herself. At her feet. Cracked and coated with dust. Her throat was parched, and she longed for a glass of water. Sweat gathered between the soles of her feet and her slippers. It made the slippers squeak. She wished she could take a bath. A cool, refreshing bath to get the filth off her. Beyond the fishy smell, she could smell herself. Almost. And what she could almost smell scared her beyond fear. And filled her with the rage of a haboob.

Alek felt like she was carrying a ton of sorghum around each ankle. Every move she made was torture. But respite was in sight. The refugee camp on the other side of the river was a six-kilometer stretch of tents. Dust. People. Soldiers guarded the camp. She could see them, smoking and swaggering. With the pomposity of people who owned the earth.

The new refugees were directed to an office to register. For the first time, she told her story to someone else: a white-haired United Nations worker who spoke through her nose like a European even though she was black. *The woman did not blink as she listened to my story*. She did not wince as Alek told how she had heard the shots that killed her parents. How the soldiers had taken turns raping her. How she had watched her brother die, his brains splattered on the walls of her parents' room. *The woman did not blink!* She handed Alek a ration card, told her it was for food. Gave her a plastic sheet for her tent. And shouted out for the next in line. Where Alek had thought that her grief would singe ears and stop the world, the woman's reaction convinced her that the camp was a collection of sad stories. Hers was nothing special. "Next!" the woman called out. Next. All the way at the end of the line, they heard her. *Nextnextnext*. She dispensed of the refugees. Doing the job she was there to do. NEXT!

At fifteen, Alek was setting up home with a bed. And a wooden table. Her dreams of going to university and becoming a doctor buried with a past that she could never get to again. Her new home a tent that she was not sure could keep out the desert sand in the face of a strong wind.

Once she could, she washed herself. Scrubbed the dust off her feet. Until it seemed they would bleed. She willed them to bleed. She would never scrub herself like this again until she moved to Antwerp. The pain of the scrubbing was cathartic. Ridding her body of the weight it carried, so that by the time she was done she felt reborn. Her feet shone, gleaming in the dark, and her ankles felt light.

That night she stood outside her tent and looked at the night sky. It was littered with stars. She smiled at the stars and had a conversation with her father about school. About how hard she would work once she could go back to school. She talked to her mother about her period, which had become painful. She had a quarrel with her brother about his shoes, which she had found in her room. "Your shoes are stinking out my room," she told him, and he pushed his tongue out at her. She was afraid to go to bed. *I was afraid of the dreams I'd have. But I did sleep.* When she slept, she dreamed of her father. When she woke up, she allowed herself to cry. Not even wiping the tears that trailed down her cheeks. It was a silent cry. Not the noisy howling that she had anticipated, the way she had cried at her grandmother's funeral years ago. The tears moved the boulder on her chest and left a cavernous hole where the boulder had been. And in the middle of that hole was the epicenter of a sandstorm.

Alek could not settle happily into life at the camp, standing in line for food and soap. Enduring the shoving of those behind her. Impatient for their turn. During the day, she went with some of the women and young children to fetch firewood for cooking. Escorted by some soldiers from the African Union Peacekeeping Force. There was something distressingly humiliating in the routine of her daily life.

Sometimes, before she fell asleep, she saw her parents lying on the floor of their bedroom. She tasted her fear as she hid in the cupboard with her brother. She heard the laughter of the soldiers as they tore her dress and squeezed her breasts. Sometimes she wished the soldiers had killed her. Having been left alive, she felt an obligation to survive, *but what kind of survival did I have, living in a tent? I hated the camp. I couldn't make friends with the other refugees.* Their singing and laughing irritated her. *As if all was well with the world!* She did not like the ease with which they adapted to camp life. She detested the sessions when the women gathered in a tent for coffee magnanimously distributed by aid workers who encouraged them to talk to one another. To tell one another about their lives in the belief that the exercise would help heal them of the trauma they had gone through. She did not want to hear their stories. To hear about Gyora, who was dragged to a tree behind her family home by two *janjaweed* soldiers. She was raped so violently that, six months later, she was still bleeding. "My body does not want me to forget the violation," she said at the end of her testimony. All the while her arms were wrapped around her waist. Protecting her from an unseen assailant. Neither did Alek want to listen to Raoda talk about being kidnapped. She and sixteen others. Soldiers on horseback. Galloping! Galloping! Took the girls to use as sex slaves. Raoda escaped. In the night. Four months pregnant. Three months later, a baby. Impatient to see the world but unable to survive in it. Alek did not want to sit down and drink coffee. And listen to the woman whose name she could never remember talk about how her fourteen-year-old son was forced to have intercourse with her. A gun at his head. Soldiers in his ear. "Touch her breasts! Put your penis in her!" Alek's body shook with the paroxysm of her rage. What good was this? All this talking. And remembering. And digging up ghosts. *I think that maybe the aid workers got perverse pleasure from listening to these stories of madness, you know?* She refused to tell hers. She had no wish to open up her heart. To lay its bleeding rawness open to strangers.

She loathed the African Union peacekeepers, who strolled around with their hands in their pockets. Kalashnikovs around their necks like musical instruments. She almost died the day she had to go and ask for a sanitary towel. Her period had started at night. *There I was, telling a total stranger I was having my period. And a soldier nearby sniggering.* It made her aware how inconsolably helpless she was.

Three months later and a month before she turned sixteen, Alek met Polycarp. A Nigerian soldier. He was accompanying the group fetching firewood. Defiant in his uniform. Under his left eye a thin scar the length of her little finger; she found herself wanting to touch it. To feel it. To hear the story that gave birth to it. Love. It did not take her long to recognize it. Here, of all places! That was what she said. *Of all the places to find love!* She had not known she had it in her. She had dreamed of marriage and children, but that was before. Before she knew the human capacity for pain and loss. Before she knew that you could go to the center of hell. And not die. Surely not. Denial. Not with a soldier. Surely not. But Polycarp was different. He never looked at the refugees with curiosity. Or with pity. Or with anything that closely resembled derision. Or a sense of superiority. His eyes were warm. His strides, when he walked, firm but modest. As if he was no better than the people he was protecting. He played with the little ones. Let them touch his uniform. Rub their hands across his gun. He pinched their cheeks. Made them squeal with a laughter that did not annoy Alek with its intensity. That did not make her question how anyone could be happy under the circumstances. It was normal for anyone around this soldier to be happy. To laugh. To recover their joie de vivre. And she wanted so very much to be touched by him. Wanted him to induce the high laughter in her as he did the children. Oh yes, she wanted that so very, very much that his face followed her. Every moment of the day.

Polycarp noticed Alek, too. He seemed to find a reason to be near her while she chopped wood. Offered to help her tie her bunch. And when their hands touched, he squeezed hers. This tiny gesture made her want to burst into an aria. When he placed the wood on her head, he touched her neck so gently that she almost missed it. Yet it made fireworks explode somewhere inside her.

Secretly, he brought her presents. A bag. A tin of sardines. A hair comb. A mirror. Some sweets. Alek hid the presents in a corner of her tent. Sometimes she brought out the mirror and surveyed her face. Whenever she did this, the face of a stranger stared back at her. A tightness at the corners of the mouth. Fine lines fanning out from the sides of the eyes. The stranger looked old. At least twenty-five, she thought. She did not think she could ever look older than she already did. What did Polycarp see in her?

He said, "Hold your hair in a bun. So I can see your neck." She giggled.

At night she dreamed of him. She dreamed of the children she would have for him. She dreamed of a life away from the camp. And she woke up with a grin on her face. Life was no longer a chore she had to get through every day. Life was a face. A beautiful scar. A hand sending ripples down the back of her neck. These days, when she talked to the stars, she told her family about Polycarp. She described him to her mother: a man so tall that he could stand on tiptoes and touch the sky. He was the color of yellow maize. Did she think anyone could be that yellow? His voice was hoarse, as if he constantly nursed a cough. *And his nose, Mama, his nose was almost beaked, it makes you think of a bird.* She laughed about how skinny Polycarp was, so skinny he could be a pencil drawing of a stick person. She told her father how Polycarp brought her presents. How he made sure she got extra food. She told her brother how much Polycarp reminded her of him. How they had the same eyes: the pupils not quite dark, a tint of gray. She told them how often she thought of marriage these days. Of being a mother and a wife. She felt like an object that had lain dormant for years and was being excavated.

One day Polycarp gave her a note. It asked her to meet him outside her tent later.

On a night made luminous by the moon, Alek followed Polycarp back to his quarters. His tent had a strange smell. A man's smell that Alek had not smelled since her father died. She must not think of her father now. Nudge the thought aside. Polycarp led her to his bed. He undressed her. Delicately, as if she were fine porcelain that might shatter. He lifted her dress over her head. Bent down and plucked her nipples with his mouth. He threw off his shirt. Guided her hand to unzip his trousers. Gently pushed her down onto the bed. The thick green army blanket scratched her back, but she did not mind. She was floating. Flying. A butterfly fluttering. She felt Polycarp between her thighs. There was no pain. No ache. Just a long, long sigh and a happiness that filled in the hollowness in her chest. Her excavation was complete. She had been dug up from deep under.

In the still of the night, she whispered to her mother, "I'm a woman now, Mother. A proper woman." Her mother would forgive her, would she not? The rules had changed. She had slept with a man without being married to him. She called up her mother's face. And the woman smiled a wide smile that included Polycarp as well. Absolving her. Totally.

Alek met Polycarp often in his quarters. Soon it became clear to her that she could not live without him. He had become as much a part of her as any other part of her body. He made her laugh. He made her forget sometimes that the only time she saw her parents and her brother was in her dreams. Polycarp had sneaked into her heart and carved out a comfortable place for himself in there.

She asked him stories about his life. She sketched his life before they met. The scar was from a lashing by his father. He was seventeen. His father had caught him smoking marijuana. The buckle of his father's leather belt left the welt. He had walked around for days with a hand covering the eye. She relived his life and felt the pain of the flogging. He was the oldest of five children. His mother ran a bakery. His father owned a print shop. He lived in Lagos before he came to Sudan. Lagos was the most crowded city on earth. Lagos was so crowded that it was impossible to breathe. The markets were wildly beautiful. She said it sounded a lot like Khartoum. Only less dusty. "One day I'll take you to Lagos. Treat you like the queen that you are." She laughed at the thought of being a queen. He kissed her and said she had a laughter that sounded like the tinkling of crystal. She laughed at that and he kissed her. And she wished they could stay like that forever. His lips marrying hers.

Two months later, Polycarp was deployed to Lagos. He took Alek with him. *About time*, she thought. Seven months in the refugee camp was a death sentence. The plastic sheeting of the tents could not keep the sandstorms at bay.

SISI

THAT NIGHT, JUST BEFORE SHE WAS SHAKEN AWAKE BY MADAM, SISI SAW her car. A Lexus lit up in such splendor that she could not look directly upon it. But she could see the driver. And it was not her. It was being driven by a headless form with a candlewick for a head. When she woke up, she snapped her fingers over her head to ward off any evil that the dream might portend and, under the gaze of Madam, opened up the bag she had been given earlier and picked out the clothes for her first night of work. The car and the wick flittered at the periphery of her mind, so that when she was not even thinking, they strayed into her mind's eye and filled her with a certain disquiet while she dressed. Determined not to turn and run (where was she running?), she tried to calm herself by dressing with a fervor she did not feel. She pulled on the skirt Madam had chosen. Clenched her teeth and reached behind to pull up the zipper. *Triiiiiiip.* She looked at the blouse. Laughed. Pulled it over her breasts with aggression. She pursed her lips and smeared on lipstick. Red. Red. Like her thoughts. Murderous thoughts that made her wish she could smash things. She had a degree, for Pete's sake. Her hands shook. She did not think she could go through with this. Dark kohl under her eyes, cloaking the sadness that she was scared to see. Obasanjo's children, were they being forced to do things just to survive? She had heard that they were in Ivy League universities in the U.S. She wiped off excessive kohl with a spit-covered finger. Why had she bothered to go to school? She thought of the flat in Ogba. Of Peter with the stalled life. Of her father folding into himself. Of the money she could make. She arched her eyelids in the color of the earth. Madam came to the door to inspect, to ask if she was ready. "Yes," she said. She was.

Sisi was a dream maker in silver and gold. These were not clothes she ever would have picked out for herself, not even for this job. The blouse hugged her intimately, sequined in silver. A gold-colored nylon skirt that showed her butt cheeks when she bent. Sisi felt like asking for a longer skirt. She felt naked, silver and gold nude. Long gold-plated earrings dangled from her ears and rested on her shoulders, thin strings of a setting sun. And on her lips, the rich red of tomato purée. Lips pouting sensually (she hoped), their redness gleaming. She tried to recapture the energy that had made her near-immortal on the drive to the airport.

She failed.

She would come close to feeling like that only once more in her life.

Madam pulled into a parking lot close to a kebab takeaway restaurant. The restaurant was open, and outside customers lined up. "This is as far as we can go by car," Madam told her. The two women got out, and Sisi wondered how she was going to go past the restaurant — with its customers wide awake, waiting for their food — sparkling in her gold and silver clothes like flashy jewelry. Her skirt rode up her thighs, and she was sure that her butt cheeks showed. Was this thing even a skirt? She pulled on it, willing it to stretch and cover her shame.

They walked past the restaurant, and Sisi did not hear the catcalls she had expected, the insults she was expecting to be thrown at her. *I could never get away with this in Lagos, but then this is not Lagos,* she thought, and was grateful. The cobbled road made walking somewhat difficult. They took a side street and came to a wide road on either side of which blocks of flats stood. The ground flats caught her attention. Huge windows like showcases, the edges of the windows lined with blue and red neon lights, and behind the windows, young women in various poses. Mostly poses that involved their chest being pushed out, eyelids fluttering, a finger beckoning. Pretty girls all in a row. Bodies clad in leather or half dressed in frilly lingerie. Boots way up the thighs. There was mainly a population of men on the street. The few women Sisi saw held their men around the waist or dragged at their hands as if to show possession, walking rapidly with their leashed men behind them. The womenless men walked slowly, pensively, yet maintaining the look of people whose presence on the street was transient. Flitting shadows whose images would fade quickly in daylight and whose temporary presence would be pandered to by the workers behind the windows. They would stop and stare at the window displays, matching the idea in their heads with the girl winking at them, urging them to come in. Sometimes they would go up to the windows and talk to the women through slightly opened doors. She saw one or two enter and disappear behind the scenes with their choice for the night.

They passed by a big building with its name lit up in neon red, the silhouette of a woman with long, long legs sitting atop one of the letters. There was something indisputably arrogant about the building. Madam noticed Sisi looking at it and said wistfully, "Villa Tinto. The queen of all brothels. Even has its own police station. It just opened a few months ago. January or February, I think it was. It used to be a warehouse before it was converted. Cost a lot for the conversion. It had to. It's a paradise inside, all high-tech. Designed by some celebrity architect. I hear the girls who work inside have panic buttons beside their beds to press when a customer gets out of hand. They have Jacuzzis. Saunas. That kind of stuff. Too costly for us. Not too many black women inside. Two. Three, tops. This is where ministers get their girls. The girls here are top class. We are going to the *Thee Potje*. No ministers there, but paying customers all the same."

At the door, a tall dark man stood guard. He had on a plain black face cap and stonewashed jeans. Sisi wondered where he was from. His darkness did not look Nigerian, but it did not have the shine of a Ghanaian complexion. Rather, it looked ashy, like a blackboard that had just been wiped but not blackened. Senegalese, perhaps. Or Gambian. He might even be from one of those Rwanda and Burundi places. She could not decide. *They do look alike, don't they, people from those countries?*

The man moved aside, gesturing them in with a hand and his upper body bowed. "Your Beautifulness," he drawled. This made Madam cackle a laugh.

Sisi walked in ahead of Madam to a surprisingly dark room. She had expected dazzling brightness. Lots of glitter and shine. Psychedelic balls of light. The café was dimly lit, and it took a few seconds for Sisi to get used to the dimness. It had a dark wooden interior, a wooden ceiling with blue, red, and orange spotlights arranged in the shape of a huge star that spanned the width of the room, with six other stars inside it, each one smaller in size than the one preceding it, like a *matryoshka*.

At first all Sisi saw was a cloud of smoke rising up to meet the lights. It was as if she had walked off the earth and stumbled into the clouds, with stars in every conceivable color. Sitting on stools along the wall to the right were eleven men, most of whom were smoking. To the left of her was the bar, behind which a portly built man in an apron washed long beer glasses. He raised a finger to Madam, and Madam nodded, smiled, and with Sisi behind her, walked up to the bar. In front of the bar was a line of about sixteen stools. Nearly every stool was occupied by a young black woman. The women were almost uniformly dressed in tight T-shirts that showed off some flesh: a bit of the stomach, some cleavage. Under the T-shirts, they wore trousers or skimpy skirts. They all had long silky weaves—in colors ranging from blond to brown—that swayed with the slightest movement. There were only three stools that Sisi could see occupied by men, drinking beer. A woman with a black tube top and denim trousers sat between the thighs of one of the men. She eyed Sisi and turned around and said something to her companion that made him laugh and shake his head.

The man behind the bar said something to Madam, who cupped her ear. "I can't hear you," she said.

"Just one moment. I be with you. One moment," he shouted above the music, raising his index finger to indicate one. He smiled at Madam.

"Okay." Madam smiled back and, leaning into the bar, said something to him in Dutch. The barman laughed. While Sisi waited, she scanned the room. In the stomach of the café were eight square tables. Each table had about four or so men. Each man had at least one female companion hanging around his neck, sitting on his lap, or simply standing behind him. Toward the back of the café was a jukebox. A young woman in tight trousers and a tank top sat on a stool beside the jukebox, tapping her feet to the music *boom-booming* into the room.

The woman had a small toylike black mobile phone in one hand and a cigarette in the other. Her hair extensions came down to way past her shoulders. Sisi wondered why she was alone. Was she also a madam? Was she patrolling her girls? Making sure they behaved? Keeping an eye on her investment? She looked young. Too young to have her own girls. But rich enough to be no one's girl.

It struck Sisi that the café was a study in opposites. Men/women. White/black. Old/young. Apart from five men, the rest of them did not look a day younger than forty. Sisi would learn later that the older men made better customers. Ama would tell her later, "Young men want lovers. Who wants to be a lover for nothing? Old men just come to be fulfilled. They are not looking for love. They pay to get what they want. Some of them are widowers. Some have wives who no longer want to give action. They come here, and we are the Viagra they need to face the world again. Young men, ah, they have energy, they have dreams. All they want is love. And love is not what we give in this job. It's not part of the job description." Ama would slap her thighs and laugh. Her laughter would ring with the hollowness of an empty shell and move Sisi close to tears.

Madam tapped Sisi on her shoulder. Lightly, like the flutter of a butterfly, but with urgency and authority. The man behind the bar had extricated himself and, to Sisi's surprise, was not as portly as he had looked while behind the counter. He was almost as slim as Segun, and Sisi realized that what had made him seem bigger was his stomach. He had a beer belly the size of an advanced pregnancy, but the rest of him was quite slender. He walked ahead of them to an of-fice at the back of the café: a door beside the toilet that Sisi had not noticed. In the glare of the office fluorescent light, Sisi saw that crumbs of something brown were stuck on his mustache. She won-dered what he had been eating. Bread, maybe? He smiled at the two women, his teeth gleaming at them. He nodded, raked his fingers through straight black hair, brought out his hand, and traced Sisi's figure.

"Very good, Madam, very good. She knows the drill? *Ja?* Here, the *klanten* . . . how you say *klanten?*" He turned to Madam, and she pro-vided the lost word. "Customers." "Yes, customers. Thank you. The customers, they come first, *ja?* Make them drink. Make them buy lots of drinks. Much much drinks. Expensive drinks. You give me busi-ness, I give you business, no?" He winked at Madam and, with an arm around Sisi, led the two women back into the café. Sisi, unused to high heels, staggered on the silver stiletto sandals that sparkled as she walked, moving her buttocks in the way that she had seen models do on TV, feeling more self-conscious than she had thought she would be. "Smile," Madam whispered furiously to her, and Sisi took a deep breath, tucked in her stomach, and donned the smile that would become her trademark in her profession.

A man in a striped shirt smiled back. He was leaning against the wall, a bottle of beer in his hand. His smile was urgent, and Madam half pushed Sisi to his table and then barreled out of the café, vanishing into the night. She had some other business to see to, she said, and Sisi was to behave herself. Sisi pulled on her skirt in a vain attempt to stretch it farther down her thighs, but the skirt stayed put, and Sisi lost her smile.

"Hello, beautiful." The man in the striped shirt grinned at her, gesturing her to an empty chair beside him. "What's your name?"

"Eh?"

"Name? Your name?" He spoke into her ear.

"Sisi."

Sisi sat down and tried to regain her smile. She stretched her lips and parted them. Like a weak flame, the smile came, faltered, and died out. She was a woman sinking. How could she smile while she sank? What on earth was she doing here? Smiling at this stranger for whom she felt nothing but who would probably have her tonight. She had slept with only two people in her entire life. Kunle, her boyfriend before Peter, when she was eighteen and experimenting, and Peter. What would Peter think if he saw her now? Tears found their way to her eyes. She was not doing this because she liked it, she reminded herself. But she was here now, and there was no going back. She clenched her teeth and tried again to smile. Her lips, as if made out of straw, cracked, and the smile splintered. "See See? Beautiful name." The man chuckled. "Beautiful name for beautiful lady. You want a drink? See See?" He said the name as though it were something scrumptious he had on his tongue and was unwilling to let go of. Sisi nodded. "Yes, a drink would be good. Something cold. Thank you."

It was hot inside the café, although on the streets you could tell it was already September: The weather was cool without being really cold. "Wait until October," Ama had warned Sisi earlier in the day. "That's when the cold sets in, and it doesn't let off until the next summer. You'll be talking, and smoke will be coming out of your mouth, as if you've eaten fire. And by the time it gets to December, I tell you, no amount of fire will keep you warm." Sisi had wanted to ask then about the snow, whether it came in December, and was it as beautiful as it looked on TV? All soft and edible, like soursop. But she had not asked. After all, she would be in Antwerp to see it whenever it came. It would be her story to tell someone else. She would be here. She would see snow and winter and meet her destiny. She had the willpower. When this man came back, she would pick up the splinters of her smile and make them whole again.

She watched him walk up to the bar. Now that he had his back turned, Sisi thought that his buttocks looked as if he had diapers on. She chuckled, the vision of the man in diapers momentarily relieving her of unease at the thought of how the night would develop further. Even if she had not had Peter, she told herself, this was not the type of man she would have slept with. She did not find him attractive at all. His face was too wide, his eyes too far apart. What sort of man would go to a prostitute, anyway? Could he not find a woman? At least she was doing it for the money. She had no other choice. What had pushed this man to seeking pleasure between the thighs of a woman he most likely would not recognize outside the café? Laziness? Too ugly to find a woman? What?

A man in a dark brown shirt open over a black singlet passed by on his way to the toilet. His female companion danced behind him, sticking her pelvis in the face of a bespectacled man sitting at one of the tables. He smiled at her. She laughed and licked her lips. "I will wait for you here," Sisi heard her shout to her companion. Twisting at the waist, she went down until her knees were on the floor. Someone applauded her. Overcome by the music, she shut her eyes, thrust her chest out, and jounced her breasts. A whistle greeted this. Her companion turned back and grinned at her before disappearing into the toilet. He had a few front teeth missing. From the back, the grayness of his ponytailed hair melted into his shirt. He could hardly walk straight, and Sisi wondered if his posture was from age or from drink.

The man with the striped shirt returned with two bottles of Stella Artois. "Come, we sit at a table."

Sisi did not usually drink beer. Apart from the fact that it had been too expensive a habit for her to cultivate back in Lagos, she did not appreciate its salty bitterness. It did not lift her to any heights. She had often wondered why people drank bottle after bottle of the stuff. Now she wondered if she would start drinking bottle after bottle to forget. But forget what? There were worse things to become, she reminded herself. She was not a robber, not a cheat, not a 419er sending deceitful e-mails to gullible Westerners. She would make her money honestly. Every cent of it would be earned by her sweat. She did not need to enjoy her job, but she would do it well. She said thank you for the drink as the man poured out some beer for her in a glass. She drank it in one gulp and hoped it would numb her senses or at least make the man before her look attractive. He smiled at her and refilled the glass, emptying the bottle. "My name is Dieter," he said as he picked up his glass and took a sip. Foam gave him a mustache on his upper lip for an instant. He did not look desirable. Sisi lifted the glass, tilted her head, and once more drained the glass in one go. Its coldness masked some of the bitterness. He still did not look desirable. Dieter got up, went to the bar, and came back with another bottle. "You don't talk much, do you, See See?" he asked, refilling her glass a third time.

"No." Sisi shook her head. She struggled to smile, but the splinters rejected her attempts to make them whole, to bring them back to life. They disintegrated like baby ghosts floating about the room and finally disappearing into the gloom.

"Your voice is beautiful. Like you," Dieter told her, reaching across the table to touch her right cheek, his palm clammy. Sisi's natural instinct was to shake it off, but in her new life common sense ruled over instinct, so she left it there. She tried to force herself to imagine that it was Peter's palm, that she and Peter were married and had simply gone out for a drink. It did not work. Dieter's hand slipped and moved to her neck. He ran his fingers down the outside of her neck, all the time muttering, "Beautiful. Beautiful." His eyes bulged out, and shifting on his chair, he moved his hand to her breast, cupping each one in turn. *I can't do this*, Sisi thought. She sat still, her glass of beer untouched before her, her heart heavy with a sadness that felt like rage. She imagined she was in a dream. But she would never let this man into her dreams. She could no longer make out which music was playing, as her ears were filled with the rush of a waterfall.

This is not me. I am not here. I am at home, sleeping in my bed. This is not me. This is not me. This is somebody else. Another body. Not mine. This is not me. This is somebody else. Another body. Dieter got up and motioned for her to follow him. *This is not me. This is not me. This is a dream. But I need the money. I can't do this. The money. Return to Lagos? Can't. Won't?* She tottered behind him, averting her eyes from his buttocks, her sadness abysmal.

This is not me. I am not here. I am at home, sleeping in my bed. This is not me. This is not me. A Lexus sparkled in her head. *Think of the money.* Then a candlewick with a human body. *God help me!*

In a men's toilet with lavender toilet paper littering the floor, soggy (with urine?), and a shiny black toilet seat, Dieter pulled his trousers down to his ankles. A flash of white boxers. A penis thundering against them. A massive pink knob. Sisi gawked. Everything she had heard about the white man's flaccidity, his penis as small as a nose (so that the greatest insult she could heap on an annoying schoolmate was that he had the penis of a white man), was smashed. He heaved and moaned; one hand tore at his boxers and the other at Sisi's skirt. His breath warm against her neck, his hands pawing every bit of her; he licked her neck. Sisi shut her eyes. Raising his head, he stuck his tongue into her ear. In. Out. In. Out. Eyes shut still, she tried to wriggle out of his embrace. She did not want to do this anymore. "I don't need this. Stop!" she said. He held her close. Pushed her against the wall, his hands cupping her buttocks, and buried his head in her breasts. "Stop," she shouted again. Eyes open, she saw his face, his mouth open and his jaws distended by an inner hunger. "Stop!" His moans swallowed her voice. His penis searched for a gap between her legs. Finding a warmth, he sighed, spluttered sperm that trickled down her legs like mucus, inaugurating Sisi into her new profession. She baptized herself into it with tears, hot and livid, down her cheeks, salty in her mouth, feeling intense pain wherever he touched, as if he were searing her with a razor blade that had just come out of a fire. Her nose filled with the stench of the room, and the stench filled her body and turned her stomach, and she did not care whether or not she threw up. But she did not. The revulsion stayed inside and expanded, and she felt a pain, a tingling, start in her toes. The pain that could not be contained began to spread out around her and rise, taking over everything else. Even the sound of her heartbeat.

ZWARTEZUSTERSTRAAT | J●YCE

THE DAY THEY GOT INTO LAGOS, POLYCARP ASKED ALEK WHAT SHE thought of it.

She thought this: Too many people. Too many houses. An excess of everything. Nothing was organized. It reminded her of a drawing by an enthusiastic child with very little talent. Houses juggled for space, standing on one another's toes, so close that Alek feared you could hear your next-door neighbor breathing. The building that housed their flat was long and small, so that even on the balcony she felt claustrophobic. Yet she knew they could have had worse. She went to Isale Eko in her first week and saw houses standing lopsided next to one another like wobbly tables knocked together by an amateur carpenter, and naked children running around with knobbly belly buttons. Polycarp had told her then that some of the houses had no bathrooms. "And this is Lagos in the twenty-first century! Lagos in 2004!" He had sniggered. "All our government is good for is stuffing their pockets. They don't care what happens to the people they are supposed to be ruling." If she had told Sisi this, she would have said that Polycarp sounded like her father.

Lagos streets were rutted, gutted, and near-impassable, yet they were jam-packed with cars: huge air-conditioned Jeeps driving tail to tail with disintegrating jalopies whose faulty exhaust pipes sent out clouds of dark smoke, making the air so thick with pollution that a constant mist hung over the city, and the bit of sky that one saw was sullied with dirt. Broken-down trucks dotted the highways, their flanks huge banners of wisdom, warnings, tidbits of information, or prayers written in bold blacks and reds, each letter a flourish with a paintbrush: ROME WAS NOT BUILT IN A DAY; WORK HARD AND YOUR DAY WILL COME. POOR MAN GO RISE ONE DAY. GIVE PEACE A CHANCE; AFTER ALL STANLEY AND LIVINGSTONE HAD TO LIVE TOGETHER. THE YOUNG SHALL GROW. GOD PLEASE MAKE ME RICH. EDUCATION PLUS BEAUTY MINUS CHRIST EQUALS HELLFIRE; SINNER REPENT. HAD I KNOWN IS THE BROTHER TO MR. LATE. ASK AND YE SHALL RECEIVE: MATTHEW 7:7.

The words were sometimes misspelled, the job shoddy splotches of paint, but it seemed to Alek that no self-respecting Lagos truck would be seen without a slogan or prayer inscribed along its side. She loved to read the slogans out loud to Polycarp as they drove around the city: "'One plus one does not always equating two.' 'The world is my oysta. I shall eat it well.' 'Saluttation is not love.'"

The trucks that did move ferried cows and goats, packed tight like sardines. "For Christmas," Polycarp said, and asked if they ought to get a goat, too. Christmas was only three weeks away. Alek said no, she preferred chicken. "You're with an Igbo man. You better start liking goat!" Polycarp responded, his laughter almost muffling his words.

On any given day, one was likely to find a corpse abandoned by the roadside, waiting for someone to claim it or for the many vultures that circled the city to devour it. Some of the dead were victims of hit-and-run drivers, most of whom were never found and brought to justice. The majority of the dead, however, Polycarp told her, were homeless people murdered by those who needed them to make money. Apparently, juju made of human blood was the best sort to ensure abundant wealth. There were many flyover loops to ease the traffic of the more than ten million people who called Lagos home.

Under the flyovers, beggars made beds out of cardboard and empty cement bags. They left their beds to harass passersby for money, touting their disability like trophies. Every sort of illness known to man was present in whole or in part in the homeless under the bridge. Alek thought it was almost a freak show, an unabashed display of anomalies. People with stumps for arms and legs sticking them at passing cars and pedestrians; blind people rapping on closed car windows and singing for money, led by children with perfect sight; people with disfigured mouths or eyeballs that were unnaturally huge; lepers with skin that looked plastered with coarse sand.

Once Alek saw a man with only a head and a torso being pushed in a wheelbarrow by an old man with the frail body of an invalid. She felt sorry for both of them, so much that at the risk of incurring Polycarp's wrath, she threw a crumpled hundred-naira note from her window to them.

Polycarp had scowled at her, *tut-tut-tutting* his disapproval. "You're just encouraging laziness. Some of these people have absolutely nothing wrong with them. If that old man can push that wheelbarrow, why isn't he doing something useful? In Mali a blind couple are successful musicians. Their music is everywhere. I even know a Canadian professor who is blind. I met him. I shook his hand, so I know what I'm talking about." In his anger, he gripped the steering wheel tighter. "I saw a TV program once where this white woman in London without arms or legs was painting with her mouth. She held the paintbrush between her teeth and one, two, *fiam*, she had finished painting this incredible picture. I saw this with my own *koro-koro* eyes. No one told me about it. I saw it. She is making money. She is making serious money. Her paintings are everywhere in London, and she is being paid for them. In this country, will it happen? No! They just get a spot under Third Mainland Bridge and wait for people to throw money into their palms. They are an eyesore. The government should get rid of all of them. Arrest them and shoot them like they did

Anini and the other armed robbers. If they don't want to make use of the lives they've been given, they should be cleaned up."

Sometimes Polycarp's views bothered Alek, but she loved him nevertheless. The same way that Lagos sometimes bothered her but she liked it still. She loved its arrogant noisiness, its dazzling colors, its fiery temperament, and its hot food that caught her by surprise initially, making her hold her throat and mime maniacally for a glass of something to drink. Polycarp had laughed at her and told her she had to try his mother's *ngwongwo*. "It's more pepper than goat meat."

Lagos was not all pollution and dirt. It had a splendid beauty that was sometimes enough to make her cry. The first time Polycarp took her to the Bar Beach on Victoria Island, the day was made to order: clear skies and a sun that shone straight onto the beach, a dazzling show of splendor. She stood on the wet, incredibly white sand, Polycarp holding her hand, and she told herself that life would not get any better than it already was. She had reached the zenith. Later, they walked along the water's edge. She held her sandals in her right hand and Polycarp's hand in her left. Under her feet the sand was moist and warm, like Polycarp's breath behind her ears when they slept. Her feet made love to the sand. It was a day of innocence: the sort of day that made people believe nothing bad could happen.

She was sure she would be happy in Lagos. Not in the way she had been in Daru, of course, but in a different way that had nothing at all to do with her former life. Her life in Daru would never come back, but she was ready to move on. No more dust clogging her lungs. She felt lucky to have been given another shot. And with Polycarp by her side, there was very little else she wanted.

The flat that Polycarp rented for them had two bedrooms and a small sitting room that she walked the width of in ten normal steps. Alek spent time decorating it. Buying curtains for the windows and pictures for the walls. She went with Polycarp to order a dining-room table from the local carpenter. Polycarp asked for a table that could sit three, for when they had the occasional visitor, he said. Alek smiled shyly and said she much preferred a table that could sit six. She was thinking ahead. To when they would have their own children. And before then, to when Polycarp's family visited. She would make sure they felt at home. She would make it clear to them that they could look upon her as a sister. Or as a daughter.

"But there is no space for that, darling," Polycarp said, reminding her that they still had to fit chairs, a TV, and a sound system into the same room. They compromised on a table for four.

Alek chose the sitting-room furniture; she picked out chairs upholstered in the softest shade of brown, with seats so deep they swallowed one's buttocks.

"These chairs, na ministerial chairs ooo," the salesman told her, slapping the arm of a sofa. "You just sit in them and you go tink say you be president sef!" Alek laughed and asked for a set of four.

They chose a bed together, and when the salesman said they had made a good choice in a mattress: a firm, solid Dunlop on which "one trial and babies will be born." Alek smiled, but Polycarp looked away, embarrassed. She hoped their babies would have their father's eyes.

What with the decoration and the new life to get used to, it took Alek a while to notice that Polycarp had not yet gone to visit his family. Or that none of them had come to see them. She asked Polycarp when she could meet his family. She was looking forward to hours of gossip with his mother, to loving the woman who had given birth to the one person alive she loved the most. He told her they lived down south, in Onitsha, and did not often make trips to Lagos. "Too long. Too many bad roads. And the bus drivers are not always careful." He counted each reason off on his fingers.

She suggested that they go and visit them. "You're a careful driver, Polycarp, and I don't mind the distance."

Polycarp told her he would think about it, but what with him being very busy at work and the distance being long, he did not know when they would be able to make it. "It's not Badagry. You just can't get up and go. You have to prepare, make arrangements."

She tried to make friends with other women, wives of officers in her neighborhood. She asked good-neighborly-wanting-to-be-friends questions.

They answered her all right. Yes, they were fine. Yes, it was hard being an officer's wife. Yes, it was impossible to sleep with the heat. Yes, Lagos had too many cars. Far too many for its own good. But they always fell still after the queries, and none invited her to their homes. And she did not have the courage to invite them to hers. Maybe she was too young for them. Most of the women had teenage children already, children who were her age. She had nothing in common with these children who still lived at home and so did not bother to seek them out. What would they talk about? School? Friends? Parties? The things she had been through had made her way older than they were. Instead of talking to them, she stood on her balcony fighting claustrophobia and dust, making henna patterns in the skies, trying to convince herself that she did not need anyone and that Polycarp was more than enough for her.

Sometimes they went to Ojay's to listen to Rolling Dollar play music that got Polycarp reminiscing about his youth. Telling her how his parents played highlife music when he was young. Sometimes they went to all-night *owambe* parties where entire streets were barred to traffic and live bands played loud music all night long and food and drinks flowed in excess. At first Alek found the idea strange. Most times they did not even know who the celebrants were or what they were celebrating, but the music would attract Polycarp, and he would tell her to dress up, another party to go to. She soon got used to the parties with deafening music, where she and Polycarp danced until their legs turned liquid and then fell exhausted into each other's arms to rediscover themselves.

• • •

ALEK BEGAN TO SUSPECT THAT THINGS WERE NOT ALL RIGHT WHEN
Polycarp stopped saying "I'll think about it" when she asked about visiting his family in Onitsha. Instead, he muttered over a newspaper
that "it was impossible at the moment" and returned to his paper.
Alek's happiness dissipated a little, but she was not entirely down. It
was like Coca-Cola that had gone flat but was still drinkable. She
asked a few more times but, getting no further than before, she decided to let it rest for a while. Her mother used to do that with her
father. "No point in nagging a man," her mother would say. "They
are like children. The more you nag, the more headstrong they are.
You ask, you withdraw, and then you ask again. It's all tactical."

*I had been living with him for almost a year and still had not met
his family. It did not seem right. So I gave him a break and then I
started nagging him about it again.*

After a restless week in which Polycarp was a lot more taciturn
than normal, he announced to Alek on a Saturday morning that he
was leaving for Onitsha to visit his parents. Alone. Alek felt the dust
worming its way into her nose, filling up her lungs, and the pain she
felt almost had her doubled up.

"Why?"

Polycarp looked at her as if she had suddenly gone insane. "Why?
What do you mean by 'why?' Do I need a reason to visit my parents?
You have been nagging, nagging: 'Polycarp, when are you going?
Polycarp, when are they coming?' Well, now I'm going."

She knew that he knew that she was asking why he was going
without her. He knew that she wanted to come along. Something
twisted in her and she looked at him, this man she had always
adored, and for the first time she wished she could hurt him in some
way. Without a word, she turned her back on him, left the kitchen,
and walked into the bedroom. She did not come out to wave him

goodbye when he said that he was on his way out. She pressed her head into the pillow and tried not to breathe in the scent of him.

At night, alone in the flat, she stood on the balcony and tried to create henna patterns in the sky, but what she produced was a farrago of dripping red and brown. And all around her a sandstorm whipped.

He came back after two days. *He said he was sorry for going off like that. He didn't know what had come over him.* Six months later, in June, he went again. Alone. In between his trips, he was the same old Polycarp. Loving her. On the weekend, he took her to Bar Beach and paid for her to go on horse rides and bought her *suya* and Sprite. In the midst of the neck-kissing-eye-searching-horse-riding-hand-holding love, the cracks that were developing had enough hiding places. *Maybe that was why I did not notice that there was something wrong.* Why she noticed his restlessness only in retrospect.

The second time he went, he returned on a hot Tuesday after-noon with an older, feminine, fuller version of himself. Where the son had a scar under his left eye, the mother had a beauty spot above hers. She had a rather agreeable structure, ample in all the right places: the arms, the bit of legs that showed under her skirt, the cheeks. But her eyes were cold, cold, cold. They got colder when Polycarp perfunctorily introduced them: "My mother. Mama, Alek," nodding to one and then to the other. And froze when Alek threw her hands around her in a welcome embrace.

Polycarp's mother, freezer eyes and hissing lips, rejected the hug with a ferocity that landed Alek on the floor, buttocks first. *Pwa!* The humiliation! The shock! And when Alek looked at Polycarp, he averted his eyes and said something in Igbo to his mother. Mother and son walked into the guest room and left Alek sitting there like a scene from a still film, her mouth opening to form a surprised, silent 'O.' Around her, she felt the stirrings of a sandstorm.

At the lunch table, Polycarp's mother spoke only to her son. They chatted in Igbo, and often the woman burst into raucous laughter, a *ke ke ke* that, in its cheeriness, sounded false to Alek, a show staged for her, although she could not tell why. She had been there for an hour and had yet to say a word to Alek. Nor had Polycarp, for that matter, brushing Alek's infuriated "What's that all about?" away with a contained "We'll talk later. I promise you." His voice not quite sounding like his.

Alek had made lunch in silence, alone, muting the kitchen radio that often kept her company. If only she knew what she had done wrong, she would swallow her pride, forget the woman's rudeness, and apologize to her. But how could she start apologizing for something she was not aware of? Where would she start? What would she be expected to say? And Polycarp saying nothing did not help matters at all.

Alek had always wanted to meet Polycarp's family. She had imagined loving them and they in turn loving her. Nothing had prepared her for such a slight. She bent her head over her plate of rice, chewing quietly, trying hard to swallow the disappointment that rose a bile inside her.

After lunch, Alek's food barely touched, mother and son retired to the sitting room and left Alek to clear up alone. They sat side by side, conspirators, speaking in soft tones even though Alek did not understand Igbo, so it would not have mattered if she had heard them.

Done with the dishes, Alek came back to the sitting room to find Polycarp alone on a chair, his hands folded behind his head, the way he always sat when he slept. Except he was not sleeping. His eyes were focused on the vase above the TV, gazing through the frieze of the plastic flowers to the wall.

"Where is your mother?" Alek sat beside him. Behind her was a gold-plated framed photograph of Polycarp and her taken at a studio in Ikeja. Polycarp straddled her, his arms around her chest. The pho-

192 I CHIKA UNIGWE

tographer had told them that he had never seen a couple so obviously
in love, so totally happy in each other's company that they had not
even needed his "cheese" to smile.

"She's gone to lie down. She's tired."

Alek sensed something uncomfortable in Polycarp's voice. Like a
ball of wool trying to stop itself from unraveling. A sandstorm trying
hard not to erupt. Alek sneezed.

She leaned forward and took his hand between hers, rubbing it,
but he claimed it back almost immediately.

And then Alek knew. She knew that she and Polycarp had come
to an end, and she did not know why.

"I'M THE OLDEST CHILD," POLYCARP BEGAN WHEN THEY LAY IN BED.
Alek pressed her nose to the wall. It smelled of dust. "I'm the oldest
son, and my parents want me to marry an Igbo girl. It's not you, Alek,
but I can't marry a foreigner. My parents will never forgive me."

He always mispronounced her name, Ah-lake, and she always corrected him, Uh-lek, but this time she ignored it. She did not care anymore how he called her. He sounded like a stranger, anyway. His
voice was faint, weakened by this speech he had begun and halted
several times already that night. He was making no sense. Talking of
loving. And forever. Of a place in my heart. And then of a father's illness. And of grief that would crush him if Polycarp did not give him
an Igbo daughter-in-law. And of obligations. First son. Culture. His
voice skittered in the dark, saying the same things over and over
again. Love you. Can't live without you. Can't live with you. Kill.
Live.

Alek curled up, a fetus with her knees under her chin. She rested
her head against the dust-smelling wall. It flattened her nose and
hurt its bridge. What could she say? What would she say? The walls
smelled of dust. The bridge of her nose hurt.

"I am sorry," he said. "I am really sorry. I tried not to go. I tried to avoid them because I knew this would happen. I—" He turned and touched her shoulder. She shrugged it off. "I know you can't go back to Sudan. You want to leave Nigeria? Go abroad? I remember you said once that your father had hoped you could all go abroad. I know a man who'll help you. I will pay him, and he can get you into London. America. Anywhere you choose."

London. America. Londonamerica. Said with ease. Londonamerica. Americalondon. Interchangeable. Alek wished she were a man. She wished she were a match, physically, for Polycarp, then she would have shown him what she thought of him and his silly proposal. She would have ripped open the scar on his face, sliced it open with her bare hands so that it hurt with a fresh pain.

In the morning the framed photograph of the two of them, hanging on the sitting room wall, was gone. The patch of wall where it had been hanging a hurtful rectangle of dusty starkness. She grabbed a kitchen towel and started to wipe the area clean.

EVEN FROM A DISTANCE, THE HOUSE, STANDING HIGH UP IN THE AIR, was majestic. It looked so out of place in Lagos that Alek wondered if somehow they had driven out of the city and she had slept through it. Not having slept much the last days, she had been seduced by the potholes rocking the car into a snoreful slumber. "You were snoring!" Polycarp chortled. Alek looked out the window and ignored him. She had not spoken to him in two weeks. Not since the night he told her that they had no future together because she was a foreigner. Yet she made his meals as if nothing had changed. Breakfast. Lunch. Supper. Eaten with smacked lips (from him) and derisive grunts (from his mother). She cleaned up after the mother, mopping the bathroom floor that she constantly flooded with water as if that was her intention, her sole purpose in taking a bath. Alek swept her bedroom, plumped her pillows. Dusted the louvers and the bedpost. Perhaps in a part of her mind she did not control, the idea had snaked in that in remaining dutiful, she may yet sway their minds. Yet it was not in the stolidity of the mother's face when she looked at Alek or in Polycarp's refusal to fight for his girlfriend that Alek saw their relationship fleeting by, fading. It was in their lovemaking: furtive and desultory yet at the same time immensely beautiful. He would never marry her. So why was she stubborn in her dutifulness? She could not tell.

The house was surrounded by a barbed-wire fence and a white gate that was wide open. As they got closer, Alek saw that there were people in the compound. Groups of young men and a few young women with brash makeup and tawdry clothes. At one side of the gate was a huge water tank, and in front of it a man in an off-white caftan sat alone, his arms wrapped around his knees. At first the men in the compound ignored the car, but the nearer it got to the gate the more their eyes became fixed on it, as if daring Polycarp to drive all the way in. Polycarp inched the car to the nose of the gate and then killed the engine. The man in the caftan slowly got up, straightened out his caftan, and walked over to the car. He yawned and poked his head into the car. "Wetin una want?" He drew out his words, stretching each one as if testing for its elasticity.

"We wan' see Oga Dele. I get appointment with am today. My name na Polycarp," Polycarp answered.

The man withdrew his head and pointed to a spot inside the compound, indicating that Polycarp should park there and wait. The man walked past them into the house and came out five minutes later and motioned with his head for them to go in. Alek could feel the eyes of the men boring into her. She tried to disregard them, fixed her gaze on her feet, and, fighting the urge to hold on to Polycarp's extended hand, took fifteen quick steps into the house. Fifteen steps and she was in a living room the size of her father's house in Daru.

The man sitting in a gray leather chair was the fattest person Alek had ever seen. He looked like he was fitted into the chair and could not shake it off no matter how much he might have wanted to. He wore a black short-sleeved linen shirt with trousers to match. His arms were short, and the hand he brought out to shake Polycarp's was podgy and sweaty. He had huge gold bracelets on both wrists. He held a brown handkerchief in one hand and repeatedly wiped sweat off his face, even though the room was air-conditioned and nobody else was sweating.

"Sit down. Sit down."

Alek and Polycarp sank into a deep green sofa that segued into the lighter green of the walls.

"Today na very busy day for me. Una see all the people outside?"

Polycarp nodded. Yes, they had indeed seen all the people outside. Alek studied the L-shaped bar behind the man, reflecting that for someone who claimed to be very busy he did not look it at all. He had a glass of wine on a side table beside him and a bowl of fried meat beside it.

The man was still talking. "Everybody wan' Senghor Dele help. My brother, life is hard." He said the last in the tone that rich people usually reserve for when they talk about how much easier life is without excessive wealth. There was something self-congratulatory about it. Alek was not impressed. She counted the different bottles of alcohol that she could see, lined up on a shelf running the length of the bar. She had gotten to twenty-one when Polycarp touched her and said Senghor Dele had just asked her a question.

"Something to drink? Fanta? Coke? Sprite? Anything. I get dem all," the man repeated.

Alek shook her head. No. She did not want a drink, thank you for asking. Polycarp asked for a beer. Star, if he had, please. Thank you.

"Ah, I no know if I get any beer oo. I dey tink make I open a church. Dat na where the money dey these days. If you wan' make big money, go become pastor, I swear. You don' see the big big cars wey dey follow these pastors when dem dey comot? De one wey I see yesterday na only Lexus and Jaguar full everywhere like *san'san'*. Some even get private jet for dis Nigeria! *Tori olowun*. I swear. I no fit have beer if I wan' become pastor oo. Pastor Dele. Hallelujah!" He belched out a laugh, and Polycarp joined in, saying mock-heatedly, "Why you go wan' make more money? Rich man like you?"

"I never rich like those pastors. I be small man."

This seemed to instigate another gust of laughter. Alek looked from one to the other. Convinced that there was nothing funny, she kept her face passive and then returned to her bottle-counting.

In the wake of the laughter dissipating, their host yelled out, "Good luck! Good luck!"

His voice boomed into the house, bounding over the chairs to drag out a young boy of about eleven with a big head and very skinny legs. He made Alek think of an ant.

"Sah!"

His voice did not belong to his legs. It belonged to his head. Big.

Dele swigged the rest of the drink on the side table, handed the empty glass to the boy, and said, "Bring us two bottles of Star and a bottle of Fanta. The Fanta is for the lady." He winked at Alek. Alek ignored the wink. The same way she ignored the drink when it arrived. She had no plan of being bullied into having a drink she had not ordered. Who did this man think he was to be bossing her about? And why did Polycarp think whatever he said was funny? She looked momentarily at Polycarp and looked away as soon as he caught her eyes.

Polycarp took a huge gulp of his beer. "Oga Dele, this is Alek. I told you already about her." His voice was almost servile.

The fat man nodded at Alek and said, "The name has to go. Alek. Sound too much like Alex. Man's name. We no wan' men. *Oti oo*. That man's name has to go, one time. Give am woman name. Fine fine name for fine gal like her." He laughed and Polycarp laughed.

Alek hated them both. "Make I see . . . Cecilia? Nicole? Joyce? I like Nicole. Wetin you tink, Polycarp? Nicole no be nice name?"

Polycarp nodded. Yes, it was a good name. Nicole was an excellent choice, he said.

Dele shook his head. "No. Not Nicole. Dat Nicole Richie too skinny. No flesh. She be like stick insect. No be good name for fine gal like dis." Another roar of head-bobbing laughter.

Polycarp laughed along. "No, Senghor Dele. Na true. Nicole no be good name for fine gal. Nicole Richie too skinny."

"Joyce. Yes. Joyce. Dat one sound like name wey dey always jolly. Joooooyyce!" He ripped out a loud laugh, a *hee-hee haw-haw* that wobbled his stomach.

Polycarp joined in, his laughter sounding noncommittal, deferential. "Yes, yes, Senghor Dele. Joyce is a much better name!"

Alek crossed her arms and looked from one man to the other. Dele pointed at her, slapped his thighs, and burst into fresh gales of laughter, holding his head in his hands as if the force of the laughter would snap it off. Anger rose in Alek's throat and threatened to make her shout, but she pushed it down. What would she say she was angry about? She had no energy left for anger. The soldiers who raped her that night in Daru had taken her strength, and Polycarp's betrayal had left her unwilling to seek it back. From now on, she resolved, she would never let her happiness depend on another's. She would never let anyone hurt her. She would play life's game, but she was determined to win. Her resolve gave her thirst, and she downed the Fanta without tasting it. She had forgotten that she had not asked for it.

She could not remember how long they stayed there, how long she sat there, her legs crossed at the ankles, while Polycarp and the fat man talked and laughed and ate heartily. Arrangements that she understood neither head nor tail of were made. She was to take passport pictures. A passport and visa would be organized. Money would be paid. Lots of it, but it did not have to be paid at once. She would be taken to Belgium.

"Make you go look after people. Nanny work," the fat man told her, his eyes bright, a brightness that Joyce would understand only in hindsight.

Polycarp added quickly, "Yes. Look after children. Dele will find you a job as a nanny in Belgium."

Alek said nothing. She did not ask why she needed a change of name to be able to babysit children. She uncrossed her legs.

"Ah ah ah, dis one dey ungrateful oo," the fat man said, his face wobbling as he shook his head disapprovingly at Alek. "She sabi how many people dey wan' opportunity like dis? I throw opportunity for her lap and she jus' sit there like *mumu* dey look de ground. Na cow she be? Na grass she dey chop?"

Polycarp gave a faint smile and said not to worry, she just had a lot on her mind. "She'll do a good job," he added, his voice smooth like a lie, as if he was afraid that the man would withdraw his help.

IN THE PASSPORT PICTURES THAT ALEK TOOK, HER FACE WAS BLANK, her eyes fixed on a spot beyond the camera, at a cobweb in a corner of the studio ceiling. She was thinking of the spider that built the web, admiring the intricacies of web building, cloning the web, transferring the clones on the back of her hand with henna that would stain the lines first orange then the reddish brown of a brick.

When Alek got her passport from Dele via Polycarp and saw that she had indeed been renamed Joyce, she did not say a word. She did not even ask Polycarp why.

Joyce Jacobs.

Nationality: Nigerian.

Place of birth: Benin City.

She was beyond asking questions, beyond asking Polycarp to explain anything at all. It would be another two days before she left the country. And in those two days she and Polycarp were two silent strangers sharing a house and a bed on which they had been promised babies would be made. Alek tried not to think of the woman who might take her place and have the babies who had been promised her. She tried to stop the dust from getting into her nose. She swore she would not cry.

When Polycarp, who drove her to the airport, tried to kiss her before she walked through the security checkpoint, she slapped him. Hard. The *tawai!* of it when her palm connected with Polycarp's cheek flabbergasted her into a sudden, loud "Oh!" She had meant it to be hard but did not know she had enough strength to deliver such a blow. Polycarp shut his eyes, and she knew that it smarted. It did not make her feel as good as she had thought it would. And when Polycarp shuffled off, taunts of "Woman wrapper!" "Slap am back!" "You no be man at all!" following him from amused onlookers, she wished his mother had never come to Lagos. The flight was long. And dark. And lonely. Alek felt like cargo with a tag: DESTINATION UNKNOWN. For what did she know about where she was going? About the children she would be babysitting?

As soon as she stepped into the house in the Zwartezusterstraat and saw the long thin mirror, she started to have doubts about the sort of job she had been brought in to do. When Madam came in to see her that first day and she asked, "Where are the children I am supposed to be looking after?" and Madam laughed so hard that tears streamed down her face, then said, "Which children? Which *yeye* children?" she felt a sandstorm whirling in her, painting the walls a dusty, murkish brown.

Madam had given her two days of "grace." And then she had to start.

"Start what?" She eyed the lingerie Madam threw at her in suspicion.

"Earning your keep. *Oya*, time to open shop! Time to work! Time to work! Chop! Chop!" A laughing-dancing-clapping Madam bullied her out of the house, into the car, and to the Schipperskwartier. No passport. No money. What was she to do?

Blue bra sprinkled with glitter and a matching G-string, boots up to her thighs, she stood behind the glass and prayed that no one would notice her. But she was noticed. Her glitter called out to a man with a conspicuous limp. That night she lay on the bed, legs clamped. How could she spread her legs for someone she did not know? She tried not to think about her mother, because she did not want to see her mother cry. She lay there and remembered the men who raped her and squeezed her legs tighter together. The man with a limp, whose face she refused to look at, thought it was all an act, part of her trick. He gushed, "Oh, I like. I like it. Very much. Just like being with a virgin. Tight. Tight. Tight! Many women. Many. Numerous. But nobody do it like you." His gush became orgasmic. "I like! I like! I like! I like! Ahhhhhhhhhh!" He marked her out and became a regular, nicknaming her "Etienne's Nubian Princess."

She arrived in Belgium a few days after Sisi did. Two weeks later, they set off to discover the country. They took their first train ride together, giggling as they walked down the streets of Leuven, taking in the sights. Madam had told them Leuven was a city worth seeing, better than Brussels, "which has only that pissing boy to recommend it."

They got on very well, Alek and Sisi. Sisi had taken Alek under her wing, adopting her as a younger sister, and it was to Sisi that she told part of her story. It was also Sisi who encouraged her on days when she needed encouragement. Sisi who often told her how lucky she was that she could keep most of her earnings, unlike the rest of them, because she had a benefactor who was paying off her debt. Madam treated Joyce differently, deferring to her in a way she never would to the others under her control. Joyce could choose her own clothes, she could knock off work earlier than the others, and when

she said she was ill Madam took her seriously, even becoming solici-
tous on occasion, cajoling her into eating soup to make her feel bet-
ter. *One more spoon, Joyce. Chicken soup to make you better.* Once
Polycarp finished paying—and he had not defaulted even once—
Joyce would become her own woman. She was saving her own
money, too. She was not sure what she would do with the freedom.
Maybe she would move back to Lagos, open up a boutique on Allen
Avenue. The idea appealed to her. She could come to Europe every
summer and shop for her boutique. She even had a name ready for it.
She would call it TOT: Talk of the Town. She had shared this dream
with Sisi, who told her that once she, Sisi, was free, she might enter
into a partnership with her.

And now Sisi was gone.

SISI

SISI DID THE *THEE POTJE* A FEW MORE NIGHTS. IN ITS DIMNESS, IT WAS hard to fake the cheerful insouciance needed to attract a man. Its gloominess was a greedy sort that sucked her decision to pretend. To accept. So she sat in a corner and watched the other girls—flirting and chatting, throwing their hips this way and that, disappearing into toilets with men, laughing a laughter that spilled out at the sides— and had a desperate wish to be more like them. When Madam brought the news that she had found Sisi a display window in the Schipperskwartier, on the Vingerlingstraat, Sisi came close to hugging her.

Working the windows was a better job. The window girls were by far classier than the café girls. Mannequins in lingerie and high boots, they exuded a confidence, an arrogance, that Sisi was sure she could master. It would be easier to do her job from the security and the privacy of a window booth. She could see her life before her: money. And more money. A return to Nigeria with a poise and a wallet that Chisom never could have had.

Sisi learned the rates pretty quickly. She always had a head for figures. Fifty euros for a P&S, a blow job. A bit more if a French kiss was required. Twice the price for half an hour of everything: P&S, French kissing, and full penetration. With a condom. Without a condom, the client paid thirty euros extra. Sisi did not like to do without—what with everything one could catch—but thirty euros was not something she found easy to turn her nose up at. It took a lot of strong will to do so.

She learned to stand in her window and pose on heels that made her two inches taller. She learned to smile, to pout, to think of nothing but the money she would be making. She learned to rap on her window, hitting her ring hard against the glass on slow days to attract stragglers. She learned to twirl to help them make up their minds, a swirling mass of chocolate mesmerizing them, making them gasp and yearn for a release from the ache between their legs; a coffee-colored dream luring them in with the promise of heaven. She let the blinking red and black neon lights of her booth comfort her with their glow and, tripping the light fantastic, lead her to the fruition of the Prophecy.

In between customers, she talked with the woman from Albania who rented the booth beside hers, a partition wall separating them. The woman was big, bigger than Dele's women, who all seemed to be more or less the same size: tall, slim (even Efe, the heaviest, was not that big), with impressive chests and buttocks that were well rounded.

They talked about their childhood. Sisi made up hers. She was sure the Albanian woman did, too. They were people without any past, people with forgotten pasts, so whatever was said would have to be made up of air. But that did not matter. The act of talking meant a lot more than what was talked about. It meant someone still saw you as more than a toy to pass the time with. Sometimes the men who came to them wanted to talk. About the weather (bad summer this year, good winter next year). About wives (my wife, I married her at twenty; nice woman, but the love is going, I think). About parents (my father has to go into a home: old people's home, you understand? You have that in Africa? I don't think so). About regrets (I should have moved to Mexico when I got the chance). About travels (last year I went with two friends to Tunisia: It's Africa; you know Tunisia?). About love (*I love you* spoken so desperately that it became alarming). Mostly, they said nothing. Wham. Bam. No thanks. Just money counted out and, if the girls were lucky, a tip thrown in. On such nights, Sisi threw her legs in the air and counted how much more until she could open her boutique. Start her car-export business. Her Internet café. All the dreams filling her head. The dreams expanding to make sure nothing else came in.

ZWARTEZUSTERSTRAAT

JOYCE IS CRYING, AND IT IS THE FIRST TIME THE WOMEN HAVE EVER seen her cry.

They do nothing. They are on unknown territory, having always had a relationship that skimmed the surface like milk. They have never stirred one another enough to find out anything deep. Joyce's tears take even her by surprise, and she hurriedly wipes them away with the back of her hand. But that does not stop the flow. She pulls her legs up to the sofa, her knees under her chin. She looks like a giant fetus. Her snot mingles with her tears. She wipes her nose on her sleeve. For a while her sniffing fills the room, a cavernous sound that devours everything, even the silence. Ama sighs and then puts a hand out and touches Joyce on her cheek. It is a warm touch, and Alek smiles through Joyce's tears. And then the sniffing tapers and completely dies.

"Some of the stories I heard at the camp, it seems ridiculous that I'd be crying for myself. You know, there was this woman who used to walk around wringing her hands and talking to herself. She told her story to anyone she saw. It did not matter if you had heard it before." Joyce bites her lower lip, takes in a deep breath, and then: "Her village had been attacked, rockets fired, but she and her husband refused to leave their land. They were farmers, growing crops and herding sheep and donkeys. They sent their children, except for the oldest, to the mountains to hide. One day her husband was away visiting family when they were attacked again. The woman and her son were at the well with their animals when they saw hundreds of *janjaweed* militia on camelback and horseback coming. People started gathering their animals and running to safety. She hurried their donkeys to a hillock. Her son was behind her with the sheep. At least that was the arrangement. But when she turned back, she realized that all the men had stayed behind. Apparently to try and protect their land and animals. It was a stupid thing to do, because the *janjaweed* outnumbered the men. She hid behind the hill and prayed. And prayed." Alek stops, looks up at the ceiling, shakes her head slightly. It looks as if she is trying hard not to cry. A sigh that is long and sad escapes her. *Hmmmmmm.* "She could hear the sounds of gunfire and screams. She prayed. And she cried. And she prayed. By nightfall, the sounds of gunfire and screaming had faded, so the woman returned to the wells to find her son. Some other women were there, too. Searching. But there was not a single man to be found. Just carcasses of animals tossed carelessly about."

Another long pause.

"In the wells were the corpses. Dismembered body parts. A leg on a head. A hand on top of another. It was in a well, the moon lighting the features for her, that she saw her son. A head. His eyes open. His upper lip framed by a mustache that was just starting to sprout. You know what she did with that head?"

No one answers.

"She said she took the head. She took the head . . ." Sniff. "She took the head and she buried it. So you see, what Polycarp did to me, it's nothing. It's nothing at all."

Another bout of silence descends upon them, but it is less claustrophobic than before. The air has also lightened somewhat, as though a huge dark cloth that had been covering them has been flung away.

Finally, Ama breaks the silence. "Of course it's something. What he did to you is not *nothing*. Men are such fucking bastards, you know. Why did he bring you all the way to Nigeria only to abandon you?"

"Why did your mother's husband rape you?" Joyce responds. "Why do people do the stuff they do? Because. He did it just because."

The territory they are charting is still slippery. They are just starting to really know one another.

"You know, every day I go to work I wonder if Polycarp was in on this. I wonder if he knew all along what Dele had in mind for me. I don't want to believe he's that heartless. But thinking of all the whys and how comes, I can't sleep at night."

"Polycarp might have known. He might not have known. You'll probably never know. But one thing is sure, Joyce. You are the one having to live with it. And it's up to you how you handle it. What did you say you promised yourself that day at Dele's?" Efe asks gently.

"That I'll never let my happiness depend on another," Joyce says.

"So there you go. Say to fucking hell with Polycarp. Banish him to the hottest part of hell. You might not have asked for this, but this is what you got. That's life. We don't always get what we bloody order. Forget Polycarp. Be the best worker you can be, make your money, and do whatever else you want to do!" Ama lets her cigarette dangle from between her lips while she talks. She removes it now. "Whatever you do with your life from this point on is up to you. Forget Polycarp. Keep your eye on your dream. Fuck Polycarp."

"Fuck Polycarp," Joyce says after Ama. She is determined that she will never again let the thoughts of what he knew, how much he knew, keep her awake at night. She will never again suffer an insomniac night on his behalf. Later, when she thinks of this conversation with Ama and Efe, she will think of it as a release from something she had not known held her hostage. Weeks later, on a Saturday morning, she will tell Efe and Ama, "I had forgotten that my destiny was in my hands. You girls reminded me of it."

"Ah, Joyce, no begin all dis so so fucking wey Ama dey use ooo. One is enough in dis house!" Efe teases. The three women laugh.

At the end of it, a thoughtful silence swallows them up. When it spits them out, it is to hear Efe say that she always wanted to be a writer.

"It was my biggest dream. I was going to write books and become famous." She laughs. "At school na so so cram I dey cram my literature books." She stands up and begins to give a performance. "'It was the best of times, it was the worst of times, it was the age of wisdom, it was the age of foolishness, it was the epoch of belief, it was the epoch of incredulity, it was the season of Light, it was the season of Darkness, it was the spring of hope, it was the winter of despair, we had everything before us, we had nothing before us, we were all going direct to Heaven, we were all going direct the other way—in short, the period was so.'"

"I like the way 'incredulity' and 'epoch' dey drip commot from the mouth. I like the way things wey dey opposite, salt and pepper, dey side by side. Best of times. Worst of times. Light and darkness. It make me tink. Tink say how dat for happen? And when I read am, I jus' wan write like dat. Words wey fine so like butterfly, fine sotay person go wan' read am again and again and again." Her voice dims and she sighs. "But dat one no go happen now."

Before today she had not even thought about it. She has amazed herself by remembering the lines, by her ability to still recite them. But she is not amazed by the happiness it brings her. At the familiar neediness it opens up in her.

Ama starts clapping for her, and Joyce joins in. Efe beams. When the clapping stops, she takes a mock bow. "Maybe I fit try fin' the book. I hear say for Brussels dem get English bookshops. It go nice to own that book again. I for like read am again."

Efe will trawl bookshops in Brussels three mornings in a row without success. On the third day, a helpful shop assistant will offer to order the book for her. It will take a week to arrive. "I don't mind. I don't mind at all," Efe will reply. The day Efe picks it up, she will lock herself in her room with it and cry at a remembered past.

Joyce says she wanted to be a doctor. "Dr. Alek, that was how I saw myself. I thought I would marry, give my parents grandchildren, work in the government hospital. Now I think I'll settle for maybe a boutique. Or a huge supermarket in Lagos."

Ama says she gave up her dream of going to the university long ago. Now, she says, she sometimes thinks of becoming a pop star. Ama does not do more than dream, because even she knows that her singing is false. Once, during a quarrel, Sisi told her that she mewed like an angry cat whenever she sang. "Every time I hear you singing, I think we are under attack from the cat next door!" Sisi had told her. But that is not enough to stop Ama from dreaming. "Sometimes, when I stand behind my window, I imagine I am standing on a podium, posing for my fans. I imagine them screaming out my name, shouting out for autographs. I imagine that my real father hears about me, his famous daughter, and reveals himself to me so I can tell him to fuck off." She laughs, joined by Efe and Joyce.

"I wonder what Sisi's dreams were," Efe says. The question changes the mood again and sucks the easy laughter of the women.

"It's not easy to believe that she is really dead. I keep thinking, what if they've made a mistake? What if she's not really dead? What if she has just gone out on one of her walks?" Ama asks.

Joyce counters, "If she's not really dead, she'd be bloody well here."

"It feels like she is here, I dey feel am," Efe says. Her voice is soft. A prayer. Perhaps even a wish.

SISI

SISI'S FIRST EPIPHANY CAME ON A WEDNESDAY NIGHT WHILE SHE WAS waiting for clients. It was so clear that she could not have been blamed for believing that, finally, the secret of the Prophecy had been revealed to her. Diaphanous, it fluttered down and slipped over her face. What she saw dipped her in such black gloom that her first client, a man with a toupee that he insisted on hanging on to, told her he felt cheated. Her performance had been so poor, he said, that he was never coming back to her. "The girl who used to stay here, she knew her job. You just waste my money! Today I have no release. No release! I have to masturbate."

This was it. The prediction meant nothing. Just the ramblings of a bungling, overindulged guest at a naming ceremony. She swore never to forgive the woman responsible. *Stupid, stupid woman who had me in search of brightness. Stupid woman who brought me to this. To this!*

Seven days after Chisom was born, at her naming ceremony, a gap-toothed soothsaying neighbor (whose reputation was solid, backed by a series of correct predictions) sucked the air between her teeth, raised the new baby up to the skies, looked deep into her future, and declared to the waiting parents, "This girl here has a bright future ahead of her ooo. You are very lucky parents oooo."

Now Sisi knew what she had seen. The woman had seen her in the bright lights of Antwerp. That was her destination. Not, as she had stupidly imagined, a transit route to an infinite betterment of her world. Blue and red lights, like Christmas lights, decorating her window, and she in the middle of all those lights, on display, waiting for buyers to admire and buy. Temporarily. That was the bright future the soothsayer had seen through the bottle of beer she was gulping. (That woman must have drunk a carton of beer that day, so happy was she with your future! You remember, Papa Chisom? How impressed she was with Chisom's life that she finished a carton of Star?) And they had not known that the bright future she had seen was literal. Not the sort of bright future that they had all thought it to be and of which her father had been certain that education was the key to and had pushed her to study. Study! Read! You'll have all the time in the world to rest once you graduate! She had studied hard, not because of her father. Or even because of the vision the neighbor had seen. But for herself. A university education guaranteed a good job. She burned candles when there was a power failure and studied in their light, straining her eyes. What had all that been for? What had all that hard work and straining and worrying about exam results gotten for her? It turned out that it was not her math teacher—who told the class at the beginning of Chisom's final year in secondary school that she was sure to be a successful career woman, "That girl has nothing but brains in that head of hers"—who had the key but Dele. Dele, the big man with an office on Randle Avenue. Dele had brought her to the brightness that was in her future. When he made the offer, she had found herself grasping it, the Prophecy assuming truth, her belief in it as unequivocal as her father's had been. If Dele could get her a passage into Europe, he would bring the soothsayer's prediction to fulfillment.

Her education had just been a waste of resources. A total waste of time and funds. And a step in the wrong direction. It had brought her nothing but misery, smoky dreams that rose and disappeared, thoughts of what might have been.

When she thought about her life now, the phrase that came to mind was *Omnes Errant*. She could not even remember where she had picked it up. Probably school. But it encapsulated her life. Her life was a series of mistakes. Always steps in the wrong direction. Those steps placed her on the Vingerlingstraat, a regular face with the black-lined eyes and lips painted in the brightest shade of red *rat-tat-tatting* on the window to help men make up their minds. And she wanted to howl forever.

On that Wednesday night, Sisi had been in Antwerp for exactly five and a half months. The revelation displaced her enthusiasm to make money. In its place came a stoicism she could never have imagined she possessed. She went to work and her smile stayed on. She greeted her clients and it did not falter. She thanked them when they tipped her. When they complimented her. When they said she was not like a lot of black prostitutes who tried to wrangle more money than was originally agreed upon. The smile stayed on. But an unhappiness permeated her skin and wound itself around her neck and forced her head down so that she walked as if something shamed her. While she had never been comfortable in her job, there was now a certain aversion added to the discomfort. She could no longer bear to look at herself, not even when she was alone. When she took a bath, she sponged her body without once looking at it. Regrets assailed her day in, day out. She smiled, but behind that smile her regret grew bigger and bigger, its shadow casting a pall over her. She began to wish she had never left home, ruing the day she met Dele. Why, oh why, had she gone to his office? Why had she been taken in by his promises of wealth and glamour and happiness that knew no bounds? When a customer asked her to lie spread-eagled, while he yelled "whore" at her and jerked off to that, she felt something akin to revulsion. Her walks into Antwerp increased in both frequency and length. She woke up early and walked along the Keyserlei and the Grote Markt. She made detours into alleyways, discovering old buildings that held no interest for her. She bought more and more stuff: bottle openers in the shape of beer bottles. Postcards of Antwerp by night. Dainty coasters of delicate lace. Tablecloths. Swelling her suitcase under the bed, so that it was difficult to close and she feared she would need to buy another one.

ZWART

ZWARTEZUSTERSTRAAT

A CHILD SHRIEKS HAPPILY OUTSIDE. A SOUND THAT SEEMS ALMOST anomalous, slithering into the room.

"It is odd, isn't it? Sisi is dead, and everything's going on as normal," Joyce says.

Ama smiles. "In my place, we have a saying: When a stranger's corpse is being carried, it is as if it is mere firewood."

"True talk," Efe agrees. "I remember when my mama die, I dey even dey angry wit' de sun wey dey shine. Like say de world suppose end."

"But even inside this house, nothing's changed. Sisi was not a stranger here!" Joyce sounds petulant.

"Not to us. But to them she probably was." Ama points her chin in the direction of Madam's and Segun's rooms.

"Dat Segun sef na stranger to himself!" Efe scoffs.

"Probably fucks himself!"

"Ama! You and your dirty mouth. You suppose use soap wash am out!" But there is a twinkle in Efe's eyes.

Segun is their favorite topic of mutual gossip. His clumsiness. His foolish look. How the only time he shines is with a hammer. Lower lip turned out, a hammer in his right hand, a nail in the other. *Klop-klop-klopping*. His hands steady, not making nervous movements like they do when he talks. Searching. Always searching for words, fists closing to hang on to the words about to slip through. "Ma . . . aa . . . d . . . am s-s-said your do . . . doo . . . dooor neee . . . eeds fix-fi . . . I mean . . . fixing!" Feet tapping. Hands moving. When Segun is working away with a hammer, hitting the nails, there is none of that. There is a fluidity to his hand rising and falling with precision that induces admiration, even. When he made a side table for Joyce at Madam's request (as a birthday present), the women watched in wonder as he produced a table so well made that they had begged Madam to commission him to make tables for them, too.

"E dey be like say he dey listen to the voice of heaven. As if de voice dey command am. Hit. Stop. Hit. Stop," Efe once said. For how could it be that this man who seems inadequate, inept, in every way, should be so flawless a workman.

Joyce's mood is broody. "Sisi was no stranger," she insists.

"Madam with her fucking nose in the air. You want her to come and sit with us here?"

"And Segun, then? You saw her in his car, didn't you?"

"Yes. But Sisi almost bit my head off for mentioning it! So maybe it was a one-off thing, you know?"

"Even so. They—" Joyce grapples with the air for the right words. Finding none, she says nothing. Just a hiss.

The child outside is no longer shrieking in delight. She is crying now with the propensity of children of a certain age to evoke sympathy with their cries. "Poor kid. I wonder what's wrong?" Joyce says, almost standing up.

"Where the fuck do you think you're going?" Ama pulls her down. "You want to go and see what's wrong with another woman's child? Haven't you learned anything here? You fucking mind your business. Look at Madam and Segun. Minding their business!"

Joyce wrings her hands. "Madam and Segun are not minding their business. They are being . . ." She draws out her rag.

"Being fucking what?"

"Dickheads!" The word falls like a surprise from Joyce.

"You don' begin dey sound like Ama!"

The child is still crying. Joyce says, "I wonder how she died. If she cried for help."

SISI

SISI HAD BARELY ANY MONEY LEFT FOR HERSELF AFTER PAYING OFF Dele. And paying her part of the rent on the Zwartezusterstraat. And paying rent on the Vingerlingstraat room she was subletting from Madam. All of Madam's girls sublet from her. Five hundred and fifty euros a week they paid. She did not see how she could do this job long enough to save anything. It would take her another two months to decide that she could not. And it would not be just the thought of being unable to save that would make her quit.

From eight o'clock at night to eight o'clock the next day, she stood, like the other girls with porcelain smiles, inside her booth, hoping to hook a big fish. She learned to keep her smile from falling and shattering. The story was still being peddled of the Ghanaian prostitute on the Falconplein—not too far from the Vingerlingstraat—who had a client fall in love with her. He was not just any client, he was a rich client. A top footballer or something, Sisi could never be sure, as the profession of the rich client changed with each storyteller, but no matter who told the story, its essence remained the same: The Ghanaian girl did good. He paid off her pimp, married her, and installed her in his villa just outside Brussels. He did everything for her (he even adopted her two children from a previous relationship and brought them over from Accra). She had everything: fancy cars, a swimming pool, designer clothes, holidays to the South of France, weekend drives to the Ardennes, holiday homes in Morocco and Barcelona, the works. Some people said she did *touch and follow* on him, the sort of juju that good medicine men made, with pubic hair and toenails clipped at dawn, to help women catch men and hold on to them. How else could she have managed to hook such a big fish? To completely transform her infinitesimal life to one of infinite power? She with the body of a rodent and the face of a horse? *Ha-ha-ha.* Anita, the Zimbabwean who worked the window a few doors away from the Ghanaian, said it was definitely *tokoloshi*, like touch and follow but stronger: a root that grows to the height of a baby and all the owner has to do is to send it out for money. "It can get money from everywhere. Even from a man's privates! I hear the man lets her handle all his accounts."

Others said she had just plain good luck. It had nothing to do with the tortoise that someone said the Ghanaian woman always had under her bed when she was with that particular client, even though it was common knowledge that a tortoise was an unmissable ingredient in touch-and-follow juju. Together with the hair and nail clippings, of course. Sisi did not care how she did it. She did not even want love. She was not looking for marriage. Just customers who would tip her enough, pay enough, to get her out of the booth, which was giving her cabin fever. She needed lots of customers if she was going to build the house she wanted for her parents. And give her dreams substance. But the customers were not always there.

The Schipperskwartier lost its vivacity in the daytime. With sunlight splashing its rays on it, it had a deserted, windblown look. It looked almost ashamed, as if the light of day exposed it in a way it did not want to be seen: very much like a woman who is not yet comfortable with a new lover being caught on the toilet letting out loud farts. The houses looked sad, on the whole, giving the area a rather desolate, mournful look. The sort of place that made one think of death. Sisi avoided it in the day, preferring to explore other parts of Antwerp that throbbed in the glare of the sun, full of the energy of a healthy toddler. She took walks alone. Telling her housemates when they asked that she was just going for a breath of air. No, thank you, she would rather go alone.

She liked the Keyserlei, with its promise of glitter: the Keyserlei Hotel with its gold facade and the lines and lines of shops. Ici Paris. H&M. United Colours of Benetton. Fashion Outlet. So many choices. She liked the rush of people, the mixing of skin colors, the noise on the streets. The Jews with their Hasidic discs and their women pushing cherubic babies in strollers with big wheels. They all made her heart race, made her feel alive, a part of this throbbing, living city.

She did not mind the dirt that littered the roads, making her think of graffiti she saw once on the walls of the Central Station: ANTWERP IS CONSTIPATED. *It is no longer constipated*, she always thought when she walked down the Keyserlei and came face-to-face with the litter that overflowed from the huge dustbin outside the McDonald's. It's *letting out its shit here*. The dirt was part of what made it familiar to her. It was a constant. As were the touts, mainly young males who hung around the eateries along the street, hands inside their coats, saying, "I've got a gold chain. Worth four hundred euros. You can have it for a hundred. Okay, how much have you got? I just stole it. Very expensive, give me what you can afford. It's a genuine article." As were the beggars, mainly East European women with young children and colorful sweaters, sitting against the walls of the entrance to the metro stations, miming to passersby that they were hungry, that their babies were hungry, and had you nothing to give them? Nothing to drop in the plastic begging bowls before their outstretched legs? Sometimes she dropped fifty-cent coins in the bowls, especially if they had crying babies. At other times she hurried past them, as if on her way to somewhere urgent, the way everybody else rushed, ignoring traffic lights and passing cars. She liked the Pelikaanstraat, with gold and diamond jewelry calling from the display windows, beckoning to customers, *Look at us, are we not pretty? Look at us, won't you buy one?* She liked the central square, with its horses and cobbled streets that made her feel like she was in one of those black-and-white films from so long ago. She liked the souvenir shops, with their laces and fancy chocolates and postcards. Sisi imagined she was a tourist, some rich woman who could afford to travel the world for leisure, taking in sights and trying the food. Sometimes she dressed for the role. A cap, sunglasses, a bum bag hanging from her waist, a camera dangling around her neck, and a Dutch phrase book in her hand. On such days she walked into shops and smiled at shopkeepers, who, eager to make a sale, smiled back, all sweetness and light. She was somebody else with a different life. She lived out her fantasies. She drooled over novelty chocolates in the shapes of penises and breasts, telling the shop assistant who sold them, "These are simply amazing. I've got to take some back."

Once she bought a pair of lace booties, telling the woman who sold them that she was visiting from Lagos and had just found out she was pregnant after five years of trying for a baby. The booties would be for her unborn child's christening. The woman had wrapped up the shoes in utter silence and reverence, stopping only to dab at her glistening eyes with a flower-embroidered handkerchief. Sisi mirrored the woman, delicately dabbing her eyes with a paper tissue, careful not to ruin her makeup.

Another time she bought two kilograms of pralines, gushing to the saleswoman about how excited she was to be in Antwerp. "Your *ciddy* is absolutely gorgeous, darling. I'm having such a wonderful time here that I am worried Paris will be a disappointment. That's my next stop. Then London on the . . . the . . . the train, the Eurostar, that's it. Doing Europe, you see. We Americans don't travel half as much as we ought to." She had giggled girlishly when the saleswoman replied that America was so big, Americans must have their hands full traveling around America, and said, "You Europeans are so smart. Your English is so good, darling. I wish I spoke another language! Anything. As long as it's foreign."

Sometimes she stopped in front of a statue—her favorite was the giant throwing a hand in the middle of the central square—and asked a passerby to take a picture of her. Phrase book open, she throttled out words, intentionally mispronouncing Dutch words and looking appropriately relieved when the passerby asked if she spoke English in impeccable English.

"Oh, yes, I do. Could you take a picture, please? Thank you." She would smile at the phrase book at her feet and take a picture that she would never develop.

She listened in rapt attention as a man who said he was a through-and-through Antwerpenaar told her the story of the statue: About five hundred years ago or so an unruly giant terrorized the inhabitants of that area, severing the hand of every boatman who could not pay the exorbitant taxes he levied on them for passing by his castle. Then a brave young man came from who knew where and killed the giant and threw his hand into the river Schelde, which ran through the city. The overjoyed inhabitants watched him throw away the hand and named the city Handwerpen, "to throw a hand away," but along the years, the name became corrupted and transformed itself to Antwerpen.

"Wow, amazing story!" She smiled, her palms on either side of her face, her eyes wide. "That's so totally amazing. Belgium has so much history for such a tiny country. Thanks ever so much for telling me that story. I'm going to treasure it. How do you say 'thank you' in Belgian, *darleen?*"

She did the Pelikaanstraat, entered shops, and coquettishly tried on gold and diamond rings she found unbearably expensive.

"My fiancé has asked me to choose an engagement ring. He's too busy to come and get one himself. Sometimes I wish he had less money and more time. It's Mexico today, Singapore the next. Oh well, I guess a girl can't have it all. Money or time, which would I rather?" She would laugh high and loud, and the shopkeepers would laugh with her, their laughter softer than hers, a thoughtful demureness that was mindful of the fact that she was the customer, a customer with lots of money who therefore should not be upstaged.

Often she would dangle a smile, bait, in front of the seller, twirling the ring on her finger, raising the finger up to the light, watching the light bounce off it in incredible sparkles of color, miniature miracles of pink and white, saying how much she liked it, turning it this way and that so that it caught the light, before declaring that maybe the stone was a bit too big. Or a tad too small. Or simply that it looked all wrong. She would watch the seller fight to maintain a smile in the face of an almost-sale that fell through, watch the clip-on smile slip, before walking out of the shop, hips and handbag swaying, imagining she was on TV.

She liked the cathedral that was so huge it made her feel small, the size of a grain of rice. She went inside and aimed her camera at paintings she found uninteresting and vulgar—really, all those huge breasts spilling out of clothes were in extremely poor taste—and pretended to take pictures. She traded conspiratorial smiles with tourists who thronged the cathedral, all solemn and wide-eyed, and whispered, "Isn't it beautiful? Rubens was a brilliant artist!"

She was anonymous to these people. She could be anyone from anywhere. She could be a married woman with a husband named Peter and a huge duplex in Ikeja: the sort of woman who could afford regular holidays abroad, living from hotel to hotel in cities across the globe, MasterCard and Visa Gold at her disposal.

She could be a professional single woman with money to burn and places to see. She was any story she wanted to be. Far away from the people she knew and who knew her.

It was only once that she bumped into Segun at a chip shop.

Segun had offered to run her home, and she, too flurried to refuse, accepted the offer, all the time worrying that he might have overheard her. What had she told the woman? Aargh! How loud had she been? Exclaiming, "I'm dying to eat Belgian fries! Quite famous back home in the U.S., you know!" She had turned around to smile at the customer behind her only to see Segun smiling down at her.

Ama had seen her get out of Segun's car, looking decidedly shifty. And Segun, walking behind her, definitely had a salacious swagger. When Sisi flared up after she asked (and she was only joking) if Segun was now her regular guy, shouting, "You're so wrong!," Ama knew that she was up to something.

"Segun and Sisi," Efe said when she heard. "That's quite something!"

There were days when Sisi had two customers. And one of the two just wanted a cheap service: "I'm on a budget. So just a blow job, sugar." The money was in delivering all the works: penetration, blow job, no condom. Black men avoided them, and Sisi initially thought that these men were embarrassed for their "sisters" in the flesh trade. But Ama corrected her on that, too. "Many black men here are just struggling to survive. They haven't got the money to pay for sex."

In all her years, Ama said, she could count the number of black customers she'd had on one hand. "And they are mainly visitors, tourists from London and America. One of them was not even proper black. He was Caribbean or something."

When business was good, Sisi did an average of fifteen men. She was diligent about her payment, walking down to the Central Station every first Friday of the month to send a payment via Western Union to Dele. Sisi still dreamed of the big house she would build, but the dream was starting to lose its urgency. When she called home, she talked in a monotone, her eyes diverted from the single bed in her room, a cigarette clutched between her fingers.

Yes, I'm fine.

Yes, I started school.

Yes, I work part-time in a nursing home.

Yes, everything here is wonderful.

Yes, I have made some friends.

Yes, they are all wonderful.

Yes, I never forget to say my prayers.

I shall send some money home soon.

Sometimes, when the night was slow, she called from her mobile phone. In her work clothes and seated on her stool behind her window, she telephoned home and tried not to think of how much it was costing her to make a long-distance call from her mobile phone. Cheaper to buy a calling card. Or, better still, to go to one of the city's many telephone shops and call from there. But sometimes the urge to call overtook everything else. Even economic good sense.

I'm calling from work, can't stay long.

I'm glad you liked the handbag I sent, Mother.

Father, I hope you're taking the vitamins I sent?

It's cold. *Oyi na-atu.* But not too cold.

Her parents always said the right things. Reminding her to pray. Thanking her for the presents she sometimes sent them. But there was an underlying flatness to their tone that filled her with such visceral anguish that she could not sleep when she knocked off work. Yet she tormented herself. She could not *not* call. That would be worse.

She had not spoken to Peter since she left. She could not bear to. Where duty demanded that she keep in touch with her family, she had no such duty toward him. She did not want to test the limits of her sadness. And what would be the use of keeping in touch with him? Best to make a permanent break. He would never have her back, not after what she had done. Besides, she was a different person, and Peter would not recognize her. She was not Chisom. She was somebody else. Rougher. Harder. Infinitely more demanding. He belonged to a past that had moved on without her.

One of the few people who made Antwerp bearable for her was Luc.

She met Luc at the Pentecostal church Efe introduced her to. A church that distributed inviting leaflets in huge black print:

LOOKING FOR A REASON? JESUS IS THE REASON.

LOOKING FOR ANSWERS? JESUS IS THE ANSWER.

LOOKING FOR A PLACE TO WORSHIP? FIRST REDEEMED
    CHURCH OF CHRIST IS THE PLACE.

JOIN US EVERY SUNDAY AND DISCOVER THE REASON FOR
    YOUR LIFE.

At the beginning Sisi had enjoyed the ambience of a church full of well-dressed, ebullient Africans (mostly) singing at the top of their voices, *Praise the Lord oh sing oh sing oh, praise the Lord. Praise His holy name, oh sing oh sing oh praise the Lord.* It reminded her of what she thought of as her age of innocence. When a balloon blown up for her was enough to make her happy. When she thought that having an education was all she needed to escape her father's sorry life.

The Ghanaian pastor was suave, his trousers ironed and creased in the right places, his jacket sitting squarely on him. He had a voice that held his audience in its grip, mesmerizing in the way it peaked and fell when he preached, calling on Holy Spirit fire to bomb evil-doers, angels in heaven to annihilate enemies with automatic rifles, assuring his congregation, "By the end of the month, money will know your names and addresses in the Lord's mighty name!," reminding them that the end was nigh. But when he made the Schipperskwartier professionals his target, raining curses on them, "evil daughters of Eve who shall certainly burn at the end," Sisi quit.

She told Efe, "When he starts acting all sanctimonious, as if he does not know that half of his female congregation are in the trade, donating tithes and paying his salary, then I can no longer be a member of his church. Every month he asks us to pay a tithe, every week he has a special donation request. Where does he think the money comes from? Who pays for his Italian shirts and his wife's Dubai trips? Who's sponsoring the new church he's opening in Turnhout?"

Efe laughed and replied, "You're very funny, Sisi. All dis big grammar because the pastor do him work? Wetin you wan' make him talk? Na him job he dey do abeg! Let him do his job *ojare*."

Luc was a thirty-year-old banker. He stood out because he belonged to that rare breed of white Belgians who attended services at African Pentecostal churches, but that was not the reason why Sisi felt pulled to him. The reason was more banal. He bore a close resemblance to Herman Brusselmans. Tall, lanky, with the same long, dry hair and radiating the same kind of understated, confident sexuality that the writer did. Not that Sisi had ever met Brusselmans. She had only ever seen him in the newspapers. A client had left behind his copy of a newspaper. Sisi had taken the paper home and, with sleep not very quick in coming, had begun to leaf through it. Her Dutch was very limited, but she enjoyed foraying into the words, searching patiently for similarities between the foreign words that danced on the pages with the English that she knew. When she saw words she recognized, she felt jubilation. A minor victory over the language she doubted she would ever be able to master. She had just celebrated "blauw" when her attention was taken by a picture on the next page. It was a very clear photograph of a man who looked at once unapproachable and irrepressibly sexy. Underneath the picture was the name Herman Brusselmans. She understood the word *schrijver*, writer, preceding the name. His eyes had a magnetic pull and his lips a stubborn set that made her want to conquer them. That was the beginning of her obsession. Often she bought newspapers and magazines just because she recognized his name on the cover. She cut out pictures of him and used them to line her cosmetic dresser so that when she moved her cosmetics to the edge of the dresser, his multiple faces stared at her as if they had been conjured up by a magician.

Sisi had felt an instant attraction to Luc but had not encouraged any relationship between them. She still thought often of Peter, and even if her heart had been free, surely nobody would want to date her.

Luc was the one to initiate a relationship. He asked her out for a coffee one day after service, and she asked him why he came to this church full of Africans. He said he liked the music. "Belgian churches are flat . . . they are like pancakes. Nothing there to make you want to go back." Sisi threw her head back and laughed.

Later, when she knew him better, he would tell her that he had stumbled into the church by mistake and the loud chanting pulled him in and kept him going back. His wife had just left him, he said, and maybe he wanted to experience joy vicariously from the singing, swaying throng.

After they became intimate, he would tell her that the faces of the congregation when they shut their eyes and prayed looked almost orgasmic in their contentment, in their happiness, and that intrigued him.

"SO, YOU'LL HAVE A DRINK WITH ME?" HE ASKED, BUT SISI TURNED HIM down. The following week he asked her out again, with the same result. He gave her a two-week hiatus. Then tried again. Again without success. When she quit the church toward the end of December, he got her telephone number from Joyce and called. He badgered her into agreeing to see him one evening in a café on the Grote Markt, but she would not commit to any date. She was not sure he knew how she made her living; she felt if he did, he would not bother with her.

For all his Brusselmans-like look, there was an obvious sense of naïveté about him. She would not be totally shocked if he were a virgin. She hoped that if she acted disinterested he would give up.

But he was persistent. "Next weekend?"

"I'll be working," Sisi said.

"The following weekend, then? Just for a drink?"

Sisi said yes to get him off her back, but she did not turn up. The phone calls did not cease.

He was becoming a distraction, and she needed to get him out of her life so she could concentrate on her work and pay off Dele to regain her freedom. An inertia was starting to spread through her body, and even Madam noticed it. "You've still got many years to work oo. Don't start slowing down now," she cautioned.

A week before she had her first epiphany, Sisi agreed to meet Luc. He had hounded her for two months. She could not decide what to wear the evening they were to meet. Her bed was piled with clothes she had chosen and discarded. Shorts, miniskirts, T-shirts with spaghetti straps. She tried not to think about why she was restless, and focused on her makeup. She could not possibly be falling for Luc. She lined her eyes. Brown lipliner defined her lips. She wore a black skirt that reached her midthigh and matched that with an off-white short-sleeved T-shirt. She wanted to dress well without looking like she had put in any effort at all.

Luc was standing at the bar, nursing a beer, when she arrived. She walked up to him. He smiled, kissed her on the cheek, and told her she looked beautiful.

"No, I don't," Sisi answered sternly. "I do ugly things, and I am not beautiful." She could not stop the images that came to her when she said this. The flat on the Vingerlingstraat with its gaudy colors, the mirror on the wall, the pictures in her room, Eric with the acne on his face who liked her sitting on him, her fingernails clawing his hair, while he let out soft groans. Casper who always asked her to kneel and cradle him, her hands around his enormous waist. How could she be beautiful? How could she be beautiful if she was tainted? How could anyone think she was beautiful? She got up to go, but Luc seemed to have anticipated it and stood up with her, spilling his glass of beer. He held her hand, and she begged him to let her go. She was aware that others in the pub were looking at them. She wondered what they must think.

"Please let me go, Luc. You don't know half the things I have done. Please, I'm begging you in the name of—"

"I don't care. I like you very much. You are very pretty," he cut in. Urgently. As though he feared that if he did not say those things he would lose his courage and never say them again. "You are the most beautiful woman I've ever seen, Sisi."

Sisi tried to free her hand, but for someone so skinny Luc had a tight grip. Her wrist manacled in the loop his right hand made, she sat back down. She could not fall in love with Luc. That would be a major upset. Her life was complicated enough; she did not intend to complicate it any more.

They drank their beer in silence. "I can't see you again," Sisi said once her beer was finished. "Just leave me alone, okay?"

Luc battered Sisi's shield with notes. He sent her postcards of hearts drawn in sand. He sent her letters expounding the theory that love was selfish and would not give up until it had conquered the object of its desire. Sisi was flattered by his attention, and it was this that softened her and made her agree to have him visit her. She imagined that once he saw her in her environment, he would no longer pursue her. That way she would be rid of him. There was no room for love in her life, not if she wanted to earn as much as she could and pay off Dele as quickly as she could. She would quash the affections she was developing for Luc, Brusselmans look-alike or not.

The day he came, Sisi tarted up. She had toyed for a while with the idea of inviting him to the Vingerlingstraat. Let him see her at the window, dressed in a thong and a matching push-up bra. That should put him off. On the other hand, it might not be a good idea to mix business with personal issues. She would see him at home, but she would be dressed for the prowl.

A short leather skirt squeezed her buttocks, and her breasts almost poured out of a body-hugging black blouse with a low neck. Her lips shone bright red, her trademark color. Her eyes, as usual, were lined with black kohl. When she let Luc in, she expected him to take a step back. Instead, he kissed her on both cheeks and stood patiently waiting for her to ask him to sit down. He had brought a fruitcake, he said, and gave her the box. The only chair in the room faced away from the framed pictures on the wall. It was Sisi's Chisom chair, for when she wanted to forget where she was and what she did. She would sit there and face the blank wall on the other side of the room.

Sisi searched Luc's face for any sign of revulsion, but it was like a stone. It revealed nothing.

"Nice room," he said, and she laughed.

"No, you don't mean that," she said, feeling self-conscious in her clothes. Maybe she should have worn something else. A blouse that was less revealing?

Luc laughed. "Okay. Maybe I don't mean it," he conceded.

Sisi got up from the bed she was sitting on and walked to the tabletop fridge beside the chair. "I have only juice," she warned while she brought out a box of orange juice. She noticed she was down to her last box and made a mental note to go to the supermarket as soon as she had some time to restock.

"Juice is okay," Luc replied, adjusting the cushion behind him for more comfort.

His ease made Sisi somewhat petulant, and before she could stop herself she asked him what he was doing visiting her. "What do you want from me? Are you looking for a woman with experience to teach you the ropes? I could be working now. Making money, you know? I have—" She broke off, shocked at her outburst. She watched Luc's face undergo many minuscule transformations, from surprise to anger and finally settling on bewilderment. He creased his eyebrows, got up, and mumbled, "Sorry," making his way to the door. Sisi blocked his path and said no, she was sorry, he had nothing to be sorry for. Nothing was his fault. She held him and covered his lips with hers.

Passion whirled them into each other's arms and dragged them down onto Sisi's bed. Later, when she thought about it, she would conclude that *that* kiss marked the beginning of a relationship that filled her with an effervescent happiness that could not be checked by pragmatic common sense. For Luc she would give up her job, she thought sometimes.

"YOU DON'T HAVE TO LIVE LIKE THIS IF YOU DON'T WANT TO, SISI," LUC sulked. They were in his house in Edegem. Outside, the streetlights glowed a tawny hue. Luc was lying in bed, and Sisi was putting on her makeup, getting ready to leave. She shook a stray braid away from her face, straightened out her modest knee-length skirt, and buttoned her blouse. Her back was turned to him.

"You know I don't like it any more than you do, Luc." She pursed her lips and examined her lipstick. It was perfect. She ran a finger under her left eye to clean up the eyeliner that had smudged a little. "Get out of bed and see me off." She half turned to him.

"So stop. All this rushing from my arms into someone else's. I don't like it." It was as if he had not heard her. "It makes me jealous. Very jealous. I want you all to myself, you know that."

From the very first time they slept together, Luc had insisted on total ownership of her body. Monopolizing her affections was not enough. "I don't like it." She did not like it, either, but what was a girl to do? she asked him. "How do I pay off my debt if I don't work, Luc?

You tell me that. Will you pay it? Can you afford it?" Her voice was close to breaking.

"We could go to the police. This man has no right to make you work for him. It is against the law, even. He has broken rules. He got you a false passport. He is the one who ought to be afraid. Not you. You are innocent."

Luc could be incredibly naïve, she thought, as she often did when he spoke about her quitting. It was exasperating explaining to him that she was as complicit as Dele. She took a deep breath. "He didn't exactly tie my hands and feet and dump me on the plane, you know. I could have chosen not to come. I was a grown woman, and he did explain the situation to me." She was weary of repeating the same things to him. It was starting to feel like déjà vu.

"That's beside the point, schat. We report him and report Madam, too. Then we can live happily. Forever." He was, as usual, insistent, his face contorted by an unusual irascibility.

Sisi was tired. "Just see me off, Luc. I am running late." She was already on the stairs before he got out of bed.

"What can they do to you, anyway? What are you so afraid of? What—" Luc's words staccatoed as Sisi said, "I am tired, please. I can't go through this now. I have to go, Luc. Really. Now is not the right time. We'll talk about this some other time. Not now. Please."

She had been seeing Luc for two months, and he asked the same questions each time. "What are you afraid of? Why don't you leave? Don't you love me enough?" On the bus, his questions boomed in her head. What was she so afraid of? What could Dele do to her from Nigeria? And what could Madam do if, as Luc promised, she would be locked up in prison? On the bus back home, she thought about it. Dele was far away. Luc would help her take care of Madam.

Luc. He wanted her. She wanted him.

Luc. It was getting more and more difficult to walk away from him into the arms of a trick. His persistence was starting to erode her insistence that his plan was not workable. It drilled holes in her and showed her just how possible it could be. *I can do this. I can just up and walk away. Start a new life with my man. I don't want to lose Luc, but how long will he hang around? How many men would wait knowing that every night their girlfriends were with other men?* When she asked Luc why he bothered with her when he could have any woman he wanted, one without her baggage, his response was simple. He loved her. And the simplicity of his words moved her. But how long would the love last if she kept her job? Even love did not have endless patience, that much she knew. Just look at what had happened to her and Peter. *What exactly do I have to lose? What am I afraid of?*

She heard Dele's "No try cross me o. Nobody dey cross Senghor Dele!" But really, what could he do from so far away? Surely she could not take that threat seriously. He probably said it to scare her. She had to admit, she was afraid.

Luc. She loved him. He loved her. He would look after her. He would make sure Dele could not touch her. They would marry, and in a few years, she would be a bona fide Belgian. She would have her own children. A different life.

The more she thought about it, the more she realized that there was very little to be afraid of. On the contrary, she stood to gain a lot: She could have a proper relationship. No more strange men in her bed. She could get another job, maybe a cleaning job. Cleaners were always in demand. And Luc had offered quite generously to give her a monthly allowance she could send to her parents. She might even be able to invite them to visit her in Belgium. She would show them the wonders of her new home. There would be no need to lie to them anymore. The lies were starting to distress her. Her parents never questioned her, never asked her to explain what it was she did. And it was this lack of curiosity, their not wanting to know, that got to her, haunting her sleep, slicing it up into miserly chunks so that she was never fully rested.

When she got home, she threw herself on the bed fully clothed. She was still lying there, her head full of thoughts, when Madam rolled in to ask why she was lying down. "What's going on, Sisi? Should you not be leaving for work? Everybody else is gone!"

She told Madam she had her period.

"How come?" Madam queried, her eyebrows joining together to form a long wavy line of suspicion. "I am sure I gave you a period break less than a month ago."

"But I am. I can't explain it. You want me to show you?"

Madam shook her head hastily, let out an annoyed hiss, and walked out of the room.

Sisi sighed in relief. For all she knew, Madam might have insisted on seeing. It would not have been out of character in a woman who sometimes inspected their underwear as if they were schoolgirls in boarding school, checking for signs of dirt or wear, telling them that her girls were always at the top of the range. "I don't want to find you wanting in any respect."

Tomorrow, Sisi told herself, she would go back to Luc and tell him she was ready to quit. They would go to the police together, and she would be a free woman. She suddenly felt weightless, as if the decision had rid her body of a physical burden. She leaned against the door, securely locked against the world, and raised a fist into the air.

"Yes! Yes! Yes!" she whispered in triumph. She looked at her bed, dressed in the white sheets Madam for some reason insisted upon, raised her eyes to the picture on the wall, whispered "Yes" again, and said to the room, as if addressing a Sisi who was separate from her, "Tomorrow it will be all over. Tomorrow you shall be free. Sisi will be dead."

She could already feel the taste of freedom rush into her mouth, intoxicating her into a rapid dance that pirouetted her round and round the room until she had to stop to catch her breath.

• • •

SISI TOSSED IN HER BED ALL NIGHT, THINKING ABOUT HER DECISION, her certainty of before gone. It occurred to her that the other women might not like it. By going to the police, she would be forcing them to give up their jobs, and she was not entirely sure she was ready to take on that responsibility. She had Luc, she had a future after this, but the rest? What did they have? Who did they have? Joyce, who had confided in her that she had no family anywhere on the face of the earth. What would happen to her? And Ama? Efe? The house on the Zwartezusterstraat was like a family home. The communal kitchen and the shared living room bound the women. They met there when they yearned for company but could always retire to their rooms for some privacy. It was where they could escape the glare of the Schipperskwartier, live a life that did not include strange men with sometimes stranger requests.

She remembered the party they went to in Brasschaat the week before. The Ghanaian community was installing a new chief; Nana something or the other, she could no longer remember, but she and the three others had sat together, a family, trading jokes and having a laugh. They had gotten the invitation through Madam, who had been invited by a friend of hers. They had their fun; she had no right to put a stop to all that just because she was fed up and in love. What would happen to Joyce's dream of owning a boutique? Luc could not assure Sisi that she would not be deported. She was an illegal immigrant, after all. And so were the rest. There was no way she could avoid implicating them if she went to the police. She lay faceup in bed and studied the cracks in the ceiling, watching them merge into whole pictures, clear as day. She put her palms under her head while she waited for the slow-coming dawn to steal across the sky and send her out of bed. Maybe she could just walk out without a forwarding address. She could move in with Luc. She would move in with Luc. *He will marry me. In five years, I'll be a citizen.* She would not have to work hard only to send her money to Dele. The man was fleecing them. How much did it cost him to get a passport? Get a visa? She was aware that he was bringing in girls almost on a monthly basis. There was no reason why she should work to line the pockets of a man whose pockets were already bulging. *Greedy man! I'll be shut of him.* Up until now she had never defaulted on her payment. And she always paid more than minimum because she wanted to be done with it in the shortest possible time. That meant that what she saved was minimal. The gold earrings and necklaces on the Pelikaanstraat were still beyond her reach, though she was one of the hardest workers in the industry. In the winter, she tried to forget the cold and displayed her body in front of her window, push-up bras and tiny thongs, rapping her gold-plated-ringed middle finger on the window to attract the men. *Rat-a-tat-tat. See me here. Let me be the one to satisfy you tonight.* She had swallowed her pride, chucked her shyness in the bin, and gotten on with her job. She was a model worker, the perfect employee, with a bit of sunshine for every client. The customer was king even when he was being obnoxious, Madam warned them, and Sisi never forgot that. "As long as he's paying for your services, his wish is your command, and you do what he wants you to. No complaints. Make him forget that he is paying for the tenderness that you are showing him. That is the secret of the game, the golden rule of the game, and you'll do well to remember it. People are funny, men especially. They're happy to pay for love as long as it does not feel like they are paying."

So when the men came, Sisi smiled and flattered and complimented. She tried to make them forget they were paying her to say those things, to do those things, like Madam said. But she never lost sight of the reward at the end of every shift. She purred:

Yes, big man, I shall take that.

Of course, big man, I shall hold it out for you.

An enema? Most definitely.

Come to me. Come to your little sweetie pie.

Come to your kitty. Your little pussy cat.

When they wanted a French kiss and were willing to pay for that extra, she delivered it with the appropriate ahhs and hmms, forcing herself to obliterate the face of the man she was kissing. Even when, as it often did, her stomach churned, she stuck at it, her tongue in a stranger's mouth, their saliva mixing. *Make him forget he's paying you for this bit of tenderness. Make him forget that you don't really care.* She held their head in her hands and arched her neck. No matter what service she delivered, her smile of straw never snapped. It stayed firm. Strong. Unmoving. A rock. One of her regulars who needed to listen to Barry White in the background got his wish. She had a nurse's uniform hanging in her cupboard. She had a waitressing apron, a drawer full of gadgets, and a head full of regrets. Apart from that one man with a toupee, she had never received a single complaint. She had more than paid her dues, and now she could reclaim her life, and by Jove she would. She would get rid of Sisi, let a fire consume Sisi, char her, and scatter her ashes.

The next morning Sisi got out of bed early, dressed, and left the house, taking nothing but her nightgown and her toothbrush. She peeped into the living room. It was empty. She stood still for a minute, as if paying obeisance to the memory of a good friend she had just learned was dead. She breathed in the smell of the room: It was the smell of all the women who lived there, mingled with the smell of incense. It was a warm smell, something familiar, comforting. It almost smelled of home. Unlike their booths in the Vingerlingstraat, it did not have the muskiness of men, the bleach smell of sperm, and, unlike their bedrooms in this house, it did not have the shadowy smell of strangers. This was where they met, their shared space, and the room they felt the most comfortable in. It did not bother them as much as their rooms did. Ama hated the white sheets in the bedrooms. Nobody knew why. As for Sisi, it was the picture of the unknown woman on the wall that she hated. The buttocks seemed to mock her. Did Madam hang up those pictures to remind the girls of their duties? The living room had no pictures, just the redness you could not escape. She breathed in, soaking up the smell, exhaled, and said a silent goodbye. Tucking in her stomach the way her home-science teacher in secondary school had taught the class, she walked out into the cold May morning, desperate for some air. Eight months was a long time to live in a world ruled by Madam and Dele.

She walked around aimlessly for a while, her yellow tote under her arm, clearing her head and mentally gathering strength for the task ahead. It had all seemed easy last night, but in the bright light of day she was once more assailed with doubts pirouetting in her head.

Could I?

Should I?

Would I?

On the bus to Edegem, the questions twirled. She imagined how the rest would feel when they realized she was not coming back. Would they miss her? She had not told them of her plan because she was not sure she would go through with it. She had left her key to the front door on top of the refrigerator in the kitchen. What would they say when they discovered it? Would Joyce feel betrayed? Was this a betrayal? Surely not. It would be a betrayal if she were to go to the police and lose them their means of livelihood. She tossed the options in her head. She knew that, more than her indecision, it was the certainty of the others not supporting her that had stopped her from breathing a word of it to them. She was worried that they would try to stop her, get her to change her mind. They had carved out semi-perfect lives for themselves here; who was she to ask them to give all that up for her?

They were getting on with their lives, preparing for lives after

Dele, mapping out the blueprint for who they wanted to be once they left the Schipperskwartier. Ama had been in Antwerp for almost six years. Efe, going on seven. They had repaid quite a huge amount of their debt to Dele. Efe believed that within the next two years she would be free of debt. She would see L.I. again. She was already talking of maybe acquiring some girls and becoming a madam herself. She would buy girls from Brussels, because it was more convenient, she said, to get girls who were already in the country. It would take Efe two years and six weeks to make her final payment. And then eighteen months to get her first lot of two girls, whom she would indeed buy at an auction presided over by a tall, good-looking Nigerian man in sunglasses and a beret. It would be in a house in Brussels, with lots to drink and soft music playing in the background. The women would enter the country with a musical band billed to perform at the *Loke-renfeest*. The man in the sunglasses was the manager of the band and had, in addition to genuine members of the band, added the names of these women who had paid him to the list he submitted at the embassy in Abuja. The women would be called into the room one at a time for the buyers to see and admire. They would all have numbers, for names were not important. Their names would be chosen by whoever bought them. Names that would be easy for white clients to pronounce. Easy enough to slide off the tongue. Nothing longer than two syllables and nothing with the odd combinations of consonants that make African names difficult for fragile tongues. "Number Three, ladies and gentlemen. Number Three is the type of woman white men like. Thin lips. Pointed nose. Sweet *Ikebe*." He slapped her on her bare buttocks. Number Three smiled.

"Imagine her inside a window. This one is material for catching plenty white men. Look at her color." Number Three's skin was the color of honey. "She is one good investment."

Number Three's smile grew wider. Efe would buy numbers Five and Seven. Number Five because she smiled easily. Number Seven because she looked docile and eager to please, the sort of girl who was grateful with little. Like Madam, Efe would have some police officers on her payroll to ensure the security of her girls and her business. She would do well in the business, buying more girls to add to her fleet.

Four years after Sisi died, Joyce would go back to Nigeria with enough capital to set up a school in Yaba. She would employ twenty-two teachers, mainly young women, and regularly make concessions for bright pupils who could not afford the school fees. She would call it *Sisi's International Primary and Secondary School*, after the friend she would never forget.

Ama, ironically, would be the one to open a boutique. She would make Mama Eko its manager. Mama Eko would tell her she always knew Ama would make it. They would never talk about Ama's years in Europe.

SISI PLACED HER TOTE ON HER LAP. DAFFODILS AGAINST THE GRASS green of her dress. One more stop and it would be hers. She reached out a hand and pressed the bell on the pole behind her.

She got off the bus and walked the three hundred meters to Luc's house. Sisi felt immortal. Unstoppable. Her world was as it should be. She liked Edegem. There was an authenticity to people there that made central Antwerp seem somewhat spurious. Here people smiled and said hello to her. Strangers she was not likely to see again asked how she was and looked like they meant it. They listened while she said she was fine, thank you. And you? People would start conversations with her at bus stops and discuss the merits of the public-transportation system over private ownership of cars: With all the pollution cars cause, people ought to be more civic-minded and take public transport, shouldn't they? They would talk about the rising cost of bread. Old women would tell of when they lived in the Congo many decades ago, talk fondly of Albertville, which had been re-named something they can never remember, something African. Ask you if you speak Lingala. What you think of Kabila. Talk of their niece who could not have a baby and adopted a beautiful little son from Rwanda. Or Burundi: "Beautiful baby, only problem is his hair. Quite difficult to comb, the *krulletjes*. I told them to try the clothes softener I use. Smells nice, and the best softener I've ever used. If it works on clothes, no reason it should not work on hair. Don't you think?"

In central Antwerp, people did not care whether you lived or died. When they said hello in shops, you could tell that it was routine, something rationed and passed out grudgingly. They said hello and looked past you, wanting to get on with their day, their lives that had no place for you. There was no emotion in the voices. There was a furious pace to the city that hindered people from stopping to smile. And at bus stops there was a general suspicion of all things conspic-uously foreign. Very often Sisi would find old women clutching their bags tighter if she stood close to them, strangling their bags under their armpits. And men quickly patted their trouser back pock-ets, assuring themselves that their wallets were safe. Even her fellow Africans did not talk to her. They had no curiosity to satisfy. Central Antwerp was a city of strangers, of anonymity. It was this anonymity that she craved sometimes.

Luc was having breakfast when she arrived and greeted her with a hug. "You are doing the right thing, *schat.*"

Life could be like this every day. *I could be a suburban housewife with croissants for breakfast on a Saturday morning,* Sisi thought. She sat down to breakfast, unable to eat anything but a thin slice of but-tered bread.

"Take some charcuterie," Luc urged, pushing the box toward her.

Sisi shook her head. "Thank you." She could never get used to all the spreads and different types of cold cuts and cheese that Luc seemed to require for one breakfast. Wouldn't breakfast be much easier without all the many choices? Besides, when Luc told her that the lean red meat that he delicately placed between bread came from a horse, she had sworn never to eat anything she could not easily identify.

When Sisi should have been at the Western Union transferring her payment to Dele, she took a bus back to central Antwerp. Luc was working and she was bored. She had five hundred euros to spend, and she was determined to enjoy it.

On the last day of Sisi's life, nothing could have prepared her for her transition. The sky was calm, and the weather was just the way she liked it: not hot enough to be uncomfortable and not cold enough for a jacket. Such weather made her think of heaven. Once, when she was young and was discovering words and worlds beyond her own, she had asked her mother what heaven was like. "Not hot like here," her mother had answered, raising an arm over her head to dry sweat off her armpit with a handkerchief. "And not cold like I hear it is overseas. Heaven has perfect weather."

Sisi walked in the perfect weather, walking Antwerp's many narrow streets. People basked on terraces and conducted conversations in loud voices, a paean to the perfect day. Sisi had a song in her heart and money in her purse. Her destination was the shopping street. She looked at Antwerp as if with new eyes. *There are so many run-down houses. And so many people. This is a city that is collapsing under the weight of its own congestion.* Every time she took the bus outside Antwerp, she was aware how easy it was to tell that one had left the city. Or had reentered. The landmarks could not be missed: houses with peeling paint and broken windows. Derelict buildings looking like life had been hard on them. They always reminded Sisi of drug users who had aged before their time, scars of hard living crisscrossing their faces like mosquito netting. Sometimes, Sisi thought, stepping over a mound of brown stool, Antwerp seemed like a huge incinerator.

She walked along the Pelikaanstraat and toward the Central Station. For no reason she could pinpoint, she entered. She loved the architecture of the station, the way it seemed to have been crafted with the utmost care, attention paid to every little detail. It did not matter how many times she went into the station, its beauty always made her gasp. It seemed built for meditation. *This should have been a cathedral. Or a museum*, she thought. *Somewhere quiet, not rowdy and filled with impatient commuters. That's the thing with Antwerp. Buildings are set up and misused.* She thought of the UCG cinema on the Annastraat. *That would do perfectly well for a train station. The cathedral looks like a museum. This city is just not planned!* She walked the length of the station and exited from the door beside the zoo. She had been to the zoo only once. With Luc. She had not found anything particularly enjoyable in walking around a park, looking at animals locked up in cages. Animals taken away from their natural habitat, only for that habitat to be artificially re-created. She thought it ridiculous that thunder and lightning should be imported for the crocodile. She walked into a huge superstore where everything from shoes to clothes went for a few euros. She turned left and walked to the front of the station. As always, here were drunks with eyes like quarter moons and throats full of stories. A middle-aged man with a long beard accosted her. He reeked of liquor, and beside him a shaggy-haired dog, fat like some medieval suzerain's eunuch, stood with its tongue out, dripping saliva. The man held out a callused palm. "*Altsublieft. Heb je iets voor me?* No Dutch? Française? Deutsch? Español? English? You've got one euro for me? Just one euro. Bus fare, please? I just lost my wallet." Sisi fished in her pocket and gave him a coin. She was in a good mood and had some money to spare.

She walked across the station and made her way to the Keyserlei, joining the throng of people that Antwerp spewed out every day. It was as if the earth itself cracked open and was hurling people onto the streets: black, yellow, white, and some a brilliant hue caused by a mixture of all three. The city tickled her senses, and for the first time in a long while she felt thrilled to be alive. No longer buffeted by indecision, she felt at ease with the world. No more promises of happiness that crumbled and turned to dust under scrutiny. Today was the beginning of a brand-new life.

She headed to the Meir. In front of her a sea of shops spread out, beckoning to her like long-lost friends. She smiled to herself and tried not to think about her housemates back on the Zwartezusterstraat, probably wondering where she had gotten to. What would they say when they found out? She stifled any insurgent feelings of guilt. *There is no reason to feel guilty. I am doing nothing wrong.* Humming James Blunt's "You're Beautiful" under her breath, she walked on. She felt beautiful. The world was beautiful. The red-haired girl distributing leaflets outside the music store was beautiful. The streets she walked on smelled beautiful. Felt beautiful. Looked beautiful. She had the world beneath her feet.

She ignored the shops she normally would have entered. The superstores that looked like massive warehouses, with clothes so cheap that with twenty euros she had once bought three new outfits: the imitation-leather miniskirt that she wore a lot in the winter, a matching jacket, a turquoise cotton caftan and matching trousers, and the long black polyester dress with an open back and a very low neck that was her coup de grâce for difficult clients. When she had the hard-to-please sort, those looking for a little something extra, she would dance in it, swinging her hips and sitting on laps. Chances were she would be left with a huge tip or a request for an extra session by the time she was done. Today she would enter other shops. She would walk down the Meir and enter shops she previously avoided.

She walked into a boutique and spent an extravagant seventy-five euros on a pantsuit. She held the gray plastic bag of the shop in such a way that its name showed. She swung into a lingerie shop with a chic name she could not pronounce and a shop assistant with spiky hair and a silver stud in her tongue. Fifty euros went on three pairs of knickers. They were nothing like she wore for work: thongs with frills and laces, huge bows suggestively trailing the front. These were sensible. The sort she imagined a schoolteacher would wear. Black and brown and cream. Elegant. Prim and proper. Like the queen's.

After a day spent in shops, she walked back to the train station, filled in a Western Union money transfer form, and sent three hundred euros to her parents. She would call them later in the day to tell them to go and pick up the money. This was the most she had sent to them at any one time. Money enough to propel her mother into a leg-throwing, hand-clapping dance. Her father would be more subdued. He would carry a smile tucked into his cheeks. And Dele? *Oh well, Dele has more than enough girls working for him; he doesn't need me.* Sisi pushed away thoughts of Dele as soon as they came. Why had she never thought of doing this before? From the train station, she floated along Pelikaanstraat, gazing into jewelry stores, exulting in the absolute beauty of the rings and bracelets behind the glass, and ultimately falling for a pair of gold earrings that she had no doubt were destined for her. She pondered how easy it was to spend five hundred euros. How many things one could get. How happiness could sometimes be bought. Whoever said that money couldn't buy happiness had never experienced the relief that came from having money to spend on whatever you wanted. Not having to send it to an exploding pimp who had more money than anyone you knew. Why was he amassing so much wealth when he must have trouble spending the amount he already had? Sisi's purse was lighter, her head turning with an unaccustomed dizziness that made her feel immortal. The money was spent and she could not retrieve it. There was no turning back now. She had defied Dele, cut all links with Madam and the house on the Zwartezusterstraat. She was ready to deal with whatever the consequences might be.

ZWART

ZWARTEZUSTERSTRAAT

A POT OF TEA HAS APPEARED AS IF BY MAGIC IN THE MIDDLE OF THE sitting-room table. A squat orange ceramic kettle in the shape of a cock that Madam bought at the flea market in Brussels one Sunday morning. It is Madam's favorite pastime. Spurred on by daytime BBC programs like *Antiques Roadshow* and *Bargain Hunt,* Madam spends Sunday mornings rummaging for bargains at the Brussels market, convinced that she will find a priceless antique she can resell and make pots of money. So far she has failed to find anything worth re-selling, but she always brings back something interesting for the house: the chimpanzee-hand ashtray, a flower vase shaped like a pair of clogs, a knitted tissue-box holder, and a cuddly cat that snores when pressed.

Somebody must have gone into the kitchen and made the tea, but who? Joyce wonders. She does not remember seeing anyone get up. She pours herself a cup of tea and halfheartedly starts to sip, holding the cup around the rim rather than by the ear. Its taste is flat, and she gives up drinking. But it as if the little she has drunk has reminded her stomach of its emptiness, because it starts to grumble and rum-ble. Maybe she should make something, rustle up something quick and easy for all of them to eat. She goes to the kitchen. She stumbles over a hammer lying on the floor. "Segun's left his hammer out again," she grumbles as she picks it up and puts it away in a kitchen cupboard. Why can't the man clean up after himself?

A thoughtful silence has descended on the women once again and is extending into the kitchen, so that even the fridge does not give out its normal whirr. Joyce opens the fridge and scans the contents. Jollof rice. Sisi made that. Joyce brings out the container and rubs her hand over it. *Sisi touched this.* She opens it and looks at the rice, faint orange grains sticking together. Cubes of green bell pepper are visible in it. And three fried snails, curled up, looking like ears. *Sisi cooked this.* She smells the rice. It is still good. *Is Sisi's body already decaying? How long does it take before a corpse starts to rot? A few hours? A few days? How long did it take for Mother and Father to rot? And my brother, Ater? They must be rotten by now. Three years is a long time for a corpse, isn't it?* She does not want to think about her family, decayed. Unidentifiable bits of matter. She returns the container to the fridge. Her appetite is gone. She is in the mood for a bit of self-pity. She thinks about her life, and it seems to her like she is being punished for something she did in a previous life. *People I love get taken away from me. Whatever it was I did, haven't I paid enough? If only I knew what sin I committed, I could make amends. I could begin to rectify it.* But she can also feel that her relationship with Ama and Efe is beginning to change. It is this change that makes her, many years later when she has her school, hang on her office wall a framed inscription—IT IS NOT THE BLOOD THAT BINDS US IN THE END—which she will find in a supermarket in Yaba.

She goes back into the sitting room just as Madam is coming in. Madam's face is less drawn than it was when she left. Her flame-orange *boubou* brightens the room like a match lit in the dark. "I have spoken to them," she says. "Everything will be all right. No need for any of you to worry." "Them" being the police. Madam has spoken to them, for lingering in the house, on the women's minds, is also the thought that they might be deported. Madam has often said that she knows enough of the right people in the police force to ensure that as long as they do not try to cheat her, the women are safe in Belgium. "Everybody has a price, even *oyibo* police! Pay the right price and you are safe. Tomorrow I want all of you back at work. I have to find a replacement for Sisi." Madam disappears into her bedroom, saying that she does not want to be disturbed. Her slippers slap against her soles as she walks. Joyce finally says what has been on her mind the entire day, gnawing away at her, eating at her like acid on paper. "Madam does not even care!"

"Of course she doesn't," Ama answers. "What did you expect?" Her voice is mocking.

Something snaps in Joyce and she shouts, perhaps louder than she intends to, "We're human beings! Why should we take it? Sisi is dead, and all Madam can think of is business. Doesn't Sisi deserve respect? What are we doing? Why should Madam treat us any way she wants and we just take it like dogs?"

"What do you suggest we do?" Ama asks, the mocking quality in her voice dissipating, making her voice a murmur. Like that of a Catholic at confession.

"We fit go to de police," Efe answers before Joyce can say anything. It shocks her, because she has never thought of it.

Ama laughs. "Madam has the police in her pocket. You heard her. We tell the police and then fucking what?"

"We're not happy here. None of us is. We work hard to make somebody else rich. Madam treats us like animals. Why are we doing this? And I don't believe that we cannot find an honest policeman. I don't believe that for a second! We report Madam, and who knows, maybe we can even get asylum here. There are always people looking for causes to support. They can support us. We can be free. Madam has no right to our bodies, and neither does Dele. I don't want to think that one day I will be dead here and all Madam will do is complain about how bad my death is for business. I don't know what will happen to us, but I want to make sure Madam and Dele get punished." Joyce pulls at the tip of the cloth hanging from the waist of her trousers.

Ama impatiently lights another cigarette, then squashes it into the ashtray immediately. She is crying. "Come here," she says to Joyce and Efe. She stands up and spreads her arms. Joyce gets up and is enclosed in Ama's embrace. Efe stands up, too, and puts one arm around each woman. Their tears mingle, and the only sound in the room is that of them sniveling. Time stands still, and Ama says, "Now we are sisters." The women hug one another tight. Years later, Ama will tell them that at that moment she knew they would be friends forever. They will never go to the police, but they do not know that now. They believe that they will, and that gives them some relief. They disentangle and sit again on the black sofa. It creaks under their weight, and someone lets out a small, high laugh. Joyce pulls the rag from her waistband and pushes it under the couch, prodding it with a finger until it is out of sight. "I wonder if I can find henna here," she says. Ama has started to say something about making lunch when the doorbell rings. The women look at one another, wondering who it can be.

Joyce gets up and opens the door to Luc, his long hair disheveled and lank, almost covering his face. It is as if someone has ringed his eyes with eyeliner. He looks like a man who has not slept in many years. She does not say a word to him. She simply turns her back and walks into the sitting room.

Luc pulls the door shut behind him and follows her in, asking, "Where's Sisi?"

SISI

BY THE TIME SISI GOT BACK TO LUC'S, THE MAY SKY WAS A SPREAD OF azure anchored by a band of pinkish red, the color of a fresh bruise on white skin, but Luc was not yet home from work. She looked at her watch. It was a quarter to six. Luc had said he would be back between six-thirty and seven; he wanted to get some shopping done. Oh, that he were already home, she thought. Her new life excited her, pleasured her into squeals of joy.

Sisi ran upstairs, dumped her shopping on the bed, and thought perhaps she ought to start cleaning the kitchen. She would clear out the breakfast plates and maybe light the candle in the middle of the table. She had just entered the kitchen when the doorbell rang.

When Sisi answered and found Segun at the door, it had her surprised but not alarmed. "Hello, do you want to come in, Segun?"

He did not want to. "But . . . bu . . . but I want you to come, I mean . . . to—to co . . . to come with me in the car. We, we, we, I mean, we . . . we . . . we have some . . . thing to dis . . . dis . . . dis . . . I mean, to discuss." Busy hands flailing all the while. Restless feet tapping on concrete.

"Discuss, *ke*? We can discuss it here," she told the lanky man. Where was Luc? *Luc, please come home now!* Maybe she should have gone to the police after all. What did Segun want with her? Where was Luc?

"No. I am sorry, Si . . . si. Not here. No . . . no . . . I mean not here. It, it, it, I mean . . . it wo—wo . . . won't take time, I promise." His voice was low. He clenched and unclenched his fists. It struck Sisi that this was the longest he had ever spoken to her.

What harm will it do? Nobody can make me go back to the Zwartezusterstraat. That part of my life is over. And certainly not this wimp of a man. This man with only half a brain whose mouth always hangs open.

She got into the car. Whatever it was he had to discuss, she hoped he would keep it short. She wanted to be home by the time Luc got in. She wanted to tell him how much fun she'd had spending her money on herself. To kiss him and tell him that she was glad he'd broken the rules and come to the church on the Koningin Astridplein. "Segun, I can't stay out too long." He nodded.

She was not scared of Segun. He was harmless, everyone knew it. So the hammer hitting into her skull had come as a shock. She had not even had time to shout. She was not yet dead when he dragged her out on the deserted road leading to the GB and pushed her into the trunk of the car, heaping her on top of a purple-and-gray plaid blanket, her ankle-length green dress riding high up her legs to expose her thighs. One of her leaf-green flat-heeled slippers fell off, and Segun picked it up and threw it nonchalantly into the trunk. It landed beside Sisi's head.

In the instant between almost dying and cold-stone dead, the instant when the soul is still able to fly, Sisi escaped her body and flew down to Lagos. First she went to the house in Ogba. When she came, her father was in the sitting room reading the *Daily Times*, thinking that when next Sisi called he would mention that at his age and with a child abroad he ought to have a car, and could she not send him one? Sisi whispered in his ears. He shooed away the fly that had perched on his right ear. She found her mother in the kitchen beside the secondhand fridge they had just bought with the money Sisi sent. She was pouring a glass of water, at the same time complaining of the heat and the power failure. "A whole week and still no light. How am I supposed to enjoy my fridge, eh?" she muttered, placing the bottle on a kitchen counter and screwing its cap back on. She lifted the glass to drink. At that moment Sisi tapped her on the shoulder, and the glass slipped from her hands, spilling water and breaking into two uneven pieces. Sisi's mother would say the next morning, when the phone call came, that she knew dropping the glass was an omen. She would wail and tell the gathered mourners that she felt a coldness in the air just before the glass slipped. "That was when my daughter died. What have I done in this life to deserve this? How have I erred? *Onye? Onye ka m ji ugwo?*" She would burst into an elegy that cracked her voice and left her hoarse for many weeks.

Her husband would not cry, for men do not cry. He would sit on the chair facing the door, so that he saw everyone who came in and everyone who left. He would sit there and look at the mourners coming and going, trying to see behind the tears those who wished him ill. For it was not normal that his daughter should die just as she was starting to do well. Only that morning she had sent them money, the largest amount ever, strengthening his resolve to ask for a car. Somebody, somebody who envied him his fortune, must have had a hand in this. So he watched the mourners with the eyes of a hawk. And when they said, "*Ndo*, sorry for your loss," he would nod, slowly, as if his head were twenty times its size, the head of a masquerade.

Once it left Ogba, Sisi's soul found its way to a house where she had never been. A house in Aje, a magnificent duplex. It was just after seven o'clock, and the Lagos sky was dark, a violent shade of black, like ink. The darkness was thick and quiet, but inside numerous lights were on, and Dele was talking loudly into a telephone.

"Yes, yes, Kate. I trust you. I trust say you go take the necessary steps. Dat gal just fin' my trouble. She cost me money. How much money you pay de police? I know. Yes. Tell de gals make dem no try insubordinate me. I warn all da gals, nobody dey mess with Senghor Dele. Nobody! You treat these gals well and wetin dey go do? Just begin misbehave. Imagine! All my gals, I treat good. I dey tell dem before dem comot. I dey dey straight wit dem. Me, I be good man. I just dey try to help poor gals. Yes, I know. Na good worker we lose but gals full *boku* for Lagos. I get three lined up. Latest next week, dem visa go ready. Dem full for front, full for back. I swear, dem go drive *oyibo* mad. Na beauty-queen statistics dem get. You sabi as my gals dey dey nah, no be gorillas I dey supply. Na beauty queens! Gals wey carry double Jennifer Lopez *nyash*. Who talk say na Jennifer Lopez get the finest buttocks? Dem never see my women." He boasted and laughed, and his breasts, which were almost womanly, shook with laughter. Two mounds of flesh going up and down. And up and down. *Humph humph humph humph.* A hippopotamus.

Sisi imagined Madam laughing at the other end of the phone, in her room, perhaps, the door shut. Sisi stood still and listened to him. He was leaning on his L-shaped bar, a glass of whiskey in his left hand, the hand that was not holding the phone. Her soul zoomed around the bar, flew beyond it, went through a door, and found itself on a stairway. It went up the stairs and turned the knob on the second door on the right of a wide corridor. In the room, there was a bunk bed. On the beds, two little girls lay asleep in pink cotton nightgowns, their braided hair on either side of them like miniature angel wings. They were chubby, the way angels were drawn in children's Bibles, and Sisi almost felt sorry for them. But then she saw the likeness of Dele in them, remembered whose daughters they were, and she went to them, first to the girl on the upper bunk, and whispered something in her ear. Then she went to the lower bunk, lifted the hair to get to the ear, and whispered the same in that ear. Anyone who knew Sisi well might say that she cursed them. They might say that she told them, "May your lives be bad. May you never enjoy love. May your father suffer as much as mine will when he hears I am gone. May you ruin him."

For Sisi was not the sort to forgive. Not even in death.

Sisi's soul bounced down the stairs and began its journey into another world.

ACKNOWLEDGMENTS

WRITING *ON BLACK SISTERS STREET* HAS BEEN A LEARNING EXPERIENCE FOR me. I am, in the first place, grateful to those whose story it is: the nameless Nigerian sex workers who allowed me into their lives, answering my questions and laughing at my ignorance.

This book was written with the help of a grant from the Het Vlaams Fonds Voor de Letteren. It would have been, undoubtedly, more difficult to concentrate if I had not had the grant. Thank you.

I am grateful in no small measure to Johan De Koning, who wanted a "big" book and reminded me of the virtues of patience. Thank you, Johan, for introducing me to Faulkner, whom I ought to have known but did not.

My parents-in-law, Jose Branders and Rene Vandenhoudt, gave me the gift I needed to get this work done: time, by taking the children off my hands. Thank you so, so much.

Thanks to Maggie Wilkinson, friend and early draft reader, who also took the children when she could.

Thanks to the Zingiziro Triumvirate: Brian Chikwava (for sending me in search of the Narrative Arc), Monica Arac de Nyeko (for refusing my thanks "because this is what friends do"), and Jackee Budesta Batanda (for *Emma's War*).

I am grateful to all those who read the earliest drafts and asked the right questions: Tolu Ogunlesi; Ike Oguine; Trevor Wadlow; Stella Okemwa; Patrick (Stella's friend); Katrien Lodewyckx; and my BFFL, Amaka Omenka (for loving the chapter on Efe and wanting to read more).

Thanks to Bart Cabanier, who checked an extract for me. And to Peter Gevers for reading and rereading and finding everything I missed.

Thanks to the Sudan connection: Gomai, David Lukudu, and John Oryem. While Daru is a fictional city, they gave me much needed insight into life in southern Sudan. I only hope that I have represented the area well. I apologize if I have not.

Thanks to Ellah Allfrey and to Harold Polis for their guidance, and for pushing me to challenge myself. Thanks to David Godwin for being the perfect agent and a wonderful man, to Millicent Bennett for being a dream editor, and to Basorun Richard Adeolu for opening my eyes to hidden things. *Ose pupo*.

Thanks to Hans Schippers for being a friend in the first instance, and for being unstinting with his time and knowledge.

And to my family: Mom and Dad, Jane, Winnie, Nnamdi, Maureen, Okey, and BG, you are the best.

And finally to Jan, for the many years we have shared and the many more ahead.

ABOUT THE AUTHOR

CHIKA UNIGWE was born in Enugu, Nigeria, and now lives in Turnhout, Belgium, with her husband and their four children.

She holds a Ph.D. from Leiden University and is the recipient of several awards for her writing, including first prize in the 2003 BBC Short
Story Competition, a Commonwealth Short Story Award, and a Flemish
literary prize for "De Smaak van Sneeuw," her first short story written in
Dutch. In 2004 she was short-listed for the Caine Prize for African Writing. Her stories have been on BBC World Service and Radio Nigeria.

Her first novel, *De Feniks*, was published in Dutch in 2005; it is the
first book of fiction written by a Flemish author of African origin.

ABOUT THE TYPE

This book was set in Electra, a typeface designed for Linotype by W. A. Dwiggins, the renowned type designer (1880–1956). Electra is a fluid typeface, avoiding contrasts of thick and thin strokes that are prevalent in most modern typefaces.